The Solace
of Autumn

a novel

Michael D. Pappas

Dead Weight Press

Dead Weight Press
www.deadweightpress.com

ISBN 979 8 9912611 2 8 (paperback)
ISBN 979 8 9912611 3 5 (dust jacket hardcover)
ISBN 979 8 9912611 1 1 (case laminate hardcover)
ISBN 979 8 9912611 0 4 (ebook)

This is a work of fiction. Names, characters, places, and incidents either are the products of the author's imagination or are used fictitiously, and any resemblance to actual persons, living or deceased, buildings, companies, or locales is entirely coincidental.

Cover design by Sarah Lahay

Author photograph by Beth Bales

First edition, 2025

The Solace
of Autumn

Chapter 1

Friday, October 9, 1987

"IT'S JUST A MATTER of time now."

Wade Thompson looked at the old man sitting across the table and knew it was true. He barely recognized him. The broad shoulders that once carried the strength and muscle of a farmer's body were nothing more than brittle bones holding up a scarecrow's outsized clothes. His skin was paper thin and pale. His once piercing blue eyes were now a dull gray. He could play a ghost without any makeup, but Wade wasn't sure Tom Richardson would make it a few more days, let alone three more weeks to Halloween.

"What are the doctors saying?" Wade asked.

Tom let out a chuckle. "They don't have to say anything."

Tom pushed a brown legal-size envelope across the table. It was thick with documents. Wade stared at it but didn't pick it up.

"I've been getting my affairs in order," Tom told him. "The details are in there. When this thing happens, you'll need to take Lily to see the lawyer. Sam Marshall is handling everything. He knows about this." Tom motioned between them with a thumb and finger.

"How much does Lily know?"

"She knows I'm dying."

"What about the rest of it?" Wade asked, pointing at the envelope.

Tom rose slowly from his chair and walked over to a small wooden liquor cabinet on the other side of the dining room. He pulled out a bottle of Jack Daniels, grabbed two glasses, and poured each of them a drink. "I'd say we should drink to my health, but we both know it's a little too late for that."

Wade managed a reluctant smile and dutifully drank down his whiskey. Tom drank his and walked back to his side of the table. Wade watched Tom ease himself into his chair. Face taut. Teeth clenched. There was pain written all over him, physical and emotional, and he let out a heavy, ragged breath when he took his seat.

"She won't hear any of it. Leaves the room whenever I bring it up. I guess we can't blame her for that."

Wade nodded. It'd been a tough life for her, losing her mother as an infant, her grandparents and her great aunt as a young child, and now her great uncle as a teenager.

"It isn't going to be easy for her," Wade said.

"That's why you're here. That's why I want you and Ginny to look after her when I'm gone. I want people in her life who will care for her and be there for her."

Wade felt a twinge of regret. Maybe more than a twinge. More like a punch in the gut that made his stomach turn in shame. Lily's mother, Emma, had been his best friend, and Wade hadn't been there for her daughter, with all she'd gone through all those years, losing one relative after another. He'd see her on occasion, when he'd visit his mother's house, and she was still living with her grandparents next door. But after she moved in with her uncle, she was out of his life. He couldn't help but feel like he'd abandoned her. What made it worse was he felt like he'd abandoned her mother, too.

"Is Lily going to be okay with that?" Wade asked. "Being looked after by people she barely knows? I'm pretty much a stranger to her now."

"I know it's a lot," Tom answered. "For you and Ginny. And for Lily. Talk to Ginny. Take some time to think about it and let me know, but don't wait too long." Tom laughed at his own sad joke.

As far as Wade was concerned, there wasn't much to think about. He wasn't going to leave that poor girl alone in the world. He wasn't going to abandon her all over again. Not this time, with no family left to turn to. Tom knocked on the table to get Wade's attention. There was a second envelope, the kind you might use to send a greeting card or a handwritten note. This one was light blue and wrinkled, like it had been opened and closed and handled often throughout the years. Tom slid it over to Wade.

"I thought you should have that."

Wade picked it up. It felt heavy in his hand. Heavier than it was or should have been. He tipped it and emptied it, and out spilled a small black-and-white photograph of a boy and girl holding hands in front of a pond. They looked ragged, like they'd been playing together all day. Shirts untucked, hair out of place, a swirl of dust surrounding them. But they looked happy. On the back, in smudged black grease pen, it read: *Emma and Wade. Elliott's Pond. 1954.*

Wade looked up from the picture and back to Tom and happened to notice another photograph, this one held in a frame and perched on a shelf on the other side of the kitchen. He got up and walked over for a closer look. It was Lily at about six years old, standing on a porch in a yellow poncho, her arms raised above her head and a wide smile splashed across her face. It reminded Wade of her mother. The face, the eyes, the mischievous grin.

"I'll talk to Ginny tonight," Wade told Tom, resolved now to make things right. "We'll take her in if that's what she wants. And we'll look after her for as long as we're alive."

"It's the way it should be, really," Tom said. "You and Lily were the two people Emma loved most in the world."

It was already dark and almost time for dinner by the time Wade got home. Ginny didn't hear him come in. Wade leaned against the side of the entryway leading into the kitchen and watched her. She was humming a tune and dancing barefoot to the rhythm of some unheard song as she prepared their dinner. She was always barefoot in the kitchen.

"I want to feel the earth when I cook," she'd once told him.

"I think you'd cook naked if you could," he'd replied.

"How do you know I don't, when you're not around?" she'd asked with a wink.

It was moments like this, when she was carefree, happy, and oblivious, that reminded him why he fell in love with her and how much he still loved her, despite all their troubles. After a couple of minutes, she turned to the island behind her and spotted Wade.

"Holy shit!" she cried out. She leaned over with both hands on the counter and let out a deep breath. "How long have you been watching me?"

"Well," he answered, "I wanted to see if you really did cook naked when I wasn't around."

Her pale blue eyes settled on him, and he felt a flash of heat run through his body. She walked over and gave him a kiss. "Don't get all riled up," she warned him. "I'm not letting this food get cold." She pulled away with a pat on his backside and left him to finish preparing their dinner.

After they ate, Wade volunteered to clear and clean the dishes while Ginny took a quick bath. He made chamomile tea for Ginny and poured out a finger of bourbon for himself. He carried the drinks into the living room where he found Ginny already waiting. She was sitting on the couch, legs folded under her, with a book propped open on her knee. Her wheat-blonde hair was down, still damp from the bath, and draped along the sides of her face. She'd washed off her makeup, revealing light freckles that dotted her cheeks and bridged across her nose, and she was dressed in a pair of pink-flowered pajamas.

Wade set down her mug and lowered himself into the armchair diagonal to her. He was thinking about Tom and Lily again, working on a plan in his head to spill it all to Ginny, so he didn't hear her calling his name. He finally noticed after what must have been her third or fourth try.

"Sorry, my mind was somewhere else," he told her.

Ginny put down her book. "What's going on, hon?"

Wade didn't respond right away. He considered the question and how she might react when he told her a seventeen-year-old girl they barely knew, Emma's daughter no less, would be coming to live with them soon. He hoped that Ginny would understand. He wouldn't blame her if she couldn't. The idea of bringing a child into their home now, even one nearing adulthood, was sobering. They'd lost one baby to miscarriage and another to illness shortly after birth. They'd named that baby Chloe Marie, and losing her almost broke their marriage.

"Ginny," he started cautiously, "I met with Tom Richardson earlier today. He's pretty sick, you know. Probably doesn't have much time left. A few weeks, maybe even days."

"Oh my God. I didn't realize." Ginny reached across the side table and took Wade's hand.

"This might be hard for you to hear, but he asked me for a favor. Actually, he asked both of us. Tom wants Lily to come live with us. He wants us to take care of her."

He stopped and waited for a reaction. A resounding *Absolutely not!* or a *How could you do this to me?* and a quick exit from the room. Instead, Ginny rose from the couch and climbed into the chair and onto his lap.

"I think that would be wonderful," she said. She leaned in and rested her head against his chest. He brushed his fingers through her hair and kissed her forehead, and he couldn't stop thinking about how lucky he was to have her.

Chapter 2

1959

WADE AND HIS OLDER brother Paul waited patiently for their mother to serve them breakfast. Paul had a fishing lure with him and was concentrating with a determined, almost angry look on a tricky knot that kept slipping when he pulled the line. His face was darkened from a summer full of sun, and his jet-black hair, conditioned in the sea-salt air, shot out in stiff strands like spindles on a wire brush. Wade had a gentler appearance. His tawny brown hair fell in soft layers over his forehead, almost covering his ocean blue eyes completely, as if hiding a secret. He peered through the strands and watched his mother stack hot biscuits in a wooden bowl. She covered them with a thin white linen cloth decorated with lemons and limes to keep in the heat. She set the bowl in the middle of the table and reached into a cupboard for a Mason jar filled with her homemade strawberry preserves.

"Okay boys," she said, as she set down the jar. "Dig in."

Paul began right away, biting eagerly into a piece of bacon before scooping a forkful of scrambled eggs into his mouth. Wade waited. He watched his mother take a seat at the table and a sip from her coffee before she started on her needlework. On most days, she was fine. On others, she couldn't get herself out of bed. On those days, the boys had to pack their own lunches and get themselves off to school. Sometimes when they came home, she'd still be in bed, and

Wade would check on her and ask her if she was all right. But today, Sarah Thompson looked happy, and that's all that mattered to Wade.

A cool breeze poured in through the screen door at the back of the kitchen, carrying with it a voice from outside. "Wade," a girl called in a singsong that lingered on the first half of the boy's name. "Wade," she called again.

Paul snickered. "Looks like your girlfriend is here for you."

"Shut up. She's not my girlfriend," Wade spit back. But, when Paul wasn't looking, Wade snuck a peek over his shoulder and saw his neighbor, Emma Parker, approach the back door. Emma knocked and cupped her hands around her face and pressed against the screen.

"There you are," she said, as if she'd just found her lost kitten.

Mrs. Thompson got up and unhooked the screen door. "Good morning, Emma. Come in and sit with the boys."

Emma brushed away a stray brown curl from her forehead, walked in, and sat down next to Wade.

"Would you like some breakfast?"

"Thanks, Mrs. Thompson. I'll just have one of these." Emma grabbed a biscuit and ripped it open.

Wade watched silently as she took the knife right off his plate and used it to smear a healthy serving of preserves across both sides. She took a big bite and smiled at him between chews.

"Today we're gonna look for a ghost," Emma started, with a mouth half full of food. "Papa says a Native woman used to live near the marsh. He says her son drowned when his canoe sank in the bay, and when she heard, she walked right out into the water and killed herself."

Emma stopped talking just long enough to take a sip of milk from Wade's glass. Wade kept staring at her.

"Sometimes you can see her out near the water looking for him." Emma turned to Wade's brother. "Paul, you can come with us if you want. But, if you do, you gotta do what I say. I'm leading this expedition."

It was as if Emma had suggested something so unreasonable and ridiculous as to merit his full contempt. Paul was thirteen years old, just three years older than Wade and Emma, but he'd been done with their childish games for a while now.

"I'm going fishing," he declared abruptly. He rose from the table, lure in hand, and left the room.

Emma finished her biscuit and shot up from her seat, pushing her chair back with a screech. "Thanks, Mrs. Thompson." She turned to Wade, who was still sitting at the table, mesmerized by Emma and her story. "Well, what are you waiting for? Let's go."

Wade got up and followed Emma outside.

"You kids be careful now," Mrs. Thompson called out through the screen door. "Stay out of the water."

The pair walked down a well-worn path along the edge of the corn-field that fronted the Thompson's house. Wade had to skip a step to keep up with Emma's hurried pace. A young yellow lab trotted along, weaving between them and occasionally darting off to chase a bird or chipmunk through the towering stalks, ripe with ears of corn, ready to be harvested.

"You haven't trained that dog very well," Emma admonished. "He shouldn't be wandering off like that."

Wade didn't answer. He shrugged his shoulders and looked over at his dog, who continued along with them, unconcerned with Emma's disapproval. Wade's father had brought the dog home for the boys a few years earlier. They named him Blue, and they took him everywhere they went. Whenever Paul went out alone, though,

Blue would stay with Wade. And whenever Wade went somewhere without Paul, Blue would follow him. Eventually, Paul gave up, and Blue became Wade's dog and Wade became Blue's human.

Emma and Wade stepped off the path and into a patch of wild grass and buttercups, following beaten trails laid down by deer that had wandered back and forth, in and out, for seasons. Emma held out her arms to feel the blades and petals, but to Wade, it looked like she was trying to take flight with the bobwhites they'd rustled awake as they traveled through the brush. Emma zig-zagged back and forth, raising one arm and dropping another like airplane wings angling up and down to quickly change direction.

"Woohoo!" Emma sang out.

Wade smiled and started flying himself. "Woohoo!" he answered. Blue bounced along with them, hopping across the path, biting at tufts of dandelion that shot in the air after them.

The crunching under their feet grew softer as the ground got sandier and reeds sprung up on either side of them like the spines of a wrought-iron fence. Some locals had laid out wooden planks to create a boardwalk along the creek that cut through the marsh. They jumped onto the walkway and travelled over tangled thicket and marsh grass. They could taste the salt and smell the sulfur from the wetlands around them. Wade was looking out over the creek to the other side of the marsh where the bleached trunks of dead trees looked like the spirits of fallen soldiers on a battlefield. An osprey swooped overhead and let out a high-pitched cry. Wade stared up as it circled above them and walked right into Emma, who had stopped to survey their progress.

"Watch where you're going!" she scolded, hands on her hips. "C'mon. We're close."

They hopped off the boardwalk and sank, the muck rising up to their ankles. It was a mixture of sand and mud and decaying plants that had the consistency of wet cement.

"Be careful," Wade said, finally uttering his first words to her.

Emma looked down and raised and lowered her feet slowly as she navigated through the sludge. The sound of it made them giggle.

After a short distance, Wade slowed and then stopped. "We don't want to go too far and get in trouble out here."

"We're only going to the point over there," she said, motioning to an unseen spot in front of her. She reached back and grabbed Wade's hand and pulled him along with her. They trudged another twenty yards or so until they emerged onto a sandy beach at the edge of the marsh, where the creek opened into the bay.

"This is it," she said confidently. "This is where it happened. I can feel it."

Wade believed her. When they were younger, Emma had invisible friends. She'd hold conversations with them when she was alone or even with other people, and many times when she was with Wade. Most people thought it was her imagination running away with her. But Wade knew they were real, at least to Emma. When she described them to Wade, they didn't just have names, they had personalities. Some of them were funny, others were sad. Some chewed their nails when they were nervous or twirled strands of hair when they felt shy. A few scared her when they got angry. She told Wade what they looked like, the color of their eyes, the shapes of their faces, the color of their skin. She knew how old they were, and some of them told her how they died. As Emma aged, the visits became less frequent, but she told Wade that she could still feel a presence in a room sitting in an empty chair or standing in a corner. Sometimes she felt an unexplained chill, or the hair on the back of her neck would stand for no apparent reason. So, it was no surprise to Wade that Emma could feel something now.

Emma sat down and stared out over the open water. Wade sat next to her and watched as Blue chased a fiddler crab back into the sand.

"Do you think people go to heaven when they die?" Emma asked, out of nowhere.

Wade turned to look at her. "That's what momma says."

"Hmm," Emma let out. "What about animals?"

Wade looked at Blue, who had laid down next to him. "I sure hope so. I'd hate to be up there without Blue."

Emma glanced over to Blue and then back out to the water. "I hope you're right, Wade," she said. "But none of it makes a whole lot of sense to me. If we were meant to live forever, why wouldn't we do it here? Why do we have to die and go someplace else? And why does your momma have to tell you that's what happens? If it was true, shouldn't we know it without anyone telling us?"

Wade picked up a stick and started drawing circles in the dark, wet sand. "I don't know, Emma. I guess some people need something to keep living. Anyway, I don't think about that too much." He put down his stick and turned to her. "I just know I like it when we're together."

"Hmm," she let out again. "Me too. I like the idea of the two of us being together forever. Here and maybe in heaven too."

Wade had felt that way for a long time. He always wanted to be with Emma. Even more than his other friends, the boys whom he ate lunch with at school and played baseball with on the weekends. Even more than his brother, who taught him how to fish and crab and do almost everything else that he knew how to do. But none of them were Emma. A sudden urge ran through him. He turned to her, closed his eyes, and kissed her.

Emma pulled away and wiped her lips with the back of her hand. Wade turned from her, hurt and ashamed, and started making circles in the sand again, this time with his finger.

Emma studied Wade like she was working a riddle. Wade reckoned she was trying to figure why he'd do such a thing.

"You're my best friend, Wade," she told him. "You just surprised me a little."

"I know," Wade replied, his eyes cast downward, trying to hide his embarrassment.

"I mean it, Wade. You're like a brother to me."

"I know," he repeated. He was squatted down, close to the sand, with his chin in his hand and his cheeks puffed out like a pouting toddler. He was still drawing his circles.

Just then a stray cloud moved slowly across the sky, blocking the sun and casting a shadow over the point and the edge of the bay. A gust of wind picked up from offshore and swept over them. Blue whimpered and shot up as if alarmed. Wade looked over at Emma. Little bumps had sprouted up her arm. She got up and walked to the edge of the water.

"Emma?" Wade called to her, but she kept walking. She was looking at something in the distance. "Emma?" he called again.

"Shush!" she yelled back. "Can you hear that?"

Wade didn't hear anything except for the wind humming across the water. Emma kept walking, into the water now, up to her ankles and then to her knees. Her short, brown hair fluttering like a sparrow's wings in the wind.

"Emma!" Wade yelled and rose to his feet.

Blue was barking and dancing excitedly at the water's edge. But Emma kept walking, farther and deeper into the bay, her eyes still fixed on a point somewhere out in front of her. Then she stopped and looked down at her feet. Wade ran after her, splashing his way through the water, which was now up to Emma's waist. By the time he reached her, the sun had escaped from behind the rogue cloud and the wind had eased.

"Emma, what happened?"

Emma didn't respond. She looked down at her feet again and searched the water. Wade looked down as well. The water had settled after his rush out to her, and they could see down to the bottom.

"Careful," she said to him. "Don't disturb the sand again." She reached down and felt around for a few seconds. She grabbed at something and pulled out her fist and raised it to Wade. "Papa told me the Assateague used to live here a couple hundred years ago, before us white people drove 'em all off. They had villages up and down the coast, and they used to hunt and fish right here."

"Did you see her?" Wade asked. "Did you see the Native woman?"

Emma shook her head. "No, but I heard a whisper when the wind blew. It was nothing I could understand, but somehow it led me to these." Emma dipped her hand back in the water to wash the sand away. She lifted her hand out again and opened it to reveal two carved arrowheads.

"There's one for each of us." She gave one of the arrowheads to Wade. "Keep that with you," she told him. "It will protect you."

"How do you know that?"

"I just know."

"What about the other one?" Wade asked her.

"I'll always keep it close. And if I ever get lost, it'll help you find me."

They walked out of the water and back onto the beach. Emma grabbed Wade's hand and spun him around to face her.

"You know, I don't have any brothers or sisters. Why can't we be brother and sister?" She opened her left hand and rubbed the edge of her arrowhead across her palm, opening a fine cut that spilled bright red blood. "Give me yours," she ordered.

Wade held out his closed hand and hesitated before opening it for her. He gritted his teeth and let out a little hiss as she cut across his palm. The blood mixed with the water and burned with the salt. Emma clasped his bloody hand in hers.

"Blood sister," she said to him.

"Blood brother," he said back, relieved that he hadn't driven her away with that one errant kiss.

They sat back down, hands still tangled together, and watched the laughing gulls dart across the horizon.

Chapter 3

Saturday, October 10, 1987

W ADE FINISHED GETTING DRESSED before the sun had chased the last star from the sky. Ginny was still asleep on her side of the bed, closest to the window. Her lips were parted slightly and curled at the edges in a hinted smile. Her hands were tucked under her head, raising it off the pillows just enough for Wade to kiss the whole of her mouth. Her smile widened, but she didn't wake. The pink-flowered pajamas Ginny had worn to bed the night before were lying on the floor in a heap, replaced above the waist with one of Wade's white tank tops, the ridges of the shirt carving familiar trails across her breasts and stomach. She pulled her knees closer to her chest, exposing the bare skin of her legs. Wade kissed the outside of her thigh and pulled the sheet back up to cover her.

It had been a while. More than a month at least, Wade figured. They'd gone out for a nice dinner. Ginny had a little too much wine, and when they got home, she pulled him right into the bedroom. The next day, he mentioned something about maybe trying to get pregnant one more time. Ginny got angry. Called him selfish. There wasn't a lot of warmth between them for a time after. Things did get better, but it took a little longer than he wanted or expected, and he'd worried that he'd lost her for good.

Wade knotted his tie in front of the mirror and caught a reflection of their three-year-old black lab hiding around the corner of the bed. Shadow usually waited until Wade was out of the house before popping into bed with Ginny, like he was keeping it a secret. But he snuck up sooner than usual this morning and gave himself away.

"I see you, you sneaky bastard," Wade whispered, pointing a scolding finger in his direction. Shadow lifted his eyes without moving his head and let out a little sigh. Wade turned and patted a spot next to Ginny's legs. Shadow lumbered in, leapt onto the bed, and curled up in a nook behind Ginny's knees, his shame gone as soon as he hit the sheets.

Wade picked up his campaign cover and his holstered Colt revolver off the dresser on his way out of the bedroom, leaving his wife and his dog snuggled together in their bed. He walked out the front door of the house, climbed into his dark brown Crown Victoria, and was on his way to the barracks when a call came over the radio.

"Sheriff Thompson. Come in, Sheriff Thompson."

Wade lifted the handset. "Good morning, Loretta."

"Good morning, Sheriff. Ocean City police called. They need you at the inlet."

"Did they say why?"

"They just told me to get you out there as soon as possible."

"Ten-four, Loretta. On my way."

Wade drove the short distance from his house, reaching the road leading into the beach town and to the inlet parking lot in a couple of minutes. As soon as Wade turned the last corner, he saw a cluster of police cars surrounding a white pickup truck, and he knew at once that Tom Richardson was dead.

Mid-morning sunlight spilled into the kitchen and bathed the mahogany plank table where Lily sat eating an English muffin and drinking her coffee. She had her knees pulled up and tucked into an oversized black t-shirt with The Cure's brooding lead singer on front staring out from his screen-printed prison. Lily massaged her temple with the heel of her hand, trying to rub out the last bits of a hangover from last night's party. Even though she was still in high school and under the legal drinking age, she wasn't new to it. They started young out on the Eastern Shore, easing in with a beer here or there at parties on the beach in Ocean City or bonfires in the razed cornfields in Bishopville, then graduating over time to beer bongs and shots and sometimes a little pot. Last night it was wine coolers, and Lily had had one too many.

Lily was glad her uncle wasn't here to see her like this. He'd surely disapprove, shaking his head with an admonishing *tsk tsk*, which would be enough to riddle her with guilt for putting him through the worry. But the house was empty by the time she got out of bed, which wasn't unusual for a weekend morning. Her uncle often woke before dawn to visit her aunt Maggie at the cemetery when he knew they'd be alone. Or he might drive across the bay to the beach to greet the sunrise along the shoreline.

When Lily heard the crunch of tires on the oyster-shell driveway, she assumed it was her uncle, but then she heard a knock. She walked to the front room, looked out the window, and found the sheriff standing on the uneven landing of the porch, hat in hand. She opened the door.

"Hello, Sheriff."

"Good morning, Lily."

"My uncle isn't here," she told him, figuring that he would only be there to see him. Then, Lily noticed a woman in uniform standing next to him. His deputy, she assumed.

"Can we come in?" the sheriff asked, the warped baseboards under his feet squeaking in pain with every shift in weight.

Lily waved them in. Sheriff Thompson and her uncle were acquainted, and she knew Sheriff Thompson and his wife Ginny a little from church, though she couldn't remember the last time she'd seen him there. She'd also known Sheriff Thompson a bit when she was a little girl and still lived in her grandmother's house. She'd see Wade and his brother Paul on occasion, when they would visit their mother at the house next door. Paul was more of a shadow in her memory, but Wade was there in full color. Sometimes Lily would amble into their backyard, chasing one of the many stray cats that liked to congregate at the Thompsons' back porch for a sip of cream or nibble of food. If Wade was there, he'd invite her to sit with him and offer her a snack—some homemade sugar cookies or a slice of banana bread and a cup of milk—or they'd play tag amongst the giant sunflowers planted in his mother's garden. He'd take her hand and walk her to the path leading to the creek and marsh, and he'd tell her fanciful stories about princesses and magic. And she believed the princess in each of those stories was her mother. But that was a long time ago, and the man that was in her living room right then was different than the man she knew from her childhood. This wasn't Wade. This was Sheriff Thompson. And there was something in his manner that made her uneasy. Something was wrong.

"What's going on?" she asked, her concern growing, realizing now that they hadn't asked about her uncle. "Is Uncle Tom all right? Where is he?" The deputy reached for Lily's hand, which shook under her touch.

Chapter 4

Sunday, October 11, 1987

A T LEAST A COUPLE of Sundays a month, Wade met his brother for breakfast. He left the house early, driving east and across the drawbridge spanning the Sinepuxent Bay into Ocean City, then north for about a block before parking his pickup in a mostly empty lot across from Sandy Mitchell's restaurant. He crossed the street, pulled open the glass door, and stepped inside.

Sandy looked up from the cash register and smiled. "Hey, Wade. You want the usual?"

"Sounds good. Thanks, Sandy."

Wade had known Sandy almost his whole life. She still had a soft, round face that preserved a youthfulness in her, even now in her late thirties, and long, straight brown hair that was a vestige of her high school hippie days. "You remember what I was like in the sixties, don't you, Wade?" she'd ask him occasionally, usually after she'd had a couple of drinks. It was an easy memory for him, and when he saw her just then, he recalled a day when he, Sandy, Emma, and some of their other friends met after class at the beach to drink some beer and smoke a cigarette or two. She'd had a pair of large, pink-shaded sunglasses propped on top of all that hair, which back then reached down to her hips. A thin leather headband tied it together near her right temple. She was wearing a brown suede tank top and faded bell bottom jeans that hugged tight to her body, with a red heart patch on her left knee and a blue peace symbol on her right thigh. If he hadn't been in love with Emma all those years, he was sure he would've fallen in love with Sandy.

"Your brother already ordered," she said now, breaking Wade's recollection. "He's over there, under the fish." She emphasized the last word with a hint of disgust and then left to take the order back to the kitchen.

Wade headed toward the white marlin mounted on the wall on the other side of the restaurant. Scattered patrons nodded as Wade crossed the room, which he acknowledged with a nod of his own. He spotted his brother in the booth and slid into the empty seat across from him.

Paul lifted his head and set his eyes on him. "You don't look too good," he said matter-of-factly.

Wade rubbed his cheek and chin, feeling out the truth of Paul's observation. He hadn't slept much the last couple of days, and he figured the fatigue and worry had taken its toll. It didn't do much to diminish his still handsome features. Square jaw and chiseled cheekbones. Blue eyes and olive skin that hinted at some ancient Mediterranean bloodline.

"There's something I need to talk to you about." He hesitated. Paul put down his fork and waited. "It's Tom Richardson. We found him at the inlet in his truck yesterday morning. He's dead."

Paul's face tightened. "Jesus Christ," he whispered. "What about the girl? What's she gonna do now?" There was genuine concern in his voice.

"That's another thing I wanted to talk to you about. I met with Tom on Friday. Believe it or not, he told me he wanted me and Ginny to look after her."

"He wanted you to take care of her?"

"There's no family left," Wade replied.

"I guess you're the closest thing, with no father around."

In another time, in another context, that comment might have stung him. There was a resentment he'd held against Emma for always choosing someone else. It was something that should've faded away a long time ago, especially after she was gone and certainly after he was with Ginny. For some reason, though, it stuck with him, but he couldn't think or feel that way now. This was about the girl, not him.

"I'm supposed to take Lily to see Tom's lawyer and go over the details of his estate. Tom was already working with him to finalize a will and get all his paperwork straight." Wade paused a second, then continued. "I don't know how Lily's going to take it." After Wade and his deputy broke the news to her, she'd crumpled to the ground crying, and he'd worried she'd never stop.

Wade felt a nervousness in his stomach. The gravity of the situation was setting in. Tom had been planning this for a while. He could've talked to Wade and Lily weeks or even months earlier. It would have given all of them time to adjust.

"Where's the girl now?" Paul asked.

"She's staying with one of her friends."

Sandy's daughter arrived with Wade's breakfast. She was the same age as Lily.

"Mom told me to make sure to give you extra strawberry jelly, Sheriff Thompson," she said as she put down the plate.

"Thank you, Holly."

"Anything else for you, Mr. Thompson?" she asked Paul.

Paul shook his head. "No. I'm good."

Holly turned and left them.

"What's Ginny saying about all this?" Paul asked.

Wade picked at his eggs and bacon but didn't take a bite. "I was worried. I didn't want to put this on her. She's handled it way better than I would've expected, although maybe I should've expected more from her to begin with."

The brothers sat quietly for a few minutes as Wade worked on his breakfast and Paul finished his. Paul wiped a napkin across his mouth and got up to leave.

"Have you been by to see Mom yet today?" Wade asked him.

"Yeah. She's having a good day. The house is clean, and she said she was going to do some baking."

"I'm going to have to break the news about Tom to her at some point," Wade told him. "I think I'll head over there this afternoon."

Paul reached into his back pocket for his wallet and dropped enough money on the table to cover both meals plus a hearty tip. "It's on me today."

As Paul left the restaurant, Sandy walked over and sat down. "Everything all right with your breakfast?" she asked, shooting a glance at Wade's half-eaten plate.

"I didn't have much of an appetite this morning." The doors to the kitchen swung open, and Holly emerged with a tray of food. It triggered a thought. "Is Holly friends with Lily Parker?" Wade asked.

"They aren't close, but they've known each other for years and hang out with some of the same people. Why are you asking?"

Wade took a breath. "Tom Richardson died yesterday."

Sandy put her hand to her mouth. "Oh no. Poor Lily."

"Yeah. She's going to need some friends to get her through all of this."

"I'll let Holly know."

Wade lifted out of the booth. Sandy followed him to the front of the restaurant.

"Let me know if there's anything else I can do," she told him.

Wade approached the front door of his childhood home. The red paint had faded to a rosy pink, and he made a mental note to add painting the door to his to-do list. He knocked but heard no response. He had a key in his hand, but before using it, he tested the knob. It was unlocked and it turned, so he pushed the door open and walked in. The smell of apple, lemon, and cinnamon immediately surrounded him.

"Mom? Hey mom, you in here?"

"In the kitchen, dear."

Her voice sounded pleasant, happy even, which wasn't always a given. He'd hate to ruin her mood and possibly send her into a depression, but it was probably best to break news like this to her on one of her better days. He followed the scent of fruit, spice, and pastry and found his mother shaking a sieve full of confectioner's sugar over the top of a cake.

"I hope you're getting ready to slice a piece of that for me."

She smiled ever so slightly and looked at him with her sad, tired eyes. They were a little brighter than usual today, but they still carried that whisper of melancholy she wore like a shadow. "I think we can share a slice or two. I was going to make some coffee."

Wade took a seat at the kitchen table and watched his mother work. She washed and cut a handful of fresh strawberries and sliced a couple of pieces of the cake from its center. Wade didn't like the ends and she didn't like them much either. She pulled out a bowl of homemade whipped cream from the refrigerator and lopped a heaping scoop onto each piece along with generous helpings of strawberries. She laid out placemats and silverware, sugar and cream. Once the pot was ready, she poured two cups of coffee and brought them to the table, and they sat together quietly for a bit and enjoyed their dessert.

"Mom, I have some news."

His mother set down her fork and refolded the napkin at her lap. She'd heard bad news from him plenty of times over the years. He figured she knew bad news was coming as soon as he walked into her kitchen.

"Tom Richardson died."

His mother let out a breath. "Was it the cancer? Or something else?"

The question didn't necessarily surprise him, and the meaning of it didn't escape him. He figured she'd entertained the possibility of ending things on her darkest days, when the pain and sorrow was so overwhelming that it took control of her body and mind and made her think about things she might not otherwise consider. She'd become a fierce critic of the convenient morality of self-righteous hypocrites and pompous know-it-alls. Wade heard her say on more than one occasion that she believed a man or woman had rights to their own reckoning. She certainly believed a man of the quality and character of Tom Richardson wouldn't find himself anywhere but the halls of Heaven, no matter the circumstances of his death, if Heaven existed at all. But he did worry how she'd take the news of the death of an old friend.

"He drove out to the inlet to watch the sunrise. The Ocean City police found him in his truck. The cancer finally got the best of him."

She nodded. "A peaceful death then," she said, stirring her coffee reflexively. "He was a fine man." She raised her cup in a toast.

"That he was," Wade agreed. He raised his cup and joined her for a drink.

"There is something else I wanted to tell you."

"Oh? What is it?" she asked guardedly.

"You remember Lily Parker? Emma's daughter?"

"Of course I remember Lily."

"Well, Tom had it in his mind that Lily would come to live with me and Ginny for a spell."

His mother smiled, which surprised him.

"Why are you smiling?" he asked her.

"I had a dream last night," she told him. "I was with your father, and we were walking on the beach. We were barefoot and our trousers were rolled up to our calves and thin sheets of water and salty foam washed up to us and covered our feet up to our ankles. We kept walking down to the pier, and we saw a man and a woman and a little girl. The girl was skipping in front of the couple, chasing the falling water, picking at shells on the sand. As we got closer, I realized it was you, Wade. It was you and Ginny and this beautiful, sparkling little girl. The three of you walked by us and smiled, and we smiled back. When I woke up, I thought maybe it was Chloe, but I think I was wrong about that. Maybe I just knew that another child would come into your life."

Chapter 5

Monday, October 12, 1987

WADE STOPPED TO PICK up a breakfast sandwich and coffee at one of his favorite spots on his way to work. Tilley's was one of those old-fashioned country stores that sold gas out front and groceries and other supplies inside. It also had a kitchen where three generations of Tilley women fashioned the tastiest biscuits, cornbread, grits, and fried chicken found anywhere in the county. Wade had been born and bred on Tilley food, and his earliest memories of the place were from trips he made with his grandfather to buy groceries and fill a basket with freshly baked biscuits and homemade apple butter for his grandmother. As soon as they were back in the truck, his grandfather would cut open a couple of biscuits and smear on a spoonful of the butter, and they would sit and eat them and giggle like little boys stealing girls' kisses on a warm summer night. "Don't tell your grammy we took 'em now, Wade," his grandfather would say to him. "This is our little secret."

The store was built from dark timber, with a wide-plank porch that held a couple of rocking chairs and a bench. There were vintage gasoline signs mounted on the front: a round white Texaco sign with a red star in the middle, an orange one with *Gulf* in blue letters, and another one with a picture of a scallop shell and *Shell Gasoline* spelled out in dark red. Wade walked in through the heavy wood doors and saw a familiar face at the counter. It was Reid Esham, son of the town doctor. He was talking to a young woman by the register. Reid said something to her, and the girl blushed and giggled. Then Reid slid something across the counter, a business card maybe, and turned to walk out of the shop. He stopped at the doorway.

"Sheriff Thompson, always a pleasure to see you."

Reid smiled and sounded sincere, but Wade knew it was the same bullshit he'd been shoveling since their teenage years.

"Morning, Reid. Give my regards to the doc."

"Will do."

Reid walked out of the store and climbed into a black BMW parked at one of the pumps. Wade watched him through a window. He was always surprised at how much he still disliked that man. Maybe it was the fights they got into after football games, when winning on the field wasn't enough to convince private school boys like Reid that their money and connections didn't mean anything to public school kids like Wade. Maybe it was the big houses on the water or the slick cars or the fancy boats. Or maybe in Reid's case, it was all the rumors about him having some sort of fling with Emma after high school.

After he arrived at the barracks, Wade stopped by his office to grab a folder off his desk, then continued to a meeting room at the end of the hallway. The three deputies already inside were standing near the front holding Styrofoam cups of coffee. They stopped their conversation and greeted Wade as he entered.

Wade walked to the lectern, flipped open his folder, and went over various pending investigations and matters with his deputies. An embezzlement at a church, a car theft in the lower part of the county, and a few other ordinary, minor complaints.

"Folks," he continued, "a family from Baltimore called the state police to report their daughter missing. She was working at the Sundancer Hotel at the beach and didn't show up for work. Her family hasn't been able to get in touch with her. State is handling the main investigation with the OCPD. We might be called in to assist, as necessary." Wade pulled some material from his folder and passed it out to the deputies. "Here's some information about the girl. Name, date of birth, approximate height and weight, and a picture."

It was a photograph of a young girl in a graduation gown. She was looking off to one side, out in the distance, responding to a cue from the photographer. She was pretty, with long, straight brown hair and a hopeful smile. The picture was at least two years old because the girl was now twenty and living on her own at the beach. Her name was Hillary Dent. The deputies took their time looking over the material and passed it back up to Wade.

"Last but not least," Wade continued, "we have Frank Brittingham."

Frank Brittingham had been a thorn in Wade's side from the time Wade joined the Sheriff's Department as a deputy almost fifteen years ago. Wade's team had responded to three domestic calls at the Brittingham house in the last year alone, though none of the complaints resulted in charges. It looked as if his wife had finally had enough.

"Vicky Brittingham has filed for a protective order and emergency petition for divorce. When we serve him, we need to be ready for anything."

He's been a son of a bitch since elementary school, Wade thought.

Lily sipped her coffee and picked at some toast in the quiet of her friend Teri's kitchen. Mr. and Mrs. Murray had left early for work, but Teri had agreed to stay home from school with Lily for a while, at least until Sheriff Thompson arrived. He'd called the day before to let her know he was going to pick her up to meet with Sam Marshall, her uncle's lawyer.

The Murrays had been kind hosts, but Lily knew this wasn't going to be a permanent arrangement, and the uncertainty of her situation amplified her despondence and anxiety. The waves of emotion hit her in random fits, a sudden rush of tears, an overwhelming sense of fear and resentment, and like angry chop on a sandbar, it bit at her unexpectedly from all sides and made her unsteady and unsure. She hoped this meeting with Mr. Marshall would bring some clarity to her situation and settle her a bit. But what was there to settle? Things were pretty damn clear. She was abandoned and alone and there was nothing that could change that now.

It also didn't help that the last month or so had been difficult for her for other reasons. She'd broken up with her boyfriend at the end of the summer and had a one-night stand with a boy she'd met at a party a few weeks later. She was drunk and he was down from Delaware and happened to be available. He had blonde hair and light gray eyes and muscles in his arms from paddling out in the surf almost every day. His name was Sean, and she knew she would never see him again. When girls are late, they usually don't sleep well until things resolve themselves, one way or another. Luckily, it was only a false alarm, but it fueled her stress in the weeks leading up to her uncle's death and led to a prolonged bout of insomnia.

When she did sleep, she had dreams that consumed her and left her drained. Last night's dream had been particularly vivid and intense. She was standing in a field of dry hay stalks at the edge of a vast pine forest. The sky was gray and threatened rain and she sought shelter among the trees. A trail emerged and she followed it toward the sound of running water. At the edge of the stream, she saw a woman, her hair unbound and flowing, wearing a white night dress that fell to her feet. Lily reached out and called to her. "Mom?" she asked. But as the woman turned to face her, Lily jolted awake, out of breath and soaked in sweat.

Lily was waiting on a rocking chair on the front porch when the sheriff arrived. She edged off the chair, peeling dried green paint chips off the seat with her, and walked to the driveway as he pulled in. He stopped the car and got out to greet her.

"Good morning, Lily," he said.

"Good morning, Sheriff Thompson," she replied somberly.

He walked around to the passenger door and opened it for her.

"Thank you, Sheriff," she said.

"You can call me Wade, Lily, like you used to when you were little."

She looked at him with a faint smile but didn't answer. They drove by the airport and after a few miles turned onto a small, backcountry road heading west. They travelled silently past harvested cornfields and chicken farms and acres of undeveloped land before they reached the outskirts of town. They turned off the road and onto a narrow street and drove past a cluster of small, nearly identical cottages that lined either side. They were modest structures, enough to hold a small family in relative comfort, all painted in a palette of pastels—light greens, blues, pinks, and yellows. Colorful flower boxes adorned the front railings, and gas-fueled lanterns lit their porches at night. It was obvious that the families who lived in these homes took pride in them.

When Lily was having a particularly tough day at school, she'd take the long route through this neighborhood on her way back home. The colors of the houses reminded her of springtime, and that usually brightened her mood a bit, but she didn't feel any of that on the drive today. Lily spotted a little boy holding a basketball at the corner of the upcoming intersection. She looked over when they stopped. The boy smiled and waved to her, and she waved back, and as soon as they drove past him, the boy dribbled the ball across the street like he was weaving through defenders on a basketball court. She felt a little something then.

Wade turned the patrol car at the next intersection onto Main Street and pulled into a parking spot behind a late nineteenth-century brick building that once housed the town's first bank. Wade and Lily exited the car, entered the building through a rear entrance, and walked up a flight of stairs to the second floor. There was a thick wooden door with an inset of amber-colored glass and the name *Sam A. Marshall, Esq.* stenciled in an arch in royal blue letters. They entered and found a woman sitting behind a desk in the waiting area readying a stapler at the corner of a stack of papers. She gripped the stapler together, but the papers didn't bind. She let out a huff of exasperation, mumbled under her breath, and returned paper and stapler back to the desk. When she looked up, curls of red hair shot off her forehead like coiled springs.

"I don't know what I'm going to do with that man, Wade. I've about had it with him," the woman said as she rose from her seat.

"Oh, Merilee, you know he can't function without you," he replied.

"We both know you're right about that," she said, nodding to emphasize her agreement.

Merilee emerged from behind the desk and hobbled toward them. Her walk reminded Lily of a duck she once kept as a pet on her uncle's farm. He was a little overweight and had lost his left foot, and he waddled around the yard on his little stump. She'd called him Pegleg.

Merilee came over to them and took Lily's hand in hers. "Hello sweet girl, you must be Lily Parker."

"Yes, ma'am."

Merilee placed her other hand on top of Lily's and pulled it to her chest. "I was so sorry to hear about your uncle, dear," she said, now patting the back of Lily's hand. "He was an old acquaintance." Merilee finally released Lily's hand. "Let me take you in to see Sam."

There was an interior office in the back corner of the room. Merilee knocked on the door and propped it open. "Sam," she announced, "Sheriff Thompson and Lily Parker are here for you."

"C'mon in," said the voice inside.

Sam was standing behind a desk littered with stacks of files and papers. He had both hands balled in fists at his hips, with a pair of spectacles poking out of the grip in his left. Two puffs of white hair drifted out from either side of his otherwise bald head like billows of smoke from the stacks of an ocean liner. A lit cigar smoldered in a ceramic ashtray, and Lily considered how quickly the room would be engulfed in flames should an errant ash land anywhere on that desk.

"Please sit," he said, and motioned Lily and Wade to the two empty chairs in front of him. Merilee closed the door behind them.

Sam sat down in the large leather chair behind his desk. He took a moment to clean off his glasses with a cloth and then placed them at the end of his nose. Lily was uneasy. She felt lost, like she was drifting helplessly in a world that wasn't hers, and all she could think of was that there was nothing left, at least nothing that mattered. Once her uncle died, the world she'd known had ended.

"Lily, I am sorry to see you under such difficult circumstances," he began. "Your uncle and I had met several times over the last half a year to ensure that we had an orderly disposition of his property and that all arrangements for your care had been finalized, or almost finalized, that is." He raised his eyebrows and peeked over the spectacles at both Lily and Wade. "We'll get into the details in a bit, Lily, but rest assured you are the sole beneficiary of Tom's estate. You will inherit all his property and belongings and you are entitled to the proceeds from his life insurance policies, which are quite significant."

Sam leaned forward in his seat, resting his forearms on the desktop and searching Lily for her reaction. Wade shifted in his chair and turned toward her. Lily was unmoved. Sam reclined and started again.

"All of his property, et cetera, has been placed in a trust to be held for your benefit and to be disbursed to you over time until you reach twenty-five years of age, at which time you will receive full custody and control of all the assets. I have been appointed to serve as the trustee for this trust and will work with you to manage the assets and to provide you with the income and support you need until you come of age."

"But what am I going to do?" Lily erupted. The sadness gathered in pools in her wide, brown eyes. "What am I going to do, Mr. Marshall?" she asked with a catch in her throat. "I don't have anyone anymore. I have lost everyone. What am I going to do?" she asked again, emphasizing every word, but this time turning to Wade.

Sam got up from behind the desk and walked to the door. He opened it and asked Merilee to bring in some water. Lily could hear Merilee's uneven steps as she shuffled away and, within a minute, she returned with a pitcher of ice water and three glasses. Sam poured a glass for Lily and handed it to her. Lily took a few slow sips and placed the glass on a small table next to her.

"Well," Sam said, "your uncle provided me with instructions to bring the two of you together to discuss that specific question." He paused and began again. "Your uncle had an idea that Wade here would serve as your guardian and that you would live with him. If you and Wade agreed, of course."

Sam and Lily both turned to Wade. His face revealed nothing, which Lily perceived as rejection. She didn't much blame him. They hardly knew each other anymore, after all. Then she heard Wade's unshaken voice rise above her.

"My wife and I would love to have you in our home, Lily. For as long as you want or need."

Lily could hear the sincerity in his voice. It was unforced and sounded as if it were a certainty. And when she looked up and into the deep blue of the sheriff's eyes, she recognized the young man she once knew from the house next door to her grandmother's, and she knew he meant every word.

After the meeting, Wade offered to take Lily to lunch, but Lily had no appetite. She leaned against the passenger window of Wade's car, trying to find comfort in the coolness of the glass. Wade turned down another road, a different route from their initial trip, and suddenly they were driving through a swamp and under a canopy of cypress trees. Ferns and spikerush, buttonbush and wax myrtle, and various species of orchids rooted within the trees and splashed them in pinks, greens, and purples. The waters of the swamp rarely reached the road, but the cypress trees still crept to the road's edges, and they towered above it to create a tunnel of branches and leaves. The light, shadows, and colors danced over them like a kaleidoscope.

"Is there anything I can do for you right now?" Wade asked.

She barely heard the question. "No thank you," she answered in a clip.

They exited the swamp and the wall of trees to an explosion of sunlight that shook her out of her trance. Her emotions were still raw. She was agitated, sad, and tired.

"We should have talked about this a long time ago," she said, angrily. "Maybe I didn't want to, but he should have tried harder. I feel like he shut me out."

"I think he was trying to protect you," Wade offered.

Lily considered that possibility. Everything her uncle did was for her, but she was unconvinced. Wade tried again.

"I think he was hoping he would go quick in the end. That he'd know the time was upon him and he could take care of all the details and then be gone. And, you know, he almost pulled it off."

"What do you mean?" she asked.

"I guess you didn't know." Wade hesitated. "I met with him on Friday. He told me he wanted you to live with us. Me and Ginny. I think he was going to give it a couple of days and get us all together to talk about it."

Lily felt betrayed. He'd mentioned something about it, sure, but it didn't register as real. He'd framed it as a hypothetical. "You've got people who'd look after you," he'd said. "The Thompsons would do it, I bet," is how he'd put it. She knew he was meeting with Wade, but she didn't know it was about living with the Thompsons. Her uncle was ready to give her away to people she hardly knew, without hardly a discussion.

"Maybe he knew exactly what he was doing," Wade continued. "Rip away the band aid, expose the wound and, hopefully, let it heal quickly."

Lily wasn't persuaded, and now she was more than just angry. She was frustrated and exhausted with all of it. "I'm not sure these wounds heal," she said.

Her words sounded as bitter as they tasted on her tongue. She was suffering. Suffering from the loss of her Uncle Tom and her Aunt Maggie, her grandmother and grandfather, and her mother. The pain was born somewhere deep inside her the day her mother disappeared. It multiplied with every lost relative. It festered inside her for years and now, with her last known relative dead and gone, it had consumed her. Bitter. That's what she was now.

"All wounds heal," he said.

She turned to him, ready to scream at him for his callousness, but she stopped herself. She noticed a deep sadness in his eyes and realized he was mourning, too. For her uncle maybe, and maybe for someone else.

"Some wounds take longer to heal," he continued. "Some of them you always feel. They might leave a scar or hurt a little, even a long time after. Sometimes pain is the ultimate memory."

Images of her life ran through her mind, snapshots set in motion by some spinning force of nature. There were days in the park with her grandparents. Trips to the beach with her aunt and uncle. Recess in the elementary school playground with her friends. Holding hands with her ex-boyfriend Jake. Lying on a blanket next to the surfer she knew for just that one night. Then she saw her mother. Reflections of her, at least, from photographs and those dreams. A smile she never really saw. A hug she never felt. A kiss she never received. Faster and faster they spun, a dizzying recall of a story with the same ending. Each memory provided a bit of happiness but was always accompanied by loss and pain.

"Sheriff," she started, "why would you be so quick to take me in? You hardly know me."

Wade turned his eyes off the road for a moment to look at her and then looked back out through the windshield and into the distance.

"I've known your family my whole life. Your mother was my best friend. I loved her like a sister. I still love her. And that means I love you too."

A tear rolled down her cheek. She didn't move to wipe it away. "I've always had people who loved me. Everyone who loves me dies."

Chapter 6

Wednesday, October 14, 1987

I T WAS FINALLY STARTING to look and feel like autumn. The leaves were turning and there was a crispness in the air that made breathing free and easy. Wade had the windows rolled down and the music turned up, Allman Brothers and Credence and Cream. He was taking the long way back from business in the western part of the county, driving quiet country roads, trying to clear his head. But Lily was on his mind, and so was her mother. He loosened his grip on the steering wheel and rubbed his thumb over the small scar on his palm. He swore he could still feel the sting of the cut, as if it were made just minutes ago.

Tom's funeral was scheduled for Friday. Lily would be moving in after that, and he wondered whether he could handle the emotion of it all, having Emma's girl living under his roof, seeing her every day, reminding him of what was missing. Emma had been gone seventeen years, disappeared off the face of the earth like she'd never been there in the first place. Wade reached under his collar and hooked the chain around his neck. His arrowhead was still with him. But where was hers? Where was she?

Wade had gone through the file a hundred times or more. There was nothing there, at least nothing he could see. Emma's car was found on a stretch of Carey Road that ran for about two miles through cornfields, pastures, and woods comprising parts of William Peterson's property. It was Mr. Peterson who discovered Emma's

Impala, unmarked and undamaged, next to an abandoned tobacco shed off the side of the road. There were no skid marks or tire
tracks or anything else to indicate loss of control or mechanical
failure. It appeared as if the car had purposely been pulled over
and parked. There were no tire treads or signs of any other vehicle,
and no footprints or evidence of Emma or anyone else. Eugene
Willis was the sheriff in those parts at the time, and he was the
one in charge of the investigation. But Wade could hardly call it
that. It was a cursory inquiry, just a few interviews really, before
Sheriff Willis ran out of ideas and interest. He had no solid leads
and little talent for the real police work necessary to chase down
and solve a case like that. The investigation sputtered to a halt.

The way his mother told it, the rumors started right away.
The matrons of the First Presbyterian Church pulled up their
elbow-length white gloves and adjusted their best church hats
and spoke in hushed whispers around the refreshment table. The
men at the American Legion traded stories between rounds of
beer and whiskey and hands of poker. People in these parts didn't
disappear unless they wanted to. When pressed, they'd spit out
something about running off to San Francisco or Greenwich
Village or some other hippie city to smoke pot, listen to music,
and live a life without care or responsibility. But Wade knew then
and now there was no way Emma would ever leave her little girl.

The radio cracked and a voice cut in, dispatch calling him to a crime
scene at the beach on Assateague Island. By the time Wade arrived,
there were three jurisdictions' worth of police cruisers in the parking
lot, along with a fire rescue truck and the medical examiner's van.
One of the local TV stations out of Salisbury also beat Wade to the
scene and had set up a remote shoot on the side of the road outside

the parking lot entrance. A park ranger manning the gate lifted it for Wade's vehicle as it approached.

Wade found one of his deputies standing with a state trooper. "What's going on, Garrett?"

Garrett Johnson's large hands were hitched into his waistband at the thumbs, his uniform stretched thin at the buttons, barely containing his thick frame. He shifted uncomfortably. "A couple of birdwatchers found the girl about a half mile up the beach."

"The girl?" Wade asked.

"The missing girl, Sheriff."

Wade started off for the trail, which wrapped around a portion of the marsh and rose above the brush and small trees into the dunes near the beach. This was familiar territory for Wade, who as a teenager used to come out to the state park with his brother or his friends, sometimes by car but usually by boat, to fish and swim or hang out. After a couple of minutes, Wade reached the beach. Small waves crashed in whispers and shot out sprays of foam. A cluster of sanderlings bustled in and out of the incoming and receding water, searching for their next meal in the shallow pools that gathered along the beach, unconcerned with Wade's approach. Wade turned north and kept walking, passing a ranger and then a couple of troopers.

"That's as bad as I've ever seen," he heard one of them say.

Another deputy met him about a hundred yards out. It was Hank Peters, tall and skinny with a sharp nose and colorless complexion, as if Death himself was greeting Wade at the scene.

"A husband and wife were taking pictures up yonder," Peters told him, pointing back with his thumb to a cluster of dunes rising above them. "They spotted something and came down to take a closer look."

They walked together for that last stretch and stood silently for a moment as they confronted the horrific sight in front of them. She barely resembled the girl in the graduation picture.

"Who would do something like that?" Peters whispered.

The girl's body was propped up against the trunk of a fallen tree that had been ripped from its roots and dropped with the tide. She was dressed in a short, see-through white nightgown, her hands folded in front of her, holding a cluster of small, yellow flowers. A crown of twisted vines and branches sat on her matted brown hair. The nightgown blew open with each puff of wind, exposing her otherwise naked body. There was bruising around her neck and ligature marks around her wrists, but there were no other wounds visible except for a small cut under each closed eye. A trail of dried blood ran from each of those cuts down to her chin.

"This is some sick shit." Wade recognized the voice. It was Rick Hampton, a state police detective out of their Criminal Investigations Bureau. Wade and Rick had worked a few cases together and had a good relationship.

Wade nodded. "You guys find anything?"

"A lot of sand," Rick said.

Wade looked out over the water. "Doesn't look like this is where it happened."

"That's our thinking, too," Rick answered.

"Must have brought her in by boat, probably a small one, as the tide was rising," Wade said. "They set her against the tree, and when the water came in it made them invisible."

"Makes sense," Rick said. "I'll leave boats and tides to the experts."

Rick's partner had walked up behind them. "We're not jumping to any conclusions," he told them.

Ken Meehan was nothing like Rick. He was abrasive and confrontational, especially where Wade was concerned. The two of them had been battling each other all the way back to their high school days. He was another one of those entitled private school kids. Ran around with Reid Esham and a few other of Wade's favorites from back in the day.

Wade surveyed all the activity. There were twenty or so troopers, detectives, police, and rangers scurrying about and another dozen or so from the rescue squad and medical examiner's office. It was a circus. This was a state police matter. He wasn't needed here.

"It looks like you guys have this in hand," he said. "Why'd you call us down here anyway?"

"Professional courtesy?" Ken quipped.

Wade didn't bite. "I'll round up my people and leave you to it, then."

Wade walked back with Peters. The sun was dropping lower in the western sky and had painted waves of purple and red as it fell behind a line of clouds right above the dunes. A shorebird darted in front of them, her wings angled back to catch the breeze. She shifted slightly and changed direction quickly, cutting across the sky and disappearing behind the dunes. Wade felt the cold edges of the arrowhead at his chest and thought back to one of his first calls as a deputy. They'd found a dead girl resting against a post under the Ocean City pier, and all she was wearing was a short, white dress.

Chapter 7

1963

WADE HAD A BEACH towel rolled under his arm and was heading out the front door when his mother called to him.

"Wade, honey, you forgot your lunch."

He stopped, turned on his heels, and walked back to his mother, who was holding a brown paper bag out in front of her. He grabbed the bag, kissed her cheek, and started out the door again to Emma's house.

"Be careful in the water," she told him.

His mother would always warn him about the water. "Watch out for rip currents" or "Wait an hour after you eat." But Wade had spent his whole life in and around the water. There were countless times jumping off his brother's boat in the bay and swimming out to sandbars or bodysurfing in the ocean. He was such a strong swimmer that he'd already planned to take the beach patrol test as soon as he turned sixteen. He'd been practicing holding his breath every night for the last year and was up to almost two minutes. He knew the ocean was a different animal and could be dangerous.

Wade found Emma's father at the top of their driveway loading his beige 1958 Ford Country Squire Wagon with beach supplies. That station wagon suited Mr. Parker's personality. Like Mr. Parker, it wasn't flashy. It was a sensible vehicle that he could use on the weekends to travel to parks and beaches and mountains with his most important people, which often included Wade. On the weekdays,

Mr. Parker shed the wagon for a red 1952 Chevrolet pickup truck that he used for his business, a feed and supply store he owned. The truck reflected this other side of Mr. Parker. It was beginning to show the wear from its hard work. The paint was fading, and it had some dings, dents, and rust, but it was dependable, resilient, and trustworthy—characteristics Wade had grown to value and appreciate from being lucky enough to be around men like Mr. Parker and his own father.

"You need some help?" Wade asked him.

"I think I have everything in here now," Mr. Parker replied. "The ladies tend to overpack on occasion, you know."

Wade chuckled. "You better not let them hear you say that."

"You're right about that," Mr. Parker responded with a serious look.

Wade dropped his sandwich bag and towel into the back seat of the wagon through an open window. When he looked back up, he saw Emma walking out of the house with her mother. Wade tried not to stare, but it was impossible. The older Emma got the more beautiful he found her. She was wearing a see-through white cover-up that fell over a pair of blue shorts and landed a couple of inches above her knees. Under it, a red, one-piece bathing suit hugged her body. Her lips were painted with a shiny pink gloss, and when the sun hit them, they flashed at him like the beacon of a lighthouse.

Emma caught him looking at her and tried to casually play it off. "Oh. Hey, Wade."

Things had changed between them in the last few years. They weren't little kids anymore, and a tension had developed. Wade was a reluctant bit player in Emma's world. He still wanted badly to be more than her friend, but that was all he was to her. Wade had hoped her feelings for him would change over time, but more and more it looked like that was all he'd ever be. Emma was spreading her wings and finding new friends and companions, including a boy or two in junior high that he heard her call her boyfriend. Wade had learned to handle the status quo, but this new trajectory worried him, and he found himself resenting her a bit.

"Hey, Emma," he replied, breaking his gaze on her. "Hello, Mrs. Parker."

"Good morning, Wade," Mrs. Parker called back. "What a beautiful day."

Wade looked up into a clear, blue sky.

"Ben," Mrs. Parker barked out to her husband, "let's get going before all the tourists take the good spots."

Ocean City was a few minutes from the house, unless the draw was up on the bridge or the tourist traffic was thick going in. Mr. Parker turned the wagon onto the main road leading into the island, which was clear through the next light and onto the bridge. They rode with the windows down, the wagon's tires buzzing like a swarm of bees when they traveled across the steel grates of the draw.

A few small boats passed under the bridge, heading to the ocean. Wade thought about his brother, who was already far out to sea working as a deckhand on a charter. The ocean was still a little rough from a passing storm, which had finally moved through and was now on its way back across the Atlantic. The offshore waters were still unsettled, though, and most charters out of the harbor remained docked. A few businessmen from D.C. were determined to get out for some tuna fishing and paid handsomely to convince Paul's boss to take them to one of the canyons where the fish were supposedly running. Paul laughed about it with Wade the night before.

"We aren't going to need any bait tomorrow," his brother had joked. "Those boys will be hanging over the rails, chumming the water with their breakfast and begging us to come back to land before we even make it to the canyon."

The road bottlenecked a bit as they pulled off the bridge and turned on the avenue heading north up the beach. There were families in sedans and station wagons and younger people riding in convertibles and coupes. The avenue was lined on either side with three- and four-story cottages, mostly built in the twenties and thirties. They held residences and rooms for rent but also restaurants and shops. There were some bigger buildings of the same vintage where, along with the grand, old oceanfront hotels on the boardwalk, the wealthy and elite used to stay when vacationing in town. Although still filled in the summers, they were an afterthought now and less sought out than the new, modern hotels and motels that were springing up to replace the relics.

They drove to a municipal lot on Seventh Street and parked the car. Wade gathered his bag and towel and walked around the back of the wagon to Mr. Parker, who handed him two yellow, aluminum-framed, fold-out beach chairs. Emma got out of the car and Wade caught himself staring again. What was it about her today that had him so wound up? One of the chairs unfurled itself, like an angry viper striking out at prey, and caught Wade in the shin. He let out a grunt, and then he heard a laugh from Emma. He ignored it and headed toward the beach.

Wade carried his load through a rush of people walking along the boardwalk and then down to the sand. He set down the chairs in an empty spot near the water a few feet from a lifeguard stand. The stand was a white, wooden tower, about eight feet tall, built with a seat and platform at the top. The lifeguard manning it was signaling to another lifeguard about a hundred yards away. Semaphore. He flashed his signal flags up and down, in and out. The fabric snapped as it ripped through the air and slapped against the guard's body.

Wade was eager to jump in the water, but he waited for the Parkers so he could help set up their spot. Mrs. Parker and Emma made their way down, each carrying a beach bag with towels, books, and lotions. Mr. Parker followed closely behind them, lugging a large and heavy-looking cooler that resembled a picnic basket. Wade hustled to Mr. Parker, grabbed one of the arms of the cooler, and helped him haul it down. After they set up the chairs and laid out a blanket, Mr. Parker decided to walk back up to a beach stand near the boardwalk to rent an umbrella for the day.

Mrs. Parker pulled out a magazine from her bag and dropped herself into one of the beach chairs. Emma shed her cover-up and then her shorts, which she pulled down her legs with a shake and a wiggle at her waist. Wade pretended not to see her, but he had a side eye on her the whole time. She picked a book out of her bag and a cold bottle of Mountain Dew from the cooler and then sat down on the blanket.

Wade emptied the contents of his paper bag into the cooler and set his towel down next to Emma. He took off his shirt and looked back out over the ocean. The waves were crashing hard on the beach and spit out great chunks of foam when they slapped against the sand. Once the waves hit, the water receded quickly and built back up into another wave that slapped itself down again. It didn't look too bad to a novice, but Wade knew a wave like that could take you down and break your neck, even if it was only chest high.

Wade noticed Emma peeking at him over her sunglasses. It wasn't the first time she'd seen him without a shirt, but this time maybe she'd noticed how broad his shoulders had become, or how muscles now ripped up his back and down his sides and in his arms, or how he'd lost that scrawny, weak-looking chest he'd had as a little boy. Working the farm with his father had had its benefits. When he wasn't throwing around bags of seed and loading bales of hay, he was punching out dozens of push-ups, sit-ups, and pull-ups to get himself ready for football tryouts. He saw Emma rub the scar on her palm against the cool glass of her soda bottle.

"You're still wearing it?" she asked him.

He felt the arrowhead at his chest. "Never take it off."

He turned and ran to the ocean and dove through a cresting wave. The Atlantic kept its chill, even in July, but it was refreshing. Wade flipped on his back and then turned again and swam out past the breakers. There was a strong current pulling him down shore, and it carried him almost a block before he turned toward land to swim back in. Swells rolled through him, and he looked back to see a large wave picking up over the horizon. He swam with it. The wave carried him up and pitched him forward, like the giant hand of a sea creature. The wave's face peaked and broke behind him. Still angry, it curled its lip and chased him down, covering him in a perfect cylinder. He was riding in the wave's mouth for a fraction of a second before it chewed him up and spit him toward the shore. As he barrel rolled in flight, he caught the blue of the sky and flashes of color from the bathing suits and beach umbrellas on shore before hitting the ground hard. The wave's lip followed him and crashed heavy into his midsection, taking his breath away. He rolled a few more times in the sand and foam before coming to rest at the feet of a little boy holding the hand of his mother. The boy looked down at Wade and then back up at his mother.

"Momma, is that boy dead?" the boy asked.

"No, baby," his mother replied, "but that's why you have to be careful in the ocean."

Wade swore the woman took the shape of his mother at that moment, but it was probably his spinning head and the sand in his eyes. He didn't care. Wiping out was part of the thrill, and it was a perfect ride right up until the end. Wade got to his hands and knees and took a few deep breaths. He stood up and jumped back in the water between waves to wash the sand from his hair and out of his shorts, and then he jogged back to Emma and her parents. Emma rose to meet him.

"Hey," she said, punching him in the side to grab his attention, or to check out his muscles, he hoped. "Let's go to Franco's. Sandy said she was working today."

Wade dried himself off and threw his towel back on the blanket. He snatched one of his orange sodas from the cooler and opened it before they set off for the boardwalk. It wasn't a long walk. Just a couple of blocks north from their spot on the beach. The smell of crust, sauce, and cheese overwhelmed Wade as they approached the pizza shop. His stomach growled, and he knew the ham sandwiches his mother packed for him wouldn't be enough to satisfy his hunger. He reached into the buttoned back pocket of his swim trunks and pulled out a wet one-dollar bill. He caught the attention of the young girl behind the register at the service window.

"Hello, Wade." It was Sophia Franco, the oldest of the shop owner's three daughters. Sophia and her sisters were true beauties like their mother. All the Franco girls had thick black hair and flawless golden-brown skin. They also matured quickly, and the boys at the high school were fond of calling the oldest of the Franco girls Sophia Loren, after the beautiful and voluptuous Italian actress.

"Oh, hello Sophia." Wade was surprised that she even knew who he was, although she was one of his brother Paul's classmates at school.

"Can I get you something?" she asked him.

"Uh," Wade stuttered. "Uh, yes, thanks. Can I get a slice of cheese pizza, please?" Wade was caught off guard by his reaction to her, particularly now, in front of Emma.

"Sure," she said, with a big smile that revealed her perfect white teeth. She pulled a piece from the pie in the warmer, placed it on a white paper plate, and handed it to Wade. Wade held out the dollar bill, but she refused it.

"It's on me," she said. "Tell your brother I said hi." She smiled again and turned to help another customer.

Wade stood motionless for a moment before a nudge from Emma stirred him awake.

"Let's go inside and look for Sandy, lover boy."

He was embarrassed but tried not to let on. They walked in and scanned the dining room for Sandy, who emerged from the kitchen holding a serving tray full of food. She saw them and nodded toward a booth in the corner. Wade and Emma walked over and took a seat to wait for her. Sandy dropped off the plates and hurried over to them.

"I can't talk for long," she said. "How's the water?"

"It's a little rough," Emma answered with a coy look at Wade.

Wade didn't know she'd seen his wipeout.

Sandy was already on to another thought. "Hey," she said, grabbing Emma's wrist with a sudden enthusiasm. "Guess who came by earlier and asked about you?"

"Who?" Emma replied suspiciously, but with a touch of curiosity.

"Brad Wilkerson," Sandy said, excitedly.

That got Wade's attention. He snuck a glance to see Emma's reaction, but she wasn't about to give up anything with Wade sitting there.

"He's the best-looking boy in the sophomore class," Sandy added eagerly. "You always get the best ones after you, Emma." She looked right at Wade when she said it. Maybe she meant it as a compliment, but that's not the way Wade took it.

Emma changed the subject, asking Sandy something about going shopping, but Wade wasn't paying much attention. He'd suddenly realized that his crush on Emma had become some kind of joke among his friends and that all of them were laughing at him. An anger swept over him, overwhelming even his jealousy. He got up abruptly, leaving Emma and Sandy at the table. They might've called after him, but if they had, he didn't hear or care. He kept walking past all the people and to the water and swam up the shore against the current.

Chapter 8

Friday, October 16, 1987

T HEY HELD TOM RICHARDSON's funeral at the First Presbyterian Church. Lily sat in the front pew with Teri Murray
and a few of her other girlfriends. All she had to do was get dressed
and show up. Mr. Marshall and Merilee were responsible for all the
arrangements. Lily felt a pang of guilt. Her uncle had sacrificed so
much for her, and she felt like she'd already forsaken him in death.

The church was packed. Tom Richardson had a lot of friends,
more than Lily remembered ever seeing, or maybe she just didn't
notice at the time. Several people got up to memorialize her uncle. A
few rambled about the *good ole days*, but others were more poignant.
Mr. Marshall followed a funny story about her uncle with a more
sentimental one about how her aunt and uncle met. Dr. Esham,
who'd delivered Lily and just about every other person in the church
under forty-five years old, told them about how Tom had shown up
at the hospital for Lily's birth and handed out cigars to everyone in
the waiting room like it was his own daughter who'd been born. That
one tore her up. The tears fell in a stream.

The reception was held in the church hall immediately after the
ceremony. She'd barely said more than a few words to anyone that
morning, including Wade and Ginny, but there they were, standing
right next to her in the receiving line. Dozens of older folks lined up
first to greet Lily and offer their condolences. She'd never met many
of them—her uncle's old classmates, friends, business acquaintances.

They all had nice things to say. *What a good man. Maggie and Tom were a lovely couple. He's going to be missed.* Lily was weary and barely heard any of it.

She happened to look up from a handshake and noticed the sheriff's brother standing near the end of the line with a cup of lemonade in his hand, waiting for the procession of well-wishers to end so he could pass along his regards and leave the scene. Lily hadn't seen him in a very long time, but she recognized him still. While he resembled his younger brother, he had harder features, rougher around the edges. And he looked uncomfortable, a little lost and out of place.

Dr. Esham was next in line. He reached out and took Lily's hand. "I'm so sorry for your loss, dear. It's always difficult to lose a loved one like that. He fought a long battle. I hope he found some peace in the end, and I hope you will too."

Dr. Esham looked straight into her eyes, which was more than some had the courage to do. Lily appreciated that. She assumed it was all the practice he'd had reassuring and comforting patients in their most trying times. He tapped the shoulder of the man standing next to him.

"My son is with me today."

Lily peered up at him. He was a little taller than his father, but they shared similar features, especially in the face and the eyes. Though the elder Esham was worn down a bit, each had well-defined cheekbones and a prominent chin. The younger Esham was closer in age to Wade and Ginny. He had dark, reddish-brown hair that was parted to the side and slicked back. He was dressed in a tailored charcoal suit that cut tight against his frame.

"Thank you for coming, Mr. Esham," she said.

"That's my father's name," he said with a smile, pointing over to the elder Esham, who was at the refreshment table engaged in an animated conversation with Mr. Marshall and Merilee. "You can call me Reid."

"Did you know my uncle?" she asked him.

"Only by reputation. I've heard nothing but good things about him. My father says he was a fine man."

"He was. Thank you."

"I'm sorry for your loss." He nodded at Wade and Ginny without speaking to them, then walked away to meet his father.

Lily needed a cup of lemonade herself, but she knew others were waiting to greet her. She looked toward the end of the line to see how many people were left and spotted Paul Thompson again. He was staring at the younger Esham. The muscles in his face were pulled tight and there was something behind his eyes that conveyed an unspoken anger. The empty cup was crushed in his fist. Paul broke his glare and turned to see Lily looking right at him. His face softened and he slipped out of line and into a hallway at the back of the church.

Lily wondered why Reid Esham evoked such a visceral reaction from him. She was getting ready to say something about it to Wade but was interrupted.

"Hey, Lily."

It was Holly Mitchell. Lily had seen her in the church earlier and had been a little surprised she'd shown up at all until she remembered that their mothers had been good friends growing up.

"Oh, Holly," she said. "Sorry, I was lost there for a second."

"That's okay." Holly waited a few beats. "Are you going back to school on Monday?"

"Yeah," Lily replied. "I need to get back. I've already missed a couple of tests. I don't want to fall too far behind."

"I think the teachers will understand," Holly reassured her. "Look, if you need anything, or need to talk to someone, let me know."

"Oh, thanks," Lily said, a little surprised that Holly would make that kind of offer. While they were cordial and had known each other since elementary school, they'd drifted apart since then and no longer considered each other friends. Lily assumed Holly's mother had put her up to it.

"You know, our moms were really good friends. Maybe we should hang out a little again. Don't you think?" Holly asked, reinforcing Lily's suspicions.

"That would be nice," Lily said, graciously. It was good of Holly to at least try, Lily thought, and there was a sincerity in the offer, even if there might be some coercion at play.

"Great." Holly puffed out a breath. "Well, I guess I'll see you on Monday," she said, then scooted off to find her parents.

Afterward, Wade, Ginny, and Mr. Marshall accompanied Lily to the cemetery. They said a prayer and placed flowers on the freshly filled grave. Her uncle was lying with her Aunt Maggie now, in a plot next to Lily's grandparents. They were all together again.

Those were better times, for sure, when they were together. She remembered visits to her aunt and uncle's farm, long ago, when she was barely out of diapers. Her grandparents would bring her over for Sunday supper. Aunt Maggie would make a whole ham or roast, served with vegetables from her garden, and homemade buttermilk biscuits. Her grandmother would bring her famous pound cake—*a county fair award winner*, as she was apt to remind them—and fresh strawberries she bought from the produce stand down the road. Sometimes she would bring a cherry or apple pie. After the meal, Lily would tug on her uncle's shirt and beg him to let her feed the animals.

He would take her by the hand and lead her through the kitchen, out the back door, and onto the back porch, where her aunt and uncle kept a pair of small yellow rubber rainboots just for her. He would help her slide them on and they would walk together to a pen a few yards from the house that held the younger animals. Usually, this included some chicks, ducklings, baby goats, and lambs. Back then, the farm was still thriving. There was so much life and happiness. Now, the pen was empty, and the fence and posts that circled the plot had fallen and lay in a tangle on the ground. The warmth of the memory slipped away, and Lily started to cry. She felt an arm on her shoulder. It was Ginny, who pulled her close.

Lily stared at the headstone next to her grandfather's, the one for her mother, presumed dead even though her body was never found. Her whole family was there in front of her, and she wondered when she would fill the empty spot next to her mother.

When they returned home, Wade dressed in his uniform and went to the sheriff's office to pick up Deputy Johnson. Wade didn't feel much like working. He'd hid his emotions the best he could through the service and at the reception, trying to stay strong for Lily, but he was unprepared for the trip to the cemetery. Seeing Emma's gravestone shook him, but he held it in until he left the house and got into his car. It was the first time he'd cried since he lost his daughter.

The district court had granted a protective order and issued a summons against Frank Brittingham. This afternoon they'd serve him with those papers and hope he would accept them peacefully. Wade was not optimistic. Frank had led a tough life, and he did his best to make the rest of the world as miserable as he was, to try and even things out. Wade wanted to be there in case things went bad.

Wade knew Frank's story. His father was a drunk who beat his son and his wife on most days for sport, so Frank enlisted in the Navy the day after he graduated high school to escape him. He came back home a few months later, dishonorably discharged. His return to the house was volatile. Frank and his father argued and fought, so he packed up again and this time just disappeared. About a year later, both his parents were dead. Frank's mother had shot and killed his father and then turned the gun on herself. Somehow, word got to Frank, and he reappeared in time to bury his parents and take over the house. He was only twenty years old.

Frank got a job at one of the seafood plants near the harbor and made enough money to scrape out a living. He met Vicky a short time later at the Sink or Swim, a locals' bar at the marina frequented by harbor workers, fisherman, and underage high school kids, among others. Frank took Vicky home and got her pregnant. She moved in with him out of convenience, they had a son, Kevin, and the family tradition of alcohol and violence continued.

Wade and Deputy Johnson pulled onto the small two-lane road heading south past the harbor. The houses in this part of the county were mostly small, shack-like structures in various stages of disrepair. Wade eased his vehicle off to the side of the road and stopped in front of Frank's. Frank was sitting in a lawn chair on the front porch, eyeing the men intently as they made their approach. He took a swig from a bottle of Miller Lite in his right hand and a drag from a Marlboro in his left.

"Hello, Sheriff." He had a thick Eastern Shore accent, which was more prominent with his drunken slur. "I see you brought your muscle with you." He tipped the bottle in Deputy Johnson's direction.

Wade slowed as he approached the stairs leading to the porch and stopped short. Johnson stood off to the side and behind him. Wade took a quick look around the property and then tried to look through the screen door and into the house. The screen was rusted and thick with grime. A shotgun was leaning against an outcropping of wood next to the front door.

"I already talked to the other boys about that girl they found out at Assateague," Frank said. "You offer a pretty girl one drink to make your wife jealous, and all of a sudden you're a murder suspect."

Wade was surprised to hear that piece of information and took a second to process it. "We're not here about that, Frank," Wade said, after a few seconds.

"Well, that's good. Maybe they should be talking to your brother anyway. He was there too."

Wade thought Frank might've been lying to provoke him, but the sudden sobriety in Frank's voice when he said it convinced Wade it was probably true. Paul was a frequent patron of the Sink or Swim. If the girl was there having a drink, chances were good that either Frank or Paul, or both, would be there too. Wade didn't think much of it. Just a coincidence.

"Is Kevin here, Frank?" Wade asked.

"He's staying with his cousin. I haven't seen him for a couple of days."

"Anyone else around?"

"I don't know, Wade. Is anyone else around?" Frank answered sarcastically, having witnessed Wade's survey of the property.

"Do you know why we're here, Frank?" Wade asked him.

Frank squinted his eyes a bit before responding. "Other than you being a self-righteous prick?"

Wade let the comment roll off him. He waved the documents in front of him. "I have some papers for you."

Frank leaned forward in his chair and flashed a mischievous grin. "Is that a marriage proposal?" he joked. "Where's my engagement ring?"

Wade propped one foot on the first step leading to the porch and rested his right hand on his holstered revolver, out of habit more than anything. Frank eyed him and leaned back in the chair.

"I reject your proposal, Wade Thompson," he said with a dismissive wave of his hand. "Now get off my property. Both of you."

"I can't do that, Frank," Wade told him. "I'm coming up there and handing these to you. And then we'll be on our way."

Frank snickered. "What did that lying bitch wife of mine say and do this time? Did she tell you I was mean? That I drink too much?" Frank tipped the bottle to his lips and emptied it. "Nah. You wouldn't be here for that. She's been spinnin' a wife-beatin' story down at the bar from what I've been hearing. Is that what this is about?" Frank slapped his knee, sending ashes in the air and to the floor. "That must be it. I can see it on your faces."

"We're not here to litigate your case," Wade told him calmly. "We're only here to give you these papers."

"Ha," Frank spit out in disgust. "She gives as good as she gets, I can tell you that." Frank pointed to a cut and bruise over his left eye. "This was from an ashtray she threw at me the other night. Did she tell you about that?"

"I don't know anything about it, Frank," Wade told him.

"That's some truth, Thompson. You don't know shit." Frank looked down from his porch and waved at them. "You're all down there looking at me like I'm some criminal. This is my goddamned house, and if you live in my house, you live by my rules. One of those rules is you don't step out on me. Not with some loser working the docks or some rich doctor or lawyer who tells you how pretty you are and buys you an expensive dinner." Frank leaned over and pulled another beer from a Styrofoam cooler near his feet. He popped the top and took a long, deep drink.

Wade shifted back on his feet and considered Frank's claims. Even though Vicky led a hard life, she was still an attractive woman. She wore her hair long and blew it out until it looked like the mane of a lion. Her skin was almost flawless, with hardly a wrinkle, and it held a tan even in the cold, sunless days of winter. She could smoke a pack of cigarettes and drink half a bottle of whiskey and then splash some water on her face, freshen up her makeup, and strap on a tight black dress, and if you squinted your eyes hard enough, you might think she looked like one of those models in those music videos on MTV. She still worked at the Sink or Swim, where rumors lingered that she'd slept with at least a few customers and a manager or two, and maybe even Ronnie Jackson, the owner, many years ago and before Ronnie suffered the first of his three heart attacks. So, it wasn't a complete shock to Wade to hear that Vicky might be running around a little, and that the news might get back to Frank. How she ended up with Frank in the first place was the big mystery. You never know what a person is living with or what they might be going through. Desperation is like a convenience store dinner. When you're hungry, you'll eat just about anything, even if it might kill you.

Frank took another hit from his cigarette and then flicked the lit stub in Wade's direction. "I guess she didn't mention anything about staying out all night and screwing her customers, did she? No, I guess she wouldn't go so far as to tell the truth about that."

"Like I said, Frank. That's not my business here today." Wade flashed the papers at Frank one more time. "Let's get this over with. I'm coming up there. Now."

Wade kept his eyes on Frank and started up the steps, slowly and calmly. When Wade approached the landing, he saw Frank's expression shift, from anger to acceptance. Frank got up, snatched the papers, and went inside.

Johnson let out a breath. "That went better than I expected."

Wade agreed, but it was also a little different than he expected. He made a mental note to follow-up with his brother about Hillary Dent.

Chapter 9

W ADE AND GINNY CAME by early on Saturday to pick up Lily from the Murrays. They drove over to her uncle's house and helped her box up her clothes and a few other items she wanted to bring with her. Wade packed it all in his pickup truck and drove it back to the house. Lily and Ginny rode together in Lily's car, a light blue Buick Riviera that her uncle had given her on her sixteenth birthday. Ginny offered to drive, and Lily let her. She just wasn't up for it.

"How about some music?" Ginny asked.

Lily nodded and Ginny turned the radio to a Top 40 station. Madonna and then Crowded House. Ginny started singing with the song.

She had a nice voice, Lily thought. And she was pretty. She was wearing jeans and a flannel shirt. She had her hair pulled back. No makeup. The kind of natural beauty that happened upon you unexpectedly.

"You know, I knew your mother a little," Ginny said.

Lily wasn't surprised. It seemed like everyone around here that was about Ginny's age had known her mother.

"I was a couple of years behind Wade and your mom in school, but I was in their math class. Your mom tried to set us up, but Wade wasn't interested. At least not back then."

"When did you get together?" Lily asked. She'd assumed that Wade and Ginny were high school sweethearts.

"It wasn't until Wade got back from Vietnam. He had a tough time over there. And then he got here and..." Ginny stopped abruptly. Lily was curious.

"And what?"

Ginny bit her lip, like she was trying to figure out how to answer. "Let's just say it was tough for him when he got back here, too. It took him some time to settle. I'd see him around every so often, sometimes at my parents' hardware store. And then one day he asked me out. The rest is history, I guess."

There was more to the story, but Lily didn't press it. A Fleetwood Mac song was playing now, and Ginny was singing again. It was nice, sitting here with her.

They got to the house and moved in her things. She'd be staying in their guestroom, which had been emptied, cleaned, and prepared for her arrival. There were brand new sheets on the bed and pretty robin's-egg blue curtains hanging on the windows, which overlooked a well-groomed fenced backyard.

Lily spent most of the day unpacking and organizing. Ginny prepared a nice lunch and then Wade got them takeout from a Mexican restaurant for dinner. It was mostly small talk all day. Music, the weather, school. By the time they finished eating, none of them could think of anything else to talk about. Really though, Lily thought, all of them were just avoiding any serious discussion. They were feeling each other out.

Lily excused herself early and went to bed, telling them she was going to do some reading, but she was ready to be alone for a bit. There wasn't much more that Wade or Ginny could have done to welcome her into their home that first day, but she was still struggling with the whole idea of it. Moving in with a family that wasn't hers, with people she hardly knew. She wondered whether it would be better for her to go back and stay by herself in her uncle's house. Her house. To try to make it on her own. It might be better to start now, anyway. Because, she figured, that day would come one way or the other.

Chapter 10

Sunday, October 18, 1987

L ILY WOKE UP TO footsteps on the hardwood of the hallway.
The Thompsons were up and moving about but she was still
lying in bed beneath the same flowered bedspread she'd slept under
for the last eight years. She had it pulled up to her chin, gripping it
with both hands like a child grabbing the top of a fence and peering
over into the mysterious unknown of a neighbor's yard. The blanket
was heavy and warm and safe, and if only she could stay under it and
on her side of the fence all morning and all day and all week, maybe
she could get her life under control.

The front door opened and closed, and then a car pulled out of
the driveway. Lily propped herself up against the headboard and
looked around her new room. The Thompsons had done their best
to make it comfortable for her. Wade brought in her dresser, desk,
and nightstand, and he hung her *Purple Rain* and Duran Duran
posters on the wall across from her bed. Prince was staring down
at her now from that wall, with a come-hither look from the perch
on his motorcycle, inviting her for a ride to or from trouble. John
Taylor and the boys from Duran Duran were up there too, but she
was getting more of a *get your shit together* kind of vibe from them
this morning, though on another day, she might interpret it a little
differently.

Lily had already filled the dresser and closet with clothes and decorated the top of her desk with the framed photograph of her and her mother. She looked at the picture of her infant self in her mother's arms and hoped she was the reason her mother looked so happy. Lily often thought of that picture in the spring when the lilacs near her uncle's house were in full bloom and she could smell them through the open windows of the kitchen. She wondered if her mother smelled like lilac and whether the scent of it triggered a memory of that day hidden somewhere inside her head.

Last night was the first since her uncle's death that she slept un-interrupted, and it was almost eleven o'clock when she finally got out of bed. She washed up in the guest bathroom and then walked down the hallway to the kitchen, where Ginny was already preparing lunch.

"Oh, there you are," Ginny said. "We didn't want to disturb you this morning. We thought you might need your rest. I guess we were right," she said with a smile.

Lily mustered a smile in response.

"Would you like some coffee or juice or anything?" Ginny asked.

"Coffee would be great."

Ginny reached into the cupboard and pulled out a mug. It had a little orange sun and a palm tree painted on the side. Ginny poured in some coffee and set the mug on the table and motioned Lily to a seat. Lily mixed in a heavy helping of cream and sugar and took a sip.

She looked around the modest kitchen, which was set at the back of the one-story brick rancher. Sunlight spilled in through the windows and filled the room. The Thompsons' hulking black lab found a spot in it near Lily. He'd taken a liking to her already, maybe because she slipped table scraps to him last night during dinner. Lily leaned down and petted his head, and he answered with a wag of his tail.

Lily could feel the heat of the sun warm her back and run through her body, relaxing the muscles in her neck and shoulders. *I will try to make myself comfortable here, for now,* she thought. She cupped her hands around the mug, closed her eyes, and took another big sip. Ginny must have been watching her.

"You don't see too many young people drinking coffee and actually enjoying it," Ginny remarked.

"I never really thought about that." Lily stared down at the mug. "My uncle used to give me these small cups in the morning with lots of cream and sugar. At that point, it wasn't really even coffee, you know what I mean?" she said with a shrug. "It was this mischievous thing for me, though. Drinking this adult drink. Doing a grown-up thing." She was looking at Ginny now. "I think he was trying to make me feel special. I guess he always tried to do that, though."

"He was a good man," Ginny said.

"Yeah, but he's not here anymore," Lily answered, with a taste of that bitterness on her tongue again.

"Just because you can't see him doesn't mean he isn't here with you," Ginny said gently. "You remembered the coffee, didn't you?"

Lily still felt as if her uncle had betrayed her, justified or not. It lingered like the smell of smoke after a burnt fire and colored every thought of him. She took a guilty sip of coffee, wishing she hadn't tarnished that memory, and hoping the resentment she felt for him would leave her soon.

⇨

After lunch, Lily decided to take a walk. The Thompsons' house was in a neighborhood near her elementary school, so she was familiar with the streets and knew the trails that led to the creek and river through the salt marsh. She wandered past the side of the school, where some children had gathered on the playground. A few girls huddled around the monkey bars and took turns climbing and racing across them. Another group of kids, boys mostly, were playing touch football in an open grass field. She did spot two girls with them, though. One was short and fast, and when they handed her the ball she darted and spun through a group of them to the end zone. The other girl was much larger, and she was responsible for laying a nasty block on a skinny redheaded boy, knocking him off his feet and springing the smaller girl for the touchdown. Lily laughed, and it caught her by surprise.

She walked through another neighborhood with houses set back on large parcels of land. Massive wrought iron gates, hundred-year-old oaks, and thick shrubbery shielded their view from the street. But she could peek through spots and see the long driveways, built with laid brick and pavers, that meandered through manicured lawns and gazebos and fountains. They landed at the foot of the massive columns and wide porches that fronted the older Greek Revival-style houses.

Lily walked past the houses and to the cul-de-sac at the end of the road, where a trail was cut into the wild marsh grass that lined the edge of the pavement. The head of the trail was marked with a sign. Lily stopped to read it even though she'd read it a dozen times before.

The Mumford Trail

This trail is dedicated to the memory of Evelyn Mumford, an educator of young minds and an advocate of nature. She fought to preserve the health of the waterways and protect its wildlife. From this trail, her favorite place on earth, she watched birds fly from their nests and heard them call to the sun, the moon, and the stars.

Lily had known Mrs. Mumford before she died. She was a kind woman who volunteered at the elementary school library when Lily was a little girl. Mrs. Mumford knew her grandmother and her mother, and when she would see Lily, she would tell her stories about them. Mrs. Mumford told her that she and Lily's grandmother would go to Lankford's Restaurant on Caroline Street when they were teenagers to drink cherry sodas and talk about boys. Another time she told Lily that her mother used to check out Nancy Drew books from the school library and would keep them past their due dates. Seeing Mrs. Mumford at school was always the highlight of Lily's day. Every story was like bringing a piece of her mother and grandmother alive.

The trail was a well-maintained boardwalk that tracked a short distance through the marsh and ended as a wide dock on the edge of a creek. Lily popped off her shoes, rolled up her jeans, and sat at the edge of the dock with her feet dangling in the water. The tide had come in and her feet sank past her ankles and almost to her knees. She leaned back onto the boards, closed her eyes, and took a deep breath of salt air.

She must have dozed off. She was aware of her surroundings, but it had to be a dream because her mother was now sitting there next to her. Her mother was still and quiet and looking out to the other side of the creek where a great blue heron had risen and swept over the open water. The bird circled them slowly, wings fully extended, spanning six or seven feet across, before landing in the marsh grass a few feet away. Lily turned to her mother. *Was she real or a ghost or just an image in her dream?* she wondered.

"Can I take you home now?" Lily asked her. "I don't want to leave you here all alone."

Her mother looked back at her. Her eyes were a grayish blue, with a hint of purple it seemed, like the slate coloring of the bird and not the brown that she'd passed down to Lily.

"I'm going to stay here," her mother said. It was the first time Lily could remember that she'd spoken. "Maybe I'll see you tomorrow. Or another day." She turned back to watch the bird, and then she disappeared.

Lily jolted awake. She sat up quickly and looked around for her mother, but the only living creature she could see anywhere near her was a blue heron walking at the edge of the creek. Unnerved by the experience, Lily gathered herself and was about to leave when she heard a voice coming down the trail.

"Toby! Toby!" a man's voice called, but the dog reached her first. The dog was a thick, handsome fellow, and he greeted Lily with some heavy panting and a few licks to the back of her hand. She went down on one knee and rubbed at his scruff, and he returned her affection with a few happy kisses to the side of her face.

"Toby. Get down boy," the man commanded from a distance. But Toby was undeterred. He nudged his nose into Lily's midsection and pushed her onto her backside. Lily hugged him as he continued to lean into her. His tail was swinging ferociously from side to side, whacking at the inside of Lily's raised knees like a marching band drummer. The man got there and grabbed Toby's thick red collar and pulled him off of Lily.

"You are a very bad dog, Toby," he admonished.

The man was dressed neatly in fitted khaki pants, leather hiking boots, and a thick, dark blue turtleneck sweater that looked heavy and warm. Lily recognized him. "Mr. Esham?" she asked.

"It's Reid, remember?" Reid offered his free hand to Lily and lifted her off the dock.

"Reid. Right. What are you doing here?"

"My dad lives in one of the houses up the street. Toby is his dog." Toby had settled a bit but was still anxious to get to her.

"He looks a lot like the Thompsons' dog." With Toby restrained, Lily slipped on her socks and shoes.

"He should," Reid told her. "They're from the same litter. They're brothers."

"Do you come down here a lot?" Lily asked. "It's familiar to him."

"Toby and my father walk the trail all the time. When I come to visit, I join them. Dad isn't feeling great, so today it's the two of us."

Toby flopped down on the dock, his front legs crossed in front of him.

Reid closed his eyes and took in a deep breath. "There's something about the air out here," he said as he exhaled. "There's a sweetness to it mixed in with the salt and the sulfur."

Lily took a breath herself. "Yeah, I smell it too. I didn't notice it before."

"Maybe it's a type of flower along the edges or something in the soil. Either way, I've never smelled anything like it anywhere else. It's unique to this spot."

Lily heard geese above her and turned her head toward the noise. The birds were flying in over a tree line behind Reid, and when she looked in that direction, she noticed Reid looking at her. It made her uncomfortable.

"Is there something wrong?" she asked him.

"Oh, no. I'm sorry, Lily. It's just...you look so much like your mother."

"My mother?" she replied. "You knew her too?"

"Yes, I did."

Before Lily could continue, Toby erupted. The geese had descended near them and landed in the shallows not far from the edge of the dock.

"Easy boy. Easy." Reid pulled his collar. "I'm going to take this monster back home." He secured Toby with his leash and yanked him away from the edge of the dock. "Maybe we can talk again soon."

"Okay. Sure." Lily waved to them. "See you next time."

Reid took a few steps back toward the path with Toby but stopped and turned again to Lily. "I take my father's boat out on the weekends sometimes. If you're ever in the mood for a ride, let me know."

"That sounds like fun," she told him.

Reid waved goodbye and pulled Toby along. Soon they disappeared back on the trail. Toby's disapproving barks echoed behind her. The geese remained in the water, unbothered by Toby's theatrics. Lily watched them drift past her in a cluster. *Someone else who knew my mother*, she thought. *Everyone knew her. Except her own daughter.*

Lily returned to the house and met Ginny in the living room. Shadow came right up to her and sniffed her legs.

"Shadow," Ginny scolded.

Sulking, Shadow edged away.

"It's okay, he probably smells his brother. I met him down at the Mumford Trail."

"You met Toby?" Ginny asked. "Was he there with Dr. Esham?"

"No," Lily answered. "His son was walking him."

Ginny looked at her warily, an eyebrow up, the side of her mouth in a hook at the corner. "Don't let Wade hear you talking about him. They didn't like each other much growing up. They still don't."

Lily recalled Paul's reaction to Reid at the funeral reception. "What about Wade's brother?"

"Paul? There might not be two brothers more different than Paul and Wade. But I can tell you this, there aren't two brothers that mean more to each other than those two. There's family, and then there's Paul and Wade. The enemy of one is the enemy of the other."

Chapter 11

Monday, October 19, 1987

WADE WALKED INTO THE barracks on Monday morning to news about Frank Brittingham. Frank had shown up at the Sink or Swim, already drunk, yelling and screaming at anyone who'd listen about his whore wife and her friend, the no-good county sheriff. A couple of Wade's deputies got the call and picked him up on a disorderly charge and threw him in the county lockup. His arraignment was scheduled for later that day, but Wade guessed he'd be held at least until the hearing on the original summons, which was set for tomorrow. He figured he should let Rick Hampton know, since they'd already interviewed Frank about Hillary Dent. If Frank was a real suspect, it was something Wade would want to know anyway.

A call to Rick would also give Wade the opportunity to tell him about that other case. He'd pulled the file from the archives to get himself reacquainted. There wasn't much in there. There was a summary about him and Sheriff Willis getting the call by mistake. Someone dialed the county number instead of the city number. They redirected to OCPD, of course, but Wade and Willis showed up anyway. There was a short write-up describing the scene. She was young. Short brown hair, pretty. Dressed in a white nightgown and nothing else. She was propped up against a post under the pier about halfway up the waterline. They found out later that her name was Lisa Harrington. She was a local girl who had fallen on tough times.

She was living in a flophouse up on Tenth Street with a bunch of druggies. They never found her killer.

Rick wasn't his usual outgoing self on the call, and that got Wade wondering if there might be something else on his mind.

"I really can't talk about it, Wade," he told him.

Wade prodded. "I hear you, Rick. I'm just wondering if there's information you might be able to share on this. We might be able to provide some help or input, like me offering up the Harrington case." There was a lengthy silence.

"You didn't hear this from me," Rick said finally.

"Okay."

"Your brother was at the bar where the girl was the night she disappeared."

"Yeah, I heard about that. Paul is at that place almost every night." Wade played it off like it was no big deal, but the seriousness in Rick's voice when he said it had him at least curious, if not concerned.

"Well, someone saw him walk out with her."

This time Wade stayed quiet. They were only doing their job, closing out all leads, is what Wade was thinking.

"Ken's got a hard-on for your brother. He's gonna play this one out."

Now Wade understood. It was Ken's doing. Anything to get back at the Thompson boys.

"I appreciate the heads-up, Rick," Wade told him. "I'll try to track down some more information on Harrington and get back to you." Wade's first order of business, though, was to go talk to Paul.

Lily saw Teri waving to her and parked her Buick in the empty spot next to Teri's yellow Beetle. Wade had offered to drive Lily to school, but Lily politely declined. She couldn't be seen pulling up to the school in a sheriff's patrol car like some convict on work release. The other kids would have a field day with that.

Teri didn't say anything when Lily got out of her car. She just gave her a big hug, grabbed her hand, and walked her through the parking lot. They walked past the line of pickup trucks and Blazers, Broncos, and Jimmys that were backed into the farthest spots from the school. Shotguns and rifles were mounted in the back windows, and surfboards topped the roofs. In this part of the state, the farmers surfed and the surfers hunted. And in the summer, they all worked side by side in the hotels, restaurants, and t-shirt shops at the beach and on the boardwalk.

Kids shuffled between cars, making conversation and waiting until the last warning bell to make their way into the school. Lily and Teri walked through the breezeway where the smokers got in their last drags before classes started. They heard Eric Dombrowski yell out, "What's up, Parker?" as he took a hit off what Lily assumed was a tobacco-filled cigarette, though she wouldn't put it past Eric to smoke a joint on school property. Teri shook her head and called him a dumbass, but Lily had a soft spot for Eric. He was a kind and gentle soul who loved his golden retriever and spent most of his free time paddling out and catching waves. Lily thought he looked like Sean Penn in *Fast Times*, with his stringy beach-blonde hair, that bump on his slightly oversized nose, and the sleeveless flannel shirts he wore that he cut just enough to show off the water-carved muscles in his arms. *Those damn surfer boys*, Lily thought. She nodded to him, and he answered with an exhale of smoke and a wink.

Lily made it through the morning of her first day back at school without too much trouble. Her first period teacher met her at the classroom door when she arrived and offered her condolences and asked how she was doing. As expected, she got a lot of that from the teachers and administrators and some of her classmates, too. She should have been more appreciative. She could have been more accepting. But it was tedious. No one knew how to act around her, especially the adults. At least with high school kids, after a quick "I'm sorry," the conversation usually shifted to another topic. Boys, girls, sports, waves, or parties, in most cases.

By lunch, she was worn out and hungry. She circled the salad bar in the cafeteria, picking up tomatoes and cucumbers and chickpeas to dress her iceberg and romaine. She poured on some Thousand Island dressing and picked up a pack of saltine crackers and carried it all on a tray with a carton of milk and some silverware. Lily scanned the room and spotted her friends sitting at a table near the back corner and close to doors that exited out to a patio at the front of the school. On nice days, the kids scarfed down their lunches and slipped out those doors to get a few minutes of fresh air before their next class. They'd kick around a hacky sack or just bullshit with each other about nothing in particular. This lunch shift was full of seniors who were looking for more distractions in a year full of them. Some of them were working on college applications and studying for one last standardized test. Some were thinking about careers as electricians, plumbers, or hairdressers, anything that could get them out of their parents' houses and into new lives. Others were coasting through without a plan or a care and figured the world would find them a place. For them it was usually at a restaurant or bar or on a fishing boat or delivery truck, where they could pocket enough money to pay rent, make a car payment, and buy a six pack whenever they felt like it. Almost all of them were done with homework and tests, though, and even on a Monday were making plans for a weekend bonfire at J.D. Cropper's place because his parents were leaving town to visit his grandmother in Harrisburg. Lily's distractions were all of that and everything else, but right now she was thinking about getting through this day and then waking up for another. She was weaving her way through the maze of tables when she heard someone calling after her.

"Lily. Hey, Lily."

It was Holly Mitchell. She was sitting tall on the bench seat of a table, her back stiff and upright, an image of perfect posture and one that had the effect of enhancing her curves and attracting the stares of several boys around her. Three other girls were sitting with Holly, all looking like a Bangle or a Go-Go, with their teased-out hair and trendy little outfits. Each of them looked up at Lily with scrunched up noses and twisted mouths like they'd bitten into a lemon or sucked on a sour candy. Stacy McPherson was in the seat right next to Holly, and it was her face, smug and indignant, that Lily focused on the most.

Lily would have walked right past them if not for Holly. Lily felt a pull to her that she hadn't felt before. She'd been thinking and dreaming a lot about her mother lately. It was like Lily and her mother were reconnecting, or maybe more like getting to know each other for the first time. With their mothers being best friends, Holly was one more link that she could build and hold on to.

"Hey, Holly." Lily didn't acknowledge the others, though she shot a brief but cold stare at Stacy.

"You want to join us for lunch?" Holly asked her.

Stacy's face shifted from disgust to shock and fear. That was satisfying, and it was almost enough to convince Lily to accept Holly's offer, but she declined. "I'm sitting with Teri and the Smiths," Lily told her. "But I appreciate the offer."

"Oh. Okay." She sounded disappointed. "I'll see you later in English?"

"Yeah. See you then."

Lily got to her table and sat next to Teri and across from the Smith twins, Alicia and Tammy. The four of them had been best friends since before high school. It was nice to be back together with them. They were as close to family as she had left.

"What was that all about?" Alicia asked in a soft voice that was almost inaudible in the din of the cafeteria chaos around them.

"Holly was trying to be nice," Lily said.

"Pfft," Tammy let out in disbelief. "That would be the first time in about four years."

For her friends, this was an unexpected change in attitude from Holly. Once they started high school, they drifted into different packs. Holly went one way, and the other four went another. They rarely spoke, and when they did, it was usually when paired for a group project at school or sometimes when they found themselves alone together by a keg at a party. There were more than a few common acquaintances. Almost the whole senior class had grown up together. But they mainly operated in separate spheres within the same world.

"Holly's trying," Lily told them. She shook her head. "I don't know. Her mom and my mom were friends growing up, and the sheriff too. Maybe she wants a fresh start."

"Or maybe her mom is forcing her to be nice," Tammy said, with a shade of resentment.

Alicia interrupted with a bite at her apple. "She was never that bad. It was always the other one that poisoned her against us." Alicia flicked her little head sideways at Holly's table and toward Stacy in particular.

"How are things going with the sheriff and his wife?" Teri asked.

Lily shrugged her shoulders. "They're nice people."

Alicia cut in again. "If you need a break, you can always stay at our house for a few days."

"Yeah," Tammy added, "maybe this Friday even. We can all go to J.D.'s together after the football game."

"That sounds like fun," Lily said. "Let's see how the week goes and I'll let you know."

Alicia lifted her eyebrows and tilted her head to a spot over Lily's left shoulder, trying to get her attention.

"Hey," said a voice next to her.

Standing at the head of the table, tall and skinny, with wavy black hair, was Lily's ex-boyfriend, Jake. He was wearing a white t-shirt with a blue wave logo on his chest and was holding a couple of books in the crook of his arm. He had a backpack strap slung over his left shoulder and the four fingers of his right hand were stuck in the front pocket of his denim blue jeans.

"Sorry to interrupt," he said in a steady voice. "Are we still good for tomorrow?"

Lily nodded. "Yeah. Four o'clock at the diner. I'll be there."

"Great."

The girls watched him quietly as he threaded his way through the cafeteria and out into the hallway.

Alicia leaned in from across the table. "Are you two getting back together?"

"No. It's nothing like that," Lily answered.

Jake had gotten the Thompsons' telephone number from Teri and had reached out to Lily over the weekend to apologize for not making it to her uncle's funeral. He asked her to meet him after school one day this week to talk, and she agreed. Lily wasn't mad at Jake about missing the funeral. She knew he was going up to Baltimore to tour Johns Hopkins with his parents. He was on his way to being valedictorian. It was a big deal for him, and she understood. There was still a little something inside her that liked the idea of spending some time with him again, even if it was only as friends. He was the sweetest boy she knew, right up until Stacy McPherson got him drunk on grain alcohol and pulled him into the back seat of her father's Firebird.

"He did do a pretty shitty thing with a pretty shitty person," Alicia said.

They looked over at Stacy McPherson, who saw them staring at her and shot back a *What's your fucking problem?* look of her own. Stacy and Jake surely deserved their fair share of the blame for what happened. Ultimately, you have to take responsibility for your own actions, which Jake had done as soon as it happened. But Lily wasn't an innocent bystander. She'd said some things, and their relationship was all but over by the time Stacy and Jake hooked up. Her friends didn't know about all of that, and they held more of a grudge against Jake than Lily did.

A plate and silverware hit the ground. Lily looked over and saw a younger boy sprawled out in the middle of the floor. Kevin Brittingham was sitting at the edge of the table across the aisle from her, laughing and pointing at the boy.

"Hey Deion," he yelled down at him, "next time, don't walk into my foot."

Lily looked down at the boy and then back at Kevin, who'd been a schoolyard bully all the way back to kindergarten. He was abrasive and vulgar, mean and unkind to everyone, including his friends, and today's target was an innocent sophomore who was just trying to get to a table and eat a quiet lunch. Lily trembled. She gripped the edges of the table to hold herself together.

Another kid sitting with Kevin swung his arm and knocked over a full carton of milk onto the fallen boy's back. "Oops," he said, sarcastically. Kevin and his companions roared with laughter.

The boy gathered to his hands and knees. Drops of blood fell from a cut on the brow of his left eye, mixing into the pool of milk on the floor to create a pinwheel of red, white, and pink. Alicia darted from the table with a handful of napkins and ran to the injured boy. She held the napkins against the cut and helped him to his feet.

"You come with me. Let's get you to the nurse's office." Alicia led him away through the mass of bodies that had gathered to observe the commotion.

"Hey. Be careful, Alicia," Kevin yelled after them. "You don't want any of that black faggot blood getting all over you."

All the emotion simmering inside Lily boiled over in an explosion of rage. She sprang out of her seat and flung herself at Kevin. She smacked him hard across the face, and then, catching him surprised and off balance, pushed him into the bench seat of his table, spilling him to the floor. The room was quiet when it happened and then blew up in a chorus of whoops and hollers. Kevin took a second to shake off the shock of the attack. There was only one way a kid like Kevin would react to such an embarrassment, and that was with anger and violence. He leapt to his feet and stepped toward Lily. She stood her ground. Several hands grabbed at Kevin to keep him back, but he shrugged them off and stuck his face right into hers.

"I'm gonna get you," he said, through clenched teeth. "I'm gonna get you and your friend, the sheriff, for what he did to my family. Just wait and see."

Lily felt the heat of his breath on her neck. She closed her eyes and turned away from him, anticipating the blow that was sure to come next. But as she readied herself for impact, she heard the voice of Mr. Dryden, the vice principal, ordering the students to clear the cafeteria and get to class. When she opened her eyes, Kevin and his friends were gone.

Wade pulled into the marina and parked in the lot by the harbor master's building. The three-story structure resembled a ship, with a large observation deck at its bow overlooking the water. It was freshly painted in a bluish green that matched the color of the water and trimmed in a crisp, bright white. A crow's nest at the top provided three-hundred-and-sixty-degree sightlines, including a full view east to Ocean City, Assateague Island, and the inlet.

Wade walked through a maze of ramps, docks, and slips until he reached his brother's two boats. He found Paul on the larger one, the trawler he used for fishing. He'd named the boat for the Greek goddess of the sea, *Amphitrite*, whom he'd read about in a book his mother had given him while he recovered from his broken leg as a child.

Wade still had nightmares about that accident. When Paul was eleven years old, he and Wade were exploring an old, abandoned fishing shanty in the dunes on the edge of the bay near his house. Paul had climbed up into the rafters when one of the support beams snapped and he fell awkwardly on his left leg, breaking it at the ankle. When Wade saw Paul's leg, with his foot pointing in the wrong direction and shards of bone protruding through his skin, he almost fainted. That moment of shock was overcome by an overwhelming fear, and Wade ran out screaming for his father the whole quarter mile back to the house.

Paul's leg was never the same, but it didn't stop him from pursuing his one true love. Paul had always wanted to be a fisherman. He bought his first skiff with his own money when he was thirteen years old. He saved what he earned from errands he ran for neighbors, odd jobs he worked when he wasn't in school, and the allowance his parents gave him for the chores he completed around the house and on the farm.

The boat was just small enough for Paul to maneuver in and out of the creeks and marsh flats and large enough to take into the river and to most parts of the bay. He would take it out to fish and to set out and retrieve crab pots and sometimes he would venture out across the bay and to the barrier island where tourists from cities and suburbs west of the Chesapeake Bay would come to vacation in the summer. He would bring home fish and crab to his family almost every night, and he sold what they didn't need or wouldn't eat to some of the restaurants on the island. He would take Wade out with him when he could. He showed him where to set out the crab pots depending on the season and where the flounder would bite depending on the tide. He taught him nautical knots, the rules of navigation, and how to dock and tie down a boat all by himself.

By the time he was sixteen, Paul was working at the marina in the harbor. It was there that Paul truly learned his craft. He started off working after school and on the weekends for the dockmaster, filling boats with gas, cleaning the docks, and manning the supply store. He would earn extra money helping on the commercial fishing boats after they returned from their fishing excursions or running other errands for the captains and their crew. Paul's reputation as a reliable and eager worker spread along the docks and Howard Hurley, one of the more genial captains among the regulars, acknowledged Paul's ambition and offered Paul an exclusive job as his deckhand. Soon, he started taking Paul out with him on his fishing trips. In the summer, Captain Hurley offered charters for tourists on one of his other boats, and Paul made runs on that one as well. Eventually, Paul served as Captain Hurley's first mate on the charter. By the time he was eighteen, Paul had earned enough money to put a down payment on a larger boat for himself. He got his captain's license and his commercial fishing license and started his own fishing and charter operation that summer. The marina and his boats became Paul's life. And whenever Wade was trying to find his brother, he knew exactly where he'd be.

Paul had his back to the dock, fiddling with a piece of equipment, and didn't see Wade approach. Wade decided to have some fun with his brother and rang the cast iron bell that was mounted on a post at the edge of the dock.

"Jesus Christ!" Paul yelled out, startled. He set down the part, cleaned off his hands, and spun around in the captain's chair to face Wade. "What the hell did you do that for?"

"I had to get your attention."

Paul waved Wade onto the boat. "Come on. If you're off duty, we can grab a beer while you tell me whatever it is you're here to tell me."

Wade climbed in and sat on a bench near the back. Paul pulled out two cans of Budweiser from a cooler on the deck and tossed one to Wade. They cracked them open and took their drinks.

"So, what's going on?" Paul asked.

"I heard Ken Meehan and the boys paid you a visit."

There was a subtle flare of a nostril. Nothing more. "Is this an interrogation?"

"Not my case."

"Then why are you asking?" Paul was never much for talking, and less so when people were trying to get into his business.

"They found that girl on the beach."

Paul nodded. "Pretty brutal stuff, from what I've been hearing."

"I heard you were at the bar the night she disappeared. She was there."

"I'm always at that bar. There were a bunch of people there."

"But you walked out with her."

Pursed lips. Furrowed brow. Wade was getting to him. He backed off.

"Look, I just want to know what happened, because I'm hearing that Ken's ready to drop twenty-five years' worth of a grudge on your ass."

"Son of a bitch," Paul mumbled. "All I did was walk out at the same time she did. She was headed to the parking lot, and I was headed back here. I had no idea that was the girl from the beach until they told me."

"That's what you told them?"

Paul nodded.

"Was she with anyone?"

"I didn't much notice. I think she was alone. Maybe she was waiting for someone. I don't know. But there were a lot of flies buzzing around her."

"Frank Brittingham?"

"Especially him. He got loud about it too. Heard him call her a stuck-up bitch."

"You told Ken all of that?"

"Yeah. And I'm sure he got the same story from everyone else who was in there."

"What about Vicky? Was she there?"

"Didn't see her."

Paul downed his beer and dropped his can into a five-gallon bucket next to him on the deck of the boat. He was through talking about it, and Wade was done asking, and it didn't much matter that Wade believed his brother was holding something back.

Paul reached into the cooler and drew out two more beers. They sat and drank and were quiet for a while. Paul's other boat, the smaller one he used for charters, was docked in the next slip. It drifted forward a bit and Wade could see its stern.

"What really happened with Sophia?" Wade asked, pointing to the name written in script on the back. "All you ever told me all these years was that things didn't work out and you broke up."

Paul let out a huff. "It's not the best memory." He pulled at the brim of the worn-out Evinrude trucker hat he was wearing and took a long drink from his beer. And then, to Wade's surprise, he started talking.

"We were still together for a couple of years after she left for school. I stayed home and worked my business while she was up at College Park. We'd see each other on breaks and over the summer, but we were both so busy and we didn't get as much time together as either of us wanted."

There was a long pause. He stared out past Wade and the other boats in the marina to some distant spot in his memory. Then he started again.

"She was so beautiful. There were always boys and men—grown-ass men—who were after her. I got so jealous. I was constantly calling her. Asking her what she was doing, who she was with. One day, I decided to drive up and surprise her. I get to her dorm and her roommate tells me she's at a fraternity party. I run over there and sneak myself in and see her with some hotshot college boy.

He's leaning in real close to her, *accidentally* rubbing against her. He's edging closer and closer. Puts his lips right up to her ear to tell her his story, I'm guessing. And then I see her laugh and smile and it sent me into a flying rage."

Wade had seen his brother angry. He'd seen his brother fight. He was the kind of strong you find in men that do real work in the world. He was the kind of tough you find in the ones that worked on the water. Wade got in a few scraps with him over the years, and he held his own against him the best he could, but he knew his brother was always holding back. Wade had seen his brother easily handle the hardest of men, and he knew that he wouldn't stand a chance against him, bad leg or not, in a fair fight.

Paul continued, more animated this time. "I rush at the guy and floor him with one punch," he said, throwing a simulated hook for effect. "He's sprawled out on the ground, unconscious, with his two front teeth laying in a pool of blood next to him. Two of his fraternity brothers see what happened and come at me. *Bam, Bam.* Two punches and I put both of those losers on the floor. I couldn't believe it. I thought I was invincible. Well, that ended pretty quick. A whole mess of 'em piled on top of me and whooped the living shit out of me. It was the worst beating I ever took. The only thing that saved me was Sophia screaming and crying. I can still hear it to this day. They finally stopped punching and kicking me, and they dragged me out onto the front lawn. Somehow, Sophia snuck me back to her room and cleaned me up. She let me stay the night, but in the morning, she told me we were through and that she never wanted to see me again. I got back home and that's how it went. I never saw her again."

Paul slumped forward, staring down at his feet. He took another drink and looked back up at Wade. "After she graduated, she followed that boy up to Baltimore and ended up marrying him. He became a dentist. Can you believe that? I'm guessing me knocking out his teeth had something to do with that." He let out a chuckle that faded softly in the air.

"Was Sophia the only girl you ever loved?" Wade asked, realizing only now, it seemed, how alone his brother had been all this time.

After a few seconds of silence, Paul spoke. "There was another girl. But that one ended worse than Sophia." He banged the empty beer can against his knee, and then tossed it against the backside of the boat.

Wade didn't remember Paul ever talking about another girl, and he thought Paul's reaction was a bit unusual, but there was no point to starting another interrogation.

A fishing boat cruised slowly through the marina, raising a small wake in the otherwise still water. The ripples reached the boat and sent it into a gentle roll. Wade stood up, rocking from side-to-side, and tossed his empty beer can in a high arc toward the bucket next to Paul. The can flew in without hitting the sides and clanked against the other empty cans at the bottom.

Wade grinned wide. "I still got it."

"Yeah, you got somethin' all right," Paul chimed back.

Wade patted his brother's shoulder on his way off the boat. He started down the dock but stopped suddenly and turned back around.

"If there was something I should know about that night the girl went missing, or anything else, you'd tell me, right?" Wade asked.

Paul met Wade's eye. An older brother's imperious stare. One that still made Wade a little uncomfortable, even as an adult.

"You'd be the first to know, little brother," Paul told him, calmly.

Wade nodded and resumed his walk back down the dock, but he wasn't convinced. His brother was hiding something, and Wade wasn't sure whether he was more worried or scared about it.

Chapter 12

Tuesday, October 20, 1987

A S WADE HAD GUESSED, Frank remained in custody up until the day's hearing, the judge having decided that Frank showing up at Vicky's place of employment, whether she was there or not, raised enough concern to deny bail. Wade settled himself near the doors at the back of the courtroom. Rick walked in and sat down about halfway up the aisle. He didn't see Wade. It might've been nothing, Rick being here. Just keeping tabs on a lead. But when Ken walked in a few seconds later, Wade started to wonder whether there was some heat on Frank about the missing girl after all.

A bailiff escorted Frank in, uncuffed. Frank was wearing civilian clothes, dark pants, and a light brown sports jacket over a white-collared dress shirt with no tie. He sat next to a lawyer waiting for him at the table. Wade noticed that Frank was clean-shaven and presentable. Vicky was at the other table with her own lawyer. She was dressed in a conservative black pantsuit and white blouse, her makeup was modest, and her hair was tame.

The proceeding went about as smoothly as could be expected under the circumstances. Frank's side quickly agreed to the terms of the protective order. He would have no contact with Vicky except through their lawyers or through the court. He agreed to stay away from the Sink or Swim, which Wade thought was a significant concession on Frank's part, considering it was as close to Frank's second home as any place could be. The judge noted that the house was Frank's and in Frank's name alone and that he was entitled to occupancy, though he provided Vicky the opportunity to object and state her case. Vicky's lawyer reported that Vicky had retrieved clothes and other necessities from the house while Frank was being held and that her preference was to move out. The lawyer noted that she had already made temporary living arrangements. Frank and Vicky agreed that Kevin would remain with his cousin for the time being but would move in with Vicky in the next few weeks.

When the conversation shifted to the divorce, Frank's lawyer objected and notified the court that Frank would be contesting Vicky's claims of abuse. "Mr. Brittingham intends to allege in his countersuit that it was Mrs. Brittingham who was abusive and that she has had more than one extramarital relationship," he told the judge. "In fact, it is our contention that Mrs. Brittingham is currently engaged in an adulterous extramarital affair."

Wade recognized Frank's lawyer from other domestic cases he'd been involved with. He was younger than Wade but had already garnered a reputation for obtaining favorable results for his clients, who were almost exclusively aggrieved husbands seeking relief from overzealous and undeserving wives. At least that's what they wanted people to believe.

Vicky's lawyer was a respected partner from one of the older law firms in town. His clientele included some of the more prominent residents of the county. Wade couldn't figure how someone of Vicky's means could afford a high-priced lawyer like that, and he began to suspect that Vicky had the backing of a benefactor. Wade considered whether Frank's claims about Vicky were true. Wade eyed Vicky and her attorney as Frank's lawyer spoke. If Vicky's counsel was surprised by the allegations of adultery and abuse, he didn't show it. While opposing counsel continued his speech, Vicky's lawyer stoically took notes on a pad in front of him. The judge heard enough to convince him that the emergency petition should be denied, and he instructed the parties to pursue their claims in the ordinary course. The hearing was adjourned, and the parties dismissed.

Frank left his table and walked to the exit at the back of the courtroom. He scowled at Wade as he passed him and pushed his way into the hallway. Ken and Rick followed up the aisle. Ken walked by without saying a word, but Rick stopped.

"You got something on Brittingham?" Wade asked.

"About as much as you've got on him." Rick stuffed a stick of Juicy Fruit in his mouth and offered one to Wade. Wade waved him off. "He's a loud-mouthed drunk who was seen interacting with the victim and then heard making derogatory statements about her. He's as good a lead as we've got."

Wade pressed him. "Anyone else you looking at? Other than my brother?"

That was a purposeful jab that caught Rick flush. "Ouch, Wade." He staggered back, as if he'd been hit. "I'll tell you what. I'll give Gail Clemmons a call over at the medical examiner's office, tell her to give you access to the autopsy report and some other info you might find interesting." He patted Wade on the shoulder and walked out.

Vicky and her attorney were still in the courtroom. Wade wanted to check on her to make sure she was settled and safe.

"Sheriff Thompson," the lawyer said, raising his palm to stop Wade's approach, "is there something we can help you with?"

Wade hesitated. "I wanted to see how Mrs. Brittingham was doing."

"While we appreciate your concern, I don't think it's a good idea for you to speak with my client at this time."

Vicky grabbed the lawyer's arm above the elbow as he spoke. "It's okay, Teddy."

Teddy lifted an eyebrow but didn't say anything. He collected the last of the papers and files on the table and slid them into his briefcase. "I'll be outside in the hall waiting," he told Vicky, then exited the courtroom.

Wade met Vicky at the table. "Looks like you've got yourself a pretty good lawyer."

Vicky tilted her head and produced a subtle, wry smile. "You don't think I deserve quality representation?"

"That's not what I was suggesting."

"Then what are you suggesting?"

Wade shifted his weight and hooked a thumb in the waistline of his pants. "Frank made some allegations here against you. He made similar allegations when I served him with his papers."

Vicky's face soured. "Is this how you treat a victim of domestic abuse, Wade? You're laying the blame on me? Like I'm the criminal?"

Wade stiffened. "You're right. I'm sorry. I just wanted to make sure you and Kevin were all right."

"Yeah. I'm sorry too." She reached down, picked up her purse, and looped it over her shoulder.

"Hang on a second." Wade decided to fish for a little information. "I'm sure you heard by now that they found that missing girl's body."

"Yeah, I heard. People get into arguments. People get killed. What does that have to do with me?"

Wade never thought Frank was a real suspect, even with Rick and Ken showing up for the hearing. The fact that Ken was messing with his brother led Wade to believe that they had no real leads. Frank was an angry, abusive drunk, but Wade doubted that Frank possessed the capacity for what he saw on the beach. He wanted to test that theory with Vicky.

"Frank talked to that girl at the bar. Is there anything I should know?"

Vicky waited a beat. "The only thing you need to know about Frank is that he is an abusive piece of shit. He deserves everything that's coming to him. But I'll tell you this. That son of a bitch is too lazy and too stupid to do anything like that."

Wade lifted his hands as if to surrender. "All right, all right. I didn't mean to get you all riled up. Just tell me that you'll be okay."

Vicky clutched her purse strap and put her hand on her hip. "I'll be fine," she said, and then she strode past Wade and out of the courtroom.

Lily's second day at school was uneventful. Everyone had moved on from her altercation with Kevin, it seemed, and that was okay with her. Holly was still being nice. That was something that might stick, and Lily was hoping that it would. She'd missed that friendship. Another good thing about her day was that Kevin ignored her at school, not that she was scared about running into him or worried about what he might do. He was always more bark than bite. It just made things a lot better knowing he wasn't interested in continuing their discussion.

The second day went by faster than the first one, and before Lily knew it, she was out of school and on her way downtown. She had some time before she had to meet Jake, so she decided to stop by to visit with Ginny at the hardware store next door to the diner. She parked her Buick and left the motor running long enough for a U2 song to finish playing on the radio. She crossed the street and walked into the store to the gentle, cascading tune of wind chimes that triggered when she opened the door. A gray cat with a tuft of black hair on his chin met her at the threshold and rubbed against her legs, purring loudly.

"I see you've met Eddie," said the man behind the cash register. Lily had been in the hardware store before, with her uncle, when she was much younger. Although she'd never been formerly introduced, she knew that this was Ginny's father.

"Eddie?" Lily asked.

"Yup. Short for Edward Teach. You know, Blackbeard, the pirate," he said, rubbing his own chin for effect.

Lily bent down and scratched Eddie on the head between his ears. The cat wrapped around one of her feet and then lay down on the ground, belly up. Lily scratched the black scruff on his chin and gave him a pat on the chest before Eddie picked himself up and scampered off toward the back of the store.

"Can I help you with something?"

"I'm here to see Ginny."

"Ahh, right. I'm sorry I didn't recognize you at first. You're Lily Parker, Hettie Parker's granddaughter."

"Yes, sir."

He walked out from behind the counter and over to Lily. He had a full head of salt-and-pepper hair parted neatly to one side. His eyebrows were bushy and the same color as his hair, and they ran almost unbroken across his forehead. His mustache was also thick and full, but mostly black. A pair of reading glasses dangled from a cord tied around his neck, and a yellow number two pencil with a point so fine Lily thought it could drive through concrete was sitting in the crook of his ear. The sleeves of his denim blue, collared shirt were rolled up above his elbows, revealing forearms that looked like ham hocks.

"I'm Dwight McCabe, Virginia's father." He shook her hand, firm but gentle. "I've heard a lot about you from my daughter. You might not remember me, but you used to come to my store with your uncle when you were a little girl."

"I remember."

Lily recalled several trips to the hardware store when she first moved in with her uncle. Her uncle was working on improvements around the house, including her new room. "I want you to be part of it," he'd told her when she asked him why he wanted her to come with him. "It's your house too." She remembered one of the first visits, when the emotions of losing her grandmother were still raw, and how Mr. McCabe had given her a lemon-flavored lollipop.

"You used to hand out lollipops to kids."

"I still do," he said, pointing over his shoulder to a large glass jar on the counter that held a rainbow variety. "You want one?"

"Sure." She smiled, almost by accident.

Mr. McCabe walked back to the counter and opened the top of the jar. "Any particular color?"

"Yellow. Yellow would be great."

Eight or so years ago, she was barely tall enough to see over the counter, and now it reached her belly button. She remembered how Mr. McCabe towered over her that day as he reached into the jar and pulled out a lollipop. That jar held so much power. It could turn a frown into a smile and change tears to laughter. Mr. McCabe pulled out another yellow lollipop now and handed it to her. She peeled the wrapper and tasted it. It was tart and sweet and it made her happy for a moment.

Ginny had come out through a swinging door at the back of the store. "Hey, Lily. This is a nice surprise." Eddie followed her to the front and jumped up on the counter, pawing at the wrapper that Lily had left behind.

"I'm meeting a friend next door and wanted to stop in to say hello," Lily told her.

"I'm so glad you did." Ginny seemed genuinely excited.

"I see you've met my father, and that he's already fed you a lollipop." She let out a little laugh.

"Oh, come on now," he replied. "You can't put a price on instant happiness, can you?"

"I guess not," Ginny answered.

Lily wondered what it must be like to have your mother or father with you almost every day. To work with them. To joke with them. To be with them. Every day. She didn't think about her father much, though. Who he was or who he might be. The concept of *father* didn't resonate with her. Her father was an incidental and inconsequential component, a flick of a match, only worth the millisecond it took to spark life into her mother's belly. As far as she could tell, the identity of her father was a mystery not just to her, but to everyone. Whenever she would ask, it was always a shrug and a *We have no idea*. With the death of her uncle, though, there was a nagging thought that she might want to find out.

"Hey, c'mon," Ginny called to Lily. "Let me show you around."

Eddie hopped to the floor and trailed them as they started their tour. Ginny pointed down at him. "He's a lover. He showed up at the back door one day a few years ago. One can of tuna and you get a friend for life."

Lily looked down at the cat, who was prancing along with them like a little soldier on parade. Ginny walked her through the aisles and to an outside section that housed garden supplies and patio furniture. Lily spotted Shadow curled up next to an Adirondack chair and bent down to pet him.

"Do you have time to sit for a few minutes before you have to meet your friend?" Ginny asked.

Lily checked her watch. "I have some time. He won't get here for another few minutes." Lily crunched at the last bits of her lollipop and stuck the white paper stick in the back pocket of her jeans before sitting in the chair nearest Shadow. The dog arched his eyebrows and let out a puff of breath but stayed in his spot.

Ginny sat down in the other chair. "He?" she asked with an eager curiosity.

Lily shrugged her shoulders. "It's no big deal. Just a friend of mine." Lily wanted to avoid this conversation. She sensed a little disappointment in Ginny when she answered, and she felt bad about that, but she wasn't comfortable enough yet with Ginny to share every intimate detail with her.

Ginny changed the subject. She reached down at a rectangular wooden box that was sitting on the floor between them and pulled open the lid. The box was insulated and full of ice and cans of soda. "You want a drink?"

"Sure," Lily answered.

Ginny reached in and pulled out two cans of Dr. Pepper and handed one to Lily. She popped the tab on her can, releasing a sizzle of carbonation, and slurped the brown foam that overflowed and covered the top. She took a long and deep drink then smacked her lips and let out a loud *ahh*.

"There's something about a cold Dr. Pepper." Ginny leaned back in her chair and eyed the can like it was a long-lost friend. "I like to keep a few of them at the store. Dad and I sit here sometimes when it's slow and enjoy the time together." She looked out through the wooden lattice fencing that surrounded the perimeter of the patio. "My mom and dad would take me to the beach on Sundays in the summer when the store was closed. They never let me drink sodas during the week, but they always let me have one as a treat on the beach." She looked down at the can again. "Funny, isn't it? The little things that take you to another time and place. Every time I take a sip of Dr. Pepper, it reminds me of the summer and the beach. And my mom."

"Your mom," Lily started, "is she..." She couldn't bear to say the words.

"She died three years ago." Ginny smiled gently and patted her chest with her free hand. "Bad heart."

Lily studied Ginny. A lock of hair had broken free from the tie at the back of her neck and dangled out in front of her face, but Lily could still see her eyes. They were clear and sharp, and they penetrated the barriers of a lost and emotionally fragile teenager. When Ginny talked about her mother, her face softened and she smiled. The memory of her mother made Ginny happy, and Lily only wished she could feel the same way when she thought about the family she had lost. Eddie jumped up onto Ginny's lap and kneaded biscuits on her leg. Ginny stroked the cat's back and Eddie purred his approval.

"He definitely isn't shy," Lily remarked.

Ginny laughed and tickled him under the chin. "Like I said, he's a lover."

The chimes rang out at the front of the store, stirring Eddie from his comfortable spot. Lily heard footsteps approaching and saw Wade making his way through the front of the store and toward the patio. He stopped at the doorway, filling it almost completely as he leaned against the frame. He cut an imposing profile standing there in full uniform.

Wade smiled and waved his arm in Ginny's direction. "I see you're hard at work out here."

Ginny pulled her foot up onto the edge of the seat of the chair. "Well, dear," Ginny started, with a smirk, "I would put my hour with Mrs. Spencer and her birdhouses and squirrel problems against any one of your arrests or investigations. It's exhausting."

She hooked the loose hairs in front of her face with her finger and pulled them behind her ear. Her eyes focused on him, and he stared back. Even in the silence, Lily thought they were communicating with each other.

Wade broke his gaze and turned to Lily. He raised a fist to his closed mouth and cleared his throat before he spoke again. "Nice to see you, Lily. What are you up to?"

"I'm meeting a friend next door. I stopped in to say hello."

"How was school today?"

"It was fine." *At least it was better than yesterday,* is what she was thinking. She hadn't felt the need to tell either of them, but Wade in particular, about what happened with Kevin Brittingham the day before. She didn't want to make a bigger deal about it than it was.

"Let us know if there's anything we can do for you," he told her. "Anything at all."

Lily checked her watch again. It was a little past four. "I need to get going," she told them.

Before she had a chance to move, Wade interrupted. "Hang on a second." His lips disappeared into a straight line. "I want you to watch yourself."

"Is this about that girl?" Lily asked. "People have been talking about it at school."

Wade's face softened. His body relaxed. "It's probably nothing. Just be careful, okay?"

There was something in Wade's manner that got to her. He wasn't talking like the sheriff. He was talking like someone who genuinely cared. Like family. And then, as Lily got up from the chair, Ginny reached across the space between them and gently squeezed her hand.

"It was nice of you to stop by. I enjoyed our little visit." Ginny's hand lingered on Lily's for a moment. Lily hesitated.

"Me too," Lily said. "It was nice to see you here with your dad." Lily choked up a bit but turned before Wade or Ginny could see her cry. She wiped a couple of tears from her face and exited through a door in the fence.

On the sidewalk outside, she took a moment to compose herself. Jake's Jeep was parked down the street, and the last thing she wanted was for him to see her crying. She looked through the diner window and saw him already sitting in a booth. A waitress hovered over him with a Coke in each hand and a couple of menus tucked under her arm. He said something to her, which made her laugh. Jake was a serious boy, more mature than other boys his age, and he interacted with adults better than any teenager she knew. When Lily's Aunt Margaret was alive, she'd tell Lily stories about her uncle as a little boy. She described him as an old soul and would often say that her uncle was always much older than his age. Lily never really understood what her aunt meant by that until she started dating Jake.

The waitress was somewhere in her late twenties, with a tired look common to people in her profession. She'd likely been on her feet all day dealing with complaining or unruly customers, maybe a farmer that got too fresh or a blue-haired old lady who didn't like the temperature of her lima beans, and now she had to manage the dinner rush with a short staff and an irritated cook. Jake could read people and somehow understood what they needed and how to give it to them. He was like that with Lily too, at least before things went bad between them. She wondered what he told the waitress to give her that moment of joy. Maybe he and Lily could be like that again. Maybe they could start over, as the friends they used to be.

The scent of freshly baked cherry and apple pies hit Lily as soon as she walked into the diner. Those were the smells of her grandmother's kitchen and Sunday afternoons after church. Lily took a deep breath and felt a tickle of sugar on her tongue, which caused her stomach to rumble and her mouth to water and made her miss her family all over again.

Jake saw her and waved her to his booth. The waitress came back over, and they each ordered a cheeseburger and french fries. They ate over some casual conversation. Jake apologized again for missing her uncle's funeral and asked her about living with the Thompsons, and she asked him how he liked Johns Hopkins. They decided to order milkshakes, and that's when Lily noticed Jake's demeanor shift a bit. He looked uncomfortable.

"Is something wrong, Jake?" she asked.

"No. Not at all. It's just that this is nice. I miss it."

Lily felt the same way. She missed being with him.

"Me too," she admitted. "We were always comfortable together." Lily regretted saying it the way she said it. Jake winced. She knew she'd stung him. "I'm sorry Jake. I didn't mean it like that."

"You don't have to apologize," he told her. "I still feel terrible about what I did. I know I hurt you and I am sorry for that, but there is something I wanted to tell you now, something that I haven't been able to tell you before. It might help you understand why I did what I did."

Lily was ready to hear it. "I'm listening."

"You remember that night on the pier, right? That first weekend after school let out."

"Sure," Lily told him. "We ate boardwalk fries and funnel cake, and you won that giant stuffed elephant playing the water gun balloon game. It's still at my uncle's house."

"Do you remember after?"

She remembered. They'd walked down from the pier and onto the beach and found a nice spot under the boards and behind the posts of the pier where no one could see them. And there they did what any number of other high school couples might do under the cover of darkness and hidden from view.

"Yes," she answered, simply.

"Do you remember what I said to you? And what you said back to me?"

Lily looked away in shame. She remembered how he'd told her that he loved her more than anyone else in the world, and that he wanted them to go away to college together and then be together after and forever. It wasn't something a normal teenage boy might say, but Jake wasn't your usual teenage boy. She remembered the pain in his eyes when she'd told him that maybe she couldn't love him like that. But that was just an excuse. She was scared. Scared of having someone love her that much. Scared of getting too close and losing him.

"I remember what we said," she told him.

"I'm not saying any of this to make you feel bad, Lily. Really, I'm not. But when you said that to me, it felt like I lost a piece of my heart. It was bothering me all that week, and I wasn't sure if we were going to be okay. In fact, I thought we were over. We pretty much were, at that point. That's why I drank so much at that party. I was trying to drown out the pain."

The waitress came back with their milkshakes, but neither Jake nor Lily moved to take a drink.

"I'm not here to ask you to forgive me or to ask you to get back together. I just wanted you to understand, and I don't want to lose you as a friend."

Lily didn't have to think about it for long. She wanted him in her life, and she was ready to forgive him and forgive herself, too. And maybe this was another step she needed to help move on with her life, with her grief—for her uncle, for her grandmother, for her mother, for all of them.

Chapter 13

Wednesday, October 21, 1987

EUGENE WILLIS LIVED WITH his wife in an old farmhouse on twenty acres of farmland and woods that bordered a stretch of the Pocomoke River. Wade found him in a rocking chair on his porch, a lit cigar in his hand and a pitcher of lemonade on a table next to him. He'd been retired almost four years now after serving the previous twenty as sheriff, and he had all but anointed Wade his heir apparent on his way out of office. As Wade approached, he heard the old sheriff's bellowing voice.

"Get on up here, boy. Dottie made us a pitcher of her fresh-squeezed."

Wade hopped up and shook his hand. "It's good to see you, Gene."

He was a little older, a little heavier, and a little balder, but he still looked to be in good health. Gene pointed to an empty glass, an invitation, and Wade poured himself a drink.

"Still as good as you remember?" Gene asked.

Wade finished half the glass. "It sure is."

Gene took a few puffs from his cigar. "What's this business you wanted to talk about?"

"We had a girl found dead out on Assateague."

Gene nodded. "I saw it in the paper."

"Did it remind you of anything?"

Gene shook his head. "Nothing comes to mind."

"How about that call we took back in '73? Lisa Harrington. The girl we found under the pier."

Gene chewed on his cigar and rolled it between his lips. "Shoot, Wade. That was a long time ago. I don't remember much. What's the connection?"

"They were both found on a beach. Killed somewhere else and placed there. Both of them naked, except for a white dress or night-gown. Both of them probably strangled."

A deer snuck out of the woods at the edge of the property. She took a few steps into the clearing, sniffing around at something on the ground. She froze when she heard the pop of floorboard beneath the old sheriff's rocking chair, then scampered away.

"That wasn't our case," Gene said. "Did you check with OCPD?"

"Not yet. I wanted to talk to you first."

Gene leaned back in his chair and rocked purposefully. "All I re-member is that she was a local girl. Her parents lived bayside, by the baseball fields. They were good people."

Wade was disappointed in the lack of helpful information, but he wasn't surprised. Eugene Willis only worried about things he needed to worry about. A dead girl on *that* beach was an Ocean City police matter. She was none of his concern or responsibility. Wade had already called the OCPD to request a copy of the Harrington file. He could get what he needed there. He decided to move on to the other reason for his visit today.

In his earliest days with the sheriff's office, Wade would occasion-ally ask for permission to reactivate Emma's case. But there was never any urgency from Sheriff Willis to reinitiate the investigation, and he always balked when Wade pressed the issue. "We did all the work that could be done," Willis told him back then. "There's nothing there. You're too close to this thing anyway. It won't be good for you or the family if you keep at it. You have to leave it be or else it will gnaw at you and eat you up." It always bothered Wade that Sheriff Willis had been so dismissive about the whole thing. He wanted to find out once and for all why Willis had given up on Emma's investigation.

"This girl on Assateague and Lisa Harrington, they got me thinking," Wade started.

Gene raised an eyebrow. "Oh yeah?"

Wade took another sip of his lemonade, doing his best to make this look and feel like a casual conversation and not an interrogation. The old sheriff might dislike this line of questioning even more than the other.

"Yeah. It got me thinking about Emma Parker."

The rocking stopped. Gene adjusted in his chair and bit at his cigar again, a little harder this time, Wade thought. "How so?"

Wade sensed the old sheriff tightening up. He decided on a different tack. "You remember Emma had a little girl?"

Gene nodded.

"She's staying with me now. She'd been living with her uncle the last few years, but he died a couple of weeks ago. He asked me to look after her."

The old sheriff's body relaxed. His face softened. "I did what I could, Wade. I really did. I tracked down the old boyfriends. I talked to her friends. They all had alibis."

Wade was unconvinced. "Why did you give it up?"

The old sheriff let out a heavy sigh. "The case went cold. We had no leads, no real suspects, no evidence. The longer it was in the news, the worse it was for tourist season. It was the middle of summer. I was getting a lot of heat from the hotel and restaurant guys down in Ocean City. And the county supervisors wanted to move on."

"Like who? And why?" Wade understood why the Ocean City people might be hot and heavy to shut it down, but not the others.

"Well, I remember Doc Esham telling me that it was time to back off. Your mother was in bad shape." Gene paused, worried perhaps about how Wade might take the comment. "He convinced me that, as long as the investigation kept going, people would keep talking about Emma, about you, and your mother had reached her limit. There was nothing more I could do. It was a dead end, so I decided to shut it down."

"I don't get it, Gene. Why would Doc Esham think that?"

Gene shrugged his shoulders. "It made sense to me at the time. You two were the best of friends. Emma was like a daughter to your mother. She already thought she'd lost you. Losing Emma was about the last straw for her."

Wade didn't buy it. "That's bullshit, Gene, and you know it. What about Emma's parents? What about her little girl? You didn't think they deserved answers?"

Gene slapped an open hand against the flat armrest of the rocking chair. "I'm done talking about it, Wade. She's gone. Disappeared. If you want to keep chasing ghosts, that's on you. But I'll tell you this, nothing good will come of it." Gene pointed his cigar at Wade. "There's no good ending to that story. All you'll find is pain and misery. Now go on and finish your lemonade. I think it's time for my afternoon nap." Gene got up out of his chair and walked into the house, leaving Wade on the porch alone.

Lily watched the clock on the wall in Mrs. Ferguson's English class slowly tick down to dismissal. The last bell finally rang, and the kids swarmed the halls in a mad dash to the parking lot. Lily, though, took her time packing her bookbag as most of the class emptied ahead of her. There were a few kids lingering about, including Holly Mitchell, and Lily got the impression Holly was waiting for her. She was still getting used to this new dynamic. Holly had even invited herself to sit at their lunch table that afternoon.

Lily finished gathering her books and supplies, looped a bookbag strap onto her shoulder, and walked toward the exit. Holly called to her as she cut through a row of desks to meet Lily at the door.

"Hey, Lily. Wait up."

Lily stopped at the front of the room and waited, thinking maybe Holly wanted to walk out with her. The remaining students slid between them and left the classroom. Mrs. Ferguson collected her purse and a bundle of papers and stopped at the door.

"Do me a favor, girls. Close the door behind you on your way out, okay? I have to rush home to the kiddies."

The girls nodded. Mrs. Ferguson smiled and left the room. The girls stood there in the empty classroom for a moment. Holly wasn't moving for the door, and Lily sensed there was something on her mind.

"What's up?" she asked her.

"What do you mean?" Holly pretended not to understand.

"Look," Lily started, "you're trying, and I appreciate it. But I really don't understand this sudden change in your attitude toward me. Why now?"

Holly let her bookbag slide down her arm. She walked over to a desk at the front of the room and sat down. Lily sat at the desk next to her.

"I didn't mean to upset you. I'm a little lost, I guess," Holly said.

"What do you mean?" Lily asked.

"I really don't know. It started when I found out about your uncle."

"I don't understand."

"The day after your uncle died, the sheriff came to my parents' restaurant. He comes in there a lot, you know. His brother too." Holly scrunched her nose. "He's an interesting character, isn't he?"

Lily remembered seeing Paul Thompson at her uncle's funeral and thinking the same thing. All those times she'd seen him and talked to him when she was living at her grandmother's house, he'd always been kind to her, but there was something different about him. She nodded in agreement.

"My mom sat me down and told me that your uncle died and that she was worried about you. She talked about your mom and how they were such good friends. They all really loved each other. My mom, your mom, the sheriff, and all their friends. It made me think, I don't have anyone like that. I have friends, but those relationships don't feel real. They're superficial, you know what I mean?"

"Yeah, I think I do," Lily said.

She thought about Holly's group, Stacy McPherson and the rest of them, a little clique that had a lot of influence on the kids in their class and even some of the younger students. It was built on good looks, gossip, and humiliation. You wanted to be one of them because they made the parties happen and they hung out with the best-looking boys, and they could make your life at school a lot easier. But if they were against you, they could isolate you and make your life miserable, like they'd almost done with Lily her freshman year. If not for Teri and the Smith twins, her transition from middle school to high school would have been much tougher. She was lucky in that respect. She did have good friends, friends she could trust and count on, friends for life.

"I don't have what my mom had with your mom and still has with the sheriff. I think I want that in my life," Holly told her. "After seeing you face up to Kevin Brittingham the other day, I started to think about things."

Holly dropped her head and picked at the sleeve of her shirt, then looked back up at Lily and continued.

"Maybe I knew I needed some change in my life a while ago. Maybe that's why I broke up with Jimmy. For good this time."

That was a surprise to Lily. Jimmy and Holly had been on and off recently, but Lily didn't know they were officially through.

"I didn't know. I've seen you two together. I didn't really notice any change."

"Yeah, we're still friends. I think Jimmy still thinks we're going to get back together. But I knew we were done. I know we *are* done." Holly paused. "What about you and Jake? Are you back together?"

"No," Lily answered. "We won't be getting back together." It was hard for Lily to say out loud, but it felt right when she said it. It was time for her to move on as well.

"That's a shame," Holly said. "Anyway, after what happened in the cafeteria, I finally realized I wasn't happy being around the people I was with. I mean, they were laughing at that poor kid as he was lying there, bleeding on the floor. Can you believe that? I don't think I like them much, Lily. Not really, anyway." Holly worked the fabric of her shirt again and sighed. "So, I am wondering if maybe we can try to be friends again. What do you think?"

Lily remembered how they used to climb the jungle gym and race across the monkey bars at recess in elementary school and how they'd practice their cartwheels and handsprings in gymnastics. And she remembered the sleepovers and birthday parties. She remembered when, soon after her grandmother died, Holly gave her the little stuffed lamb that was lying on her bed right now. She decided she wanted more of that happiness in her life, and if Holly was offering another friendship, she was ready to take it. Lily resolved to take another step today. She'd let Holly Mitchell back into her life, and maybe she'd open up to the others around her too.

"I think it's a great idea," Lily told her, more certain about it than Holly even seemed, perhaps.

Holly grabbed a piece of Lily's sweater at the arm and pulled at it like she was roping in a boat. She pulled until they were shoulder-to-shoulder in their chairs and Holly could get both her arms around Lily's neck. She hugged Lily and Lily hugged her back, and to Lily it all felt right.

Chapter 14

WADE HAD A RESTLESS night. Emma wouldn't visit often, but when she did, her visits were intense. That's not to say he didn't dream about her. He dreamed about her all the time. But there was a difference between a dream and a visit. The dreams were adventures in the woods and in the marsh and on the beach. They were their younger selves, playing in the mud or sand or swimming in the Atlantic or skating on a frozen Elliot's Pond. Sometimes they were a lunch together in the high school cafeteria or a walk on the boardwalk or a slice of pizza. And every once in a while, they were projections of a life they could have had. A small house on the marsh with a deck out to the water and a boat tied to the dock. A little girl in the front yard picking dandelions and playing with her yellow lab. A walk along the beach, bundled in thick sweaters, gray-haired and wrinkled, hand in hand.

The visits were different. She would come to him like a white-hot flash of light. He could see her clearly. She was real and alive in his mind, and usually there was some kind of message. Most of it he didn't comprehend. Every so often, he understood. Last night, she held out an arrowhead and the message was clear: *Find me.*

Wade left the house as the sun broke, before the girls had stirred from their beds. He drove out to the Ocean City Police Department, picked up his copy of the Harrington file, then headed for the barracks. As soon as Wade got there, he called Ken Meehan and left him a message. He was reopening the Emma Parker investigation, effective immediately.

Ken showed up a little before noon, storming through the entrance and rushing down the hall and into Wade's office. He slammed the door behind him.

"Who the hell do you think you are?" Ken demanded.

"I'm the sheriff of this county, Ken."

"You smug son of a bitch. You're going to jeopardize the Dent investigation over a lost cause and wild goose chase. We have a real killer on the loose and you're creating a diversion."

"I don't think it's a diversion. It's an open case that merits another look, especially now. Maybe there's something that can help with the Dent investigation. Maybe there's a connection."

"That's pure speculation. You have no evidence." Ken paced around Wade's office. "We're working with the FBI, tracking leads up in Philly. There might be something there that's worth a real look."

"I'm sure there is," Wade said. "What you and the FBI decide to investigate regarding Hilary Dent and whatever you're looking at up in Philly is up to you and the FBI. You've made that very clear. What I decide to do about Emma Parker is totally up to me. It's within my jurisdiction and I'm reopening the case."

"Based on what? There's no link. You're making it up in your head."

"Maybe. And maybe there's more here than you or anyone else realizes."

Ken shoved a chair into the corner of Wade's desk and tipped over a plastic cup full of paper clips. The clips spilled across the desk in a rattle, and a few fell to the floor.

Ken pointed a finger at Wade. "You stay out of our way." He spun around and pushed out of Wade's office, brushing by Deputy

Johnson, who'd staked himself outside Wade's door when he heard the commotion.

Wade thought Ken was a little hotter about all of this than he should've been. Maybe he was telling the truth about why he didn't want this investigation, or maybe it was something else. Maybe he was trying to protect someone. Wade saw Deputy Johnson and waved him in.

"Come on in here, Garrett. I have an assignment for you."

Wade was sitting in a fold-out chair in the corner of one of Gail Clemmons's examination rooms. He'd been waiting there alone for about ten minutes, ushered in unceremoniously by one of Gail's assistants. The room smelled of formaldehyde, and it made Wade's empty stomach uneasy. He got up off the chair and poured himself a cup of coffee from a pot on the counter. He took a couple of sips. It was old and stale and took his stomach for a spin. He spilled the rest in the sink and slumped back in the chair.

Gail strode through the door a few minutes later. She was a small woman, barely five feet tall, with salt-and-pepper hair gathered in a twist at the back of her neck. Her white lab coat reached down to her knees and swallowed her completely. "Sorry to keep you waiting, Wade." She sounded exasperated.

Wade played with the empty paper cup still in his hands. "No problem, Gail."

She wrinkled her nose. "You didn't drink any of that coffee, did you? It's from this morning."

"Yeah? Well, it tasted like last week," he said, jokingly.

Gail looked at him like his mother used to when he was a little boy, after he got in a fight with his brother or when he hurt himself rough-housing with his friends. Gail was a tough woman doing the work she was doing and seeing the things she'd seen as the Chief Medical Examiner in this part of the state. But she had a tender side to her, for sure. Wade had seen it at crime scenes with the family members of victims and bystanders and even cops, when in the middle of the chaos, with blood on the walls and bodies on the floor, she would put a hand on the shoulder of an officer or whisper a few words into the ear of a crying mother. But then, her face turned serious, and Wade knew she was ready to get down to business.

"What have you got for me?" he asked her.

Gail grabbed a rolling stool near one of the examination tables and slid it along with her across the floor and over to Wade. She sat down and shuffled through the folder. Her glasses were propped on top of her head and Wade could see the crow's feet on the sides of her exposed eyes, the result of long days working tough cases.

"The Dent girl was sexually assaulted, postmortem, but no semen. Her body was cleaned thoroughly. No hair, no fibers, no fingerprints. There was nothing we could detect on her nightgown other than sand and seawater." Gail delivered the news unemotionally. This was the scientist and clinician talking now.

Gail pulled out several photographs from the folder and laid them out on the counter. Wade rose, stood next to Gail, and looked down at the pictures of the girl. He saw her again as she was on the beach and then laid out in the examination room, with various angles of her body before and during the autopsy. There she was in five-by-sevens and eight-by-tens, shadows and colors, flesh and bone.

Wade pointed at one of the pictures. "But he left the trail of blood under her eyes. Like he drew down her face with his finger."

"Yes. That was her blood," she told him. "We believe he made those cuts under her eyes before he killed her, or contemporaneous to the killing, with a precision instrument. A scalpel, perhaps. They were small cuts that wouldn't have spilled a great deal of blood. Just enough for him to do that."

"I assume he wore a glove or something when he did it."

"I think so. The streaks were smooth and straight. There were no striations or other imperfections."

"Anything you could gather from the ligature marks?"

"We found them on the wrists and ankles. The markings suggest some sort of nylon cord or rope," she answered. "The bruising indicates that she was alive when he tied her. We also identified discoloration around the mouth, which suggests he used duct tape or some other adhesive. She also had bruising on her neck and the autopsy confirmed strangulation as the cause of death."

Gail collected the photographs and placed them back into the folder. Wade watched and thought about how this girl's life and death had been reduced to some ministerial function, just words on paper and chemicals on film, filed away and forgotten. It was all so detached from the flesh and blood and the experiences and memories of real life.

He thought about Lisa Harrington. How she'd been used and discarded just like this girl. He agonized over Emma and hoped that she didn't suffer a similar fate. Then his mind shifted to the women currently in his life, Ginny, his mother, Lily, and his immediate inclination was to do anything and everything in his power to keep them safe. Rick had sent him here for a reason. There was more to this story.

"Rick suggested that you might have some other information for me?" Wade asked.

"Yes. When we met earlier this week, they told me that the FBI was getting involved."

"I heard about that today from Ken Meehan."

"They've had other cases, apparently. One near Wilmington and another in Philadelphia. Young women gone missing and turning up dead. There are enough similarities that they're looking into a possible link."

"What cases?" Wade asked. "I haven't heard about them."

"They aren't recent," she said. "The Wilmington case happened around four years ago. A young college student disappeared after a frat party. They found her body a few days later propped up against a wooden post on a dock on the river. She was naked except for a plain white top."

"What about Philadelphia?"

"That one was about seven years ago," she told him. "The girl disappeared after leaving work. They found her in a park, near a river. She was laid out on a strip of grass, dressed in white."

Wade's stomach took another turn. Two other cases, just like Dent. "Was there any other evidence? Hair? Fingerprints?"

"You'll have to get with Rick and Ken or the FBI. They didn't give me any other details. Just a little background information while I worked up this case. From what I understand, they had no active leads and there had been no developments for some time. Until now, perhaps."

Wade became more certain of a possible connection between Dent and Harrington, and there might be something in all of this that traced back to Emma. He'd made a copy of the Harrington file and brought it with him. He slid a folder holding the report over to Gail. "I have something for you."

She opened it and flipped through the pages. Her eyebrows peaked. Her jaw dropped. "This was before my time." She flipped back to the first page. "Nineteen seventy-three."

"Old Sheriff Willis and I were there." Wade pulled a sheet out with an image of the crime scene. "Young. White dress. Strangled. Near a body of water."

Gail studied the picture. "Nineteen seventy-three," she repeated. "I'd like a copy of this."

Wade slid the page back into the folder and handed it to her. "I already made one for you. Go through it and let me know what you think."

Outside, the last traces of sunlight had already slipped behind rooftops, sending the last long shadows into the night and the temperature dropping fast. Wade tested his breath against the chill, releasing a barely noticeable wisp into the darkening sky. He stood by his car and considered the events unfolding in front of him.

It appeared possible, and even likely, that the same person was responsible for the murders of Lisa Harrington, Hillary Dent, and these other two women. The four bodies were found within one hundred fifty miles or so in a straight line from Assateague to Philadelphia. The first and last of those bodies were found within maybe a five-mile stretch. There was more than an even chance that the person responsible was local, or at least a frequent visitor, operating in the area at least as early as 1973.

While there was no direct, tangible evidence, Wade had convinced himself that Emma's disappearance was somehow connected to these murders. She could've been an earlier victim. Maybe even the first.

A test case for this killer, or maybe the trigger. And now, after his visit with Sheriff Willis, Ken's outburst, and his meeting with Gail, Wade was more determined to prove his theory. Someone who knew Emma had killed her, and that person just might be responsible for these other girls' deaths too.

Chapter 15

1965

W ADE WALKED ALONG THE brick pathway leading to the
front of Sandy's house. He climbed the flat stone steps and
reached for the brass knocker hanging at the center of the oak front
door. Three quick raps against wood. He stepped back and waited,
fidgeting from side to side, adjusting the knot on his tie, and shaking
the box in his left hand that held her homecoming corsage. The door
opened.

"Good evening, Wade." It was Sandy's mother. She had the same
warm smile that Wade remembered from his days in her elementary
school music class. Somewhere inside a classical composition of vio-
lin and other string instruments played on a record player.

"Hello, Mrs. Carter."

Mrs. Carter reached out and gently touched the side of his face,
which was bruised from chin to cheek. "Tough game last night,
huh?"

"It looks a lot worse than it feels," he told her. The truth was that
he could still feel the ache in his jaw and up through his cheekbone
and the sharp jab in his chest whenever he breathed.

"If you say so," she said, unconvinced. She stepped to the side and
opened the door wide to invite him in. "Come in. Sandy's still getting
ready upstairs. You can wait in the study with Chuck."

Wade followed Sandy's mother through the foyer and down the
hall in the direction of the music. They found Mr. Carter in a brown

leather chair in the corner of the room. He had a book propped open on his lap and was sipping a whiskey on the rocks from a thick crystal tumbler. Mr. Carter peeked over the reading glasses perched on the bridge of his nose.

"Hello, Wade." Mr. Carter scanned him up and down. "You're looking mighty sharp tonight."

"Thanks, Mr. Carter." Wade glanced at Paul's hand-me-down suit, which was tight in the shoulders and a little short in the arms and legs. Wade had outgrown all his Sunday clothes and now barely fit into his older brother's.

"You boys get comfortable," Mrs. Carter told them. "I'm going to help Sandy upstairs."

Mr. Carter set down his drink on a table next to him. "Come in and take a seat," he said, waving Wade to the sofa opposite his chair.

Wade dropped himself onto the couch and scanned the room, which, in addition to the furniture, held a variety of instruments. Mr. Carter was a salesman for a wholesale distributor of musical instruments and sold them new and used to shops and schools all over Delaware, Maryland, and Virginia. Because he worked out of his home, he often had a full orchestra's worth strewn throughout the rooms of his house. Wade spotted a couple of guitars on stands off to one side of the room, a trumpet and saxophone on shelving along a wall, and a baby grand piano in another corner. There were also several cases that held flutes and French horns and other wind instruments, and almost every flat surface was covered with sheet music or books.

Mr. Carter took off his glasses and twirled them in his hand. "Pat Flanagan over at the grocery store said you were all over the field last night. He said you played one hell of a game."

Wade looked down at the box still in his hands. "Ah, thanks, Mr. Carter." He shuffled the box from side to side and looked up again. "The team played well."

"How's school going?" Mr. Carter asked.

"Decent, I guess," Wade responded.

"That's good to hear," Mr. Carter said. "I wish I could say the same about Sandy. She's not much for studying, and she doesn't have much of an interest in music. She's started and stopped playing more instruments than all the kids in Nancy's classes combined."

The clapping of high heels against the wood stairs in the foyer interrupted their conversation. A few seconds later, Sandy stepped through the entryway and into the room.

"Are you talking about me, Daddy?"

Sandy was wearing a simple, sleeveless pale lavender dress that fit tight to her waist and blossomed out like the petals of a tulip down to the floor. She had a string of pearls around her neck and pearl studs in her earlobes, and her long brown hair was pulled up in a neat ball at the top of her head. Wade hoped his bruised face and tired suit wouldn't detract from her beauty.

"Wow, Sandy, you look great," he told her.

Sandy tried to brush off the compliment, but the blush on her cheeks gave her away. "Jeez, Wade, don't act all surprised," she said, coyly. "You don't look half bad yourself."

Mr. Carter rose to his feet and gave Sandy a peck on the cheek. "You look beautiful, sweetheart."

"Thanks, Dad," she responded with a smile.

Wade fumbled open the box, pulled out a delicate, ivory rose wrist corsage, and slid it onto Sandy's wrist. She turned it on her arm and admired it against her dress. There was another flower in the box, which she took out and pinned to Wade's lapel.

Mr. Carter picked up a camera from one of the tables and pointed the couple to the corner. "All right you two. Get over by the piano for a picture."

Wade ran a hand through his hair and adjusted his jacket. His face was smooth and clean but for the bruises, and it held the hint of summer sun even this late into the fall. Sandy stood next to him, almost reaching him in height in her high-heeled shoes and the couple of inches of hair propped up at the top of her head. She weaved her arm through Wade's and nestled close into him. They posed for a few shots, and then Wade offered to take a couple of pictures of Sandy and her parents. The family gathered at the front of the piano, but before they settled, Mrs. Carter licked her fingers and ran them across a few hairs spraying out in a tuft at Mr. Carter's temple. Mr. Carter playfully swiped at Mrs. Carter's hand.

"For crying out loud, Nancy. I'm not seven years old."

Mrs. Carter waved him away and went over to the other side of their daughter. Wade snapped the shutter and wound the film, then turned the camera for a vertical shot and took another one.

"I think I got it," Wade told them. "You guys look great."

"You kids have fun, and be safe," Mrs. Carter told them.

"We will, Mom," Sandy replied. "Don't forget that a bunch of us are staying at Tiffany's house tonight after the dance."

Sandy picked up the bag of clothes she had packed earlier, and she and Wade walked out of the house. Sandy wobbled a bit on the uneven walkway, so Wade offered his elbow, which Sandy took with her free hand, and guided her along the herringbone brick to the edge of the street and to his father's sky-blue 1960 Ford Falcon. They drove out of the neighborhood and headed to the school. Sandy leaned over and turned on the radio, which was dialed to their favorite station and playing "Yesterday." By the time they got through

"California Dreamin'" and "19th Nervous Breakdown," they were already pulling into the school parking lot.

They got out of the car and headed toward the gym entrance along with a handful of other kids who were loitering in the lot and on the sidewalks waiting for their friends to arrive. Wade and Sandy walked in, arm in arm, and weaved their way through the crowd and to a table off to the side near the stage where their friends were already gathered.

One of the boys stood up and pointed at Wade as he approached the table. "There he is!" he shouted excitedly. Timmy Finch was short and muscular, and his shirt was so tight at the collar that his veins were popping out and climbing along his thick neck like tangled vines on a birch tree.

Wade greeted him with a hand slap and a wide smile. "Hey, Timmy."

Tiffany Quinn, a thin redhead who was at least two or three inches taller than Timmy, put her arm around Sandy. "How does it feel to have a football star as your date?" she said, motioning to Wade with a cup full of punch in her hand. "I wouldn't know, of course. I'm stuck here with Timmy."

The table broke out in laughter. Timmy tried to defend himself.

"I got in a few plays and made a few tackles. Wade knows how to share the glory."

"Don't be so hard on him, Tiff," his friend Dave said. "It's tough when you're five foot two and slower than molasses."

"Oh, screw you, Dave." Timmy threw a couple of light punches into Dave's midsection.

"Easy killer," Dave said, patting Timmy's head like he was trying to calm a rambunctious puppy. "I'm gonna spill my drink."

Dave was taller and wider than Wade, and his hand was so big that it swallowed the whole crown of Timmy's head. He was the team's left tackle and one of their defensive ends, and quite possibly the strongest teenager in the state. He'd lift two-hundred-pound linemen off their feet and toss them aside like a toddler's bean bag. Wade loved it when he had the ball and they ran left. He'd follow Dave around the edge and usually over a linebacker or two that Dave had mauled to the ground. Despite his violent tendencies on the football field, David Miller was the gentlest of souls, and he could turn a stranger into a friend before they finished their handshake. He spoke with a tinge of a southern accent that filled your ears like spilt honey.

Dave's date, Claire, pulled him away from Timmy's jabs and closer to her side. "Don't get Timmy all riled up. You know how he is once he gets going." She flicked her head to the side, swinging a curtain of wavy, brown hair back over her shoulder, and turned to Sandy. "Hey, have you heard from Emma today?"

Before answering, Sandy peeked over to Wade, probably checking on his reaction to the question. There was a jealousy that had festered in Wade ever since Emma started dating Brad Wilkerson early in their freshman year. Emma was so focused on Brad, she'd all but forgotten about Wade. They'd still talk every so often. They shared friends and classes and a front yard. But it wasn't the same for Wade. At least when he was younger, there was a reasonable chance that he and Emma might get together at some point. Now that she was with Brad, those chances had narrowed to almost zero.

"I haven't heard from her today," Sandy answered. "I'm assuming she'll be here soon. Brad's up for homecoming king. He wouldn't miss that."

"Not with his ego, that's for sure," Dave said with a knowing smirk.

Sandy reached for Wade's hand and gave it a gentle squeeze. She looked over at Tiffany and the other girl at the table. "Hey, let's get these losers on the dance floor."

Tiffany grabbed Timmy by the collar. "That's a great idea," she said, pulling Timmy along at the scruff like a mother cat with one of her kittens. Dave and Claire followed them out, but Wade hesitated.

Sandy leaned into him. The soft touch of her lips brushed against the edge of his ear. The little hairs on the back of his neck stiffened. "C'mon, Wade," she whispered. "Come dance with me." Wade closed his eyes and let her lead him out onto the floor.

They danced to the Beach Boys and the Four Tops and The Ronettes' "Be My Baby." When "Can't Help Falling in Love" started playing, Wade began his retreat to the table, but Sandy pulled him back. She draped her arms around his neck and nestled her chin in the crook of his shoulder. He could smell the sweet scent of her perspiration and feel the gentle curves of her body against his as they drifted slowly across the room. For a moment, he forgot about Emma.

They got back to their table right as Brad and his posse crashed through the gym doors. A crew of older boys and girls greeted them at the entrance as if they were Hollywood movie stars, and it captured the attention of most of the crowd in the gym, who turned at the commotion. Wade looked over in disgust, and his irritation only grew at the sight of Emma following in tow like some pitiful lapdog. But she was stunning in her pink, tea-length dress. Her hair was elegant. Her lips were full and red. A fuel of rage and lust burned inside him.

Timmy cozied up to Wade and pulled a flask from the inside of his jacket. He opened it and poured out some liquid into Wade's cup of punch. "Here, buddy. Looks like you might need a little magic water tonight."

Wade stirred the cup and took a drink. "Thanks, man."

"No problem, compadre."

Emma saw Wade and the others and snuck away from her group while Brad and his boys were backslapping and glad-handing.

Claire met her as she approached. "We were wondering when you'd show up." She reached out and took Emma's hands. "You look fantastic."

"Thanks, Claire. So do you." Emma squeezed Claire's hands anxiously. "You all look great. Even Timmy." Most of the table laughed when she said it, though Wade wasn't one of them.

"Sit with us for a little while." Claire pulled Emma to the table.

Emma sat down in an open seat across from Wade. Their eyes met, but Wade couldn't stand it for more than a second. He shifted his focus down to his drink, lifted the cup, and gulped down its contents.

"Is Brad okay with you hanging out with us?" Wade asked her gruffly.

"Leave her alone," Tiffany said, slapping at Wade's hand. "Let us have our time with her."

"Hey boys," Dave said, motioning to them with an empty cup. "Let's get some punch and leave the ladies to their gossip. Timmy, bring the flask."

Timmy sprung out of his chair and patted the outside of his jacket. "Wouldn't go anywhere without it."

Dave grabbed Wade and pulled him out of his seat. Wade left the girls without saying another word. He was angry. Angry that Emma still had that kind of grip on him. Angry that her presence made him dismiss how he'd felt with Sandy on the dance floor. Angry at Brad.

They snuck out of the gym through the boys' locker room and huddled in an unlit area off to the side of the building, drinking the cocktail from their cups. Wade was beginning to feel the effects of the alcohol. The warmth ran through his chest and out to his fingers and toes, and a slight fog had settled in his head right behind his eyes, clouding his senses just a bit. Like magic, the pain in his ribs and jaw disappeared.

Dave guzzled down the rest of the liquid in his cup and motioned to the empty flask in Timmy's hand. "You got any more of that in your car?"

"You know it, brother," Timmy told him.

"Well," Dave said, "why are you still here?"

Timmy smiled and ran off toward the parking lot.

Dave turned back to Wade. "You gonna be all right, partner?"

Wade looked at Dave. He was annoyed. "Why is everyone so worried about me all of a sudden?"

"Because every time you see Emma with Wilkerson, your eyes catch fire, and it looks like you're about to kill someone."

Wade tipped his head back, mouth wide open, and tried to spill the last few drops of spiked punch from his cup into his mouth.

"There ain't nothin' left in there, stud. Timmy will be here with reinforcements soon."

Timmy was back a few seconds later and the boys took turns taking swigs of liquor from the flask until they'd emptied it out again. By the time they made it back into the gym, they were well on their way to drunk. When they got to their table, they faced three angry dates.

"Where the heck did you guys run off to?" Tiffany asked all of them, though she saved her best glare for Timmy. "You missed the crowning ceremony."

Timmy shrugged his shoulders and gave her that goofy grin she'd seen from him before. It was the one that usually meant that a little fun and maybe a little trouble would be on the agenda for the evening.

"Who won?" he asked sheepishly.

"Wade's pal Brad is homecoming king," Claire told them. "Barbara Jenkins got queen."

"I guess my write-in campaign for Dave for queen didn't work, eh?" Timmy said, giggling like a little kid hearing his first dirty joke.

Wade wasn't laughing. He was staring over at Brad and Emma and their group of friends.

"C'mon guys," Sandy said to all of them. "Let's get out of here."

The others began collecting their things and started heading toward the door. Wade didn't move. Years of pent-up anger and frustration were boiling up inside him. Dave put his arm around Wade and shook him from his stupor.

"Let's go, big guy. It's time to head to Tiff's."

Brad and his crew were crowded near the exit. He was wearing a red coronation mantle trimmed in faux white fur and a puffy red and gold crown. He was holding a fake gold scepter in one hand and he had his other arm draped around Emma's hip. Wade thought he looked like a clown.

When Brad saw Wade and the others approach, he spun around to face them, yanking Emma around with him. "Hey, Thompson," he yelled out. "One day, all this could be yours."

He held his arms high above his head and waved them as if the gym and the people were the spoils of his reign. But Wade knew that, more than anything else, he was talking about Emma.

The crowd around them laughed and Sandy did her best to pull Wade toward the door and out of the gym, but Wade stopped and wrestled his arm from Sandy's grasp. He walked over to Brad, his nostrils flaring, and poked his finger into Brad's chest.

"Why don't you take that staff and shove it up your ass, Wilkerson. And if you can't do it yourself, we can go outside right now and I'll do it for you."

Brad smacked at Wade's finger. "I'm ready, Thompson. Let's go."

Brad shrugged off the cloak and handed the staff and crown to one of the boys next to him. Wade stormed out the doors, pulling off his jacket in one quick motion and throwing it into a patch of grass near the sidewalk. He loosened his tie quickly and yanked it, still looped, over his head. He was rolling up his sleeves when Brad emerged with his entourage. Kids poured out of the gym and gathered around them.

"I'm gonna give you the ass kicking you've been asking for, Thompson."

Wade waved him forward. "Bring it on."

Brad lowered his head and charged at Wade. Wade dipped to avoid him and threw a left cross into the right side of Brad's face. Brad stumbled but caught his balance and charged at him again, this time launching a wild right-hand haymaker, trying to end the fight with one big punch. Wade anticipated Brad's move, bobbing below the assault and shifting slightly to the left. Wade caught Brad in the nose with two quick left jabs, then followed them with a right cross to the other side of Brad's face. Brad stumbled back this time and Wade followed, landing a left into Brad's gut and then a right cross at his eye. Brad staggered to the ground as Wade rained overhand rights into the side of Brad's face. Brad was trying to shield himself from the blows, but the punches were falling so fast and hard he couldn't prevent them from making contact. The fight was over almost before it even began.

Timmy and Dave pulled Wade off Brad, who was laying on the pavement with blood running from his nose and mouth. There was a cut over Brad's left eye, and it was already starting to swell shut. Wade breathed heavily through gritted teeth. Any pain he might have felt earlier had washed away in a flush of alcohol, anger, and adrenaline. He looked up and saw Emma in the background, her face twisted. Brad pushed himself off the ground. Emma reached for Brad's arm, but he brushed it away.

"Don't touch me," he said to her, angrily, before stumbling through the crowd.

Emma hesitated. She looked over at Wade, her wide brown eyes set sternly upon his, before going after Brad. Wade saw her disappointment, and he suddenly felt a wave of regret. He stood there frozen, the voices of teachers and administrators barely registering as they made their way out of the gym. Dave quickly hooked Wade underneath his armpits, lifting him and dragging him away from the skirmish and toward the parking lot. Sandy picked up Wade's jacket and tie and followed Dave to the car.

"Put him in the passenger seat, Dave," Sandy told him. "I'm driving."

"Yes, ma'am," Dave answered dutifully. He released Wade and leaned him against the side of the car. "Give me the keys, Wade." Wade reached into his pocket, pulled out the keys and handed them to Dave. Dave opened the door and pushed Wade into the vehicle, then tossed the keys to Sandy. "I'll see you two at the house," he said before leaving.

Sandy settled behind the steering wheel and turned to Wade, who was slumped and leaning against the glass of the passenger side door.

"When is it going to stop?" she asked him.

"When is what going to stop?"

"You know exactly what I'm talking about. You have to move on. You aren't anything more than a friend to her."

Wade looked down at the scar that marked the palm of his hand. "That's not true."

"It is true. You have to snap out of this funk, Wade. You are more than Emma Parker." Sandy put the car in gear and pulled out of the parking lot. "I know you love her. I do. But this isn't a healthy thing. For you or for her. All you are doing is causing both of you pain and misery."

Wade rubbed the scar and let out a heavy breath. He remembered what Emma said to him that day on the marsh after he kissed her. *You're like a brother to me.* That's the way it was then, and that's the way it was now. Nothing more than a brother. Nothing more than friends. If he wasn't careful, he might lose that too.

"Maybe you're right," he said reluctantly.

"I know I'm right." She reached over and grabbed Wade's hand. "It's time to move on. Starting tonight."

"Okay. Okay. I'm done. I'm done loving her." Wade said the words, hoping they were true but knowing they weren't. He couldn't stop loving Emma any more than he could stop the beating of his heart.

When they got to Tiffany's, Dave and Timmy had already left for the beach to work on the bonfire. Wade and Sandy changed out of their dress clothes, grabbed a couple of blankets, and headed to the beach with Claire and Tiffany. Flames and smoke were lifting from the logs when they arrived, and Dave and Timmy already had open beers in their hands.

"Here comes that crazy bastard!" Timmy barked as Wade approached. He grabbed a Schlitz from the cooler and tossed it over to Wade. Wade peeled off the tab and sucked up the foam that erupted from the top of the can.

The girls laid out the blankets and settled in. Timmy handed each of them a beer, and he and the other boys sat down with them.

Timmy raised his can in the air. "Here's to a good fight, a good night, and great company."

"Hear, hear!" Dave said, raising his beer to meet the toast. He chugged it down in one take and crushed the empty can on his knee. "Toss me another one, Timmy."

Claire nudged his shoulder. "Take it easy there, big fella. I don't want you too drunk tonight."

"It's gonna take a whole lot more than a little liquor and a couple of beers," he told her.

Dave reached over and patted Wade's back. "You settled down?"

Wade nodded. "Yeah, I'm good."

"Good," Dave said. "Now let's get down to business." He reached into the pocket on the front of his shirt and pulled out a hand-rolled marijuana cigarette.

Timmy smiled. "Whatcha got there, big boy?"

"Just a bit of something to take the edge off, little buddy."

Dave put the joint in his mouth and struck a match. He held the flame to the end of the cigarette and took a few puffs to get it started. Once it sparked, he inhaled deeply and held the smoke in his lungs, then blew it out to the sky.

"Pass that puppy over here," Timmy told him. Timmy took a long drag and then sent it around the circle, where the rest of them took turns taking a hit, until it got to Wade.

"I don't want any of that," he said, waving it off. It wasn't something Wade did very often, and he wasn't quite in the mood for it now.

"Listen, man," Dave started, "there ain't nothing wrong with a little Mary Jane every now and again. It'll even take away some of that pain," he said, pointing right at Wade's heart.

"Dave's right, Wade," Timmy added. "And if you don't trust us, surely you'd trust the greatest poet and prophet of our time?"

"Oh yeah? Who might that be?" Wade asked.

"Bob Dylan of course."

They all laughed at that, even Wade.

"All right," Wade said, taking the cigarette from Tiffany. "One hit." He put the joint to his lips, pulled in a deep breath, and held it in his lungs until he started coughing.

"Woohoo!" Timmy yelled. "That's my boy."

Wade took more than that one hit, and the alcohol and pot started working their magic on him. He felt more relaxed and at ease, and he was having a good time with his friends, especially Sandy. She had always been there for him, and he was beginning to realize that he'd taken her for granted. She was beautiful and smart. She was carefree, fun, and full of energy. She was everything a boy could ever want in a girl.

They sat around for a little longer, drinking their beers and smoking their joints, before finally deciding it was time to wrap things up and head back to the house. Dave emptied the remaining ice from the cooler, and Claire and Tiffany pulled up their blankets. When Wade started to lift himself off the sand, Sandy reached up and grabbed him.

"I want to stay down here a little longer," she said to him. "Will you stay with me, for a little while?"

Wade fell back onto the blanket. "Sure."

Sandy looked up to Claire and Tiffany. "You guys go ahead. We'll be up soon." The girls nodded and followed Timmy and Dave off the beach and to the house.

Wade leaned back on his elbows and looked over the still smoldering logs into the darkness of the ocean. The heat of the fire had diminished, and he could feel the chill in the air through his flannel shirt. Sandy leaned in close to him and wrapped her arms around his midsection. She was wearing a thick cable sweater and was still warm from the fire. It made him feel safe and comfortable and surprisingly at peace. The moon was out. It was less than full, but it was still bright in the sky, and its reflection spread out in front of them like milk spilled across the black of the open sea. The quiet of the night was broken only by the crackling embers of the fire and the rhythmic cascade of crashing waves.

A light breeze kicked in and blew a plume of smoke into Wade's face. He closed his eyes to take away the sting. He felt Sandy's hand, balled into a fist in the cuff of her sweater, wipe away a tear that was rolling down the side of his face. Then he felt her lips against his cheek. He opened his eyes and turned to her. She lifted her head and kissed him. He held her head in his hands and kissed her back. She pulled away and lifted the sweater off her body and over her head. He touched the bare skin of her shoulder as she worked the buttons of his shirt. They kissed again and laid themselves down on the blanket.

Chapter 16

Friday, October 23, 1987

T HE MITCHELLS' RESTAURANT WAS near the corner where the road leading into Ocean City joined the main south-to-north thoroughfare. On any given summer evening, vehicles entering the resort town would almost certainly pass the building. After a long day at the beach, the occupants of those vehicles might remember the bright yellow paint of the place or the big red sign on the roof that lit up at night bright enough to be seen at least six or seven blocks up or down the road. They might recall the smell of charbroiled steaks cooking from the gas grill at the front and convince themselves that a steak off that grill was worth the $7.99 that was advertised on the plate glass window when they passed it the day before. But this late in the year, with the town virtually empty of visitors, it being the offseason and maybe because a missing girl's body had just been found on the island across the inlet, there wasn't enough business to justify the expense of running the place for a few extra days in late October. The restaurant was only open for breakfast on weekends after Labor Day anyway, so Sandy's husband Billy decided to shut it down a little early, and he and Sandy shifted to their offseason work.

Billy drove a mixing truck for the concrete plant. Sandy worked part-time as a clerk at the district court. It wasn't too bad for them. They could both walk to work if they wanted, and the jobs gave them enough income to float them through the fall and winter and get them to Memorial Day when the tourists returned.

Wade had called Sandy the day before and asked if he could come over to the family's apartment to talk, and they'd arranged an early morning meeting for the next day. The place would be empty and quiet with Holly at school and Billy already at the plant or on the road. Wade arrived and climbed up the narrow staircase to the second floor above the restaurant. From the landing on the porch, he could see the drawbridge and the cement silos of the plant rising to the sky to the west next to the bay. He pulled open a weather-worn screen door and knocked against the faded blue door behind it. There was a shuffle of footsteps and the rustle of a chain before the door opened and Sandy appeared.

She was wearing an oversized white fisherman's sweater that reached down about midthigh over a pair of washed-out denim blue jeans. Wade thought it might be the same sweater he remembered her wearing on the beach that one night many years ago.

"Hey, Wade." She had a hint of a southern drawl that came out of her when she was sleepy or a little drunk. "Come in."

She rubbed her eye with the back of her hand, which was tucked in the sleeve of the sweater, like a little kid might after waking from a nap. She stepped back and let Wade pass into the living area of the apartment. Her hair was messy and looked to have been quickly gathered into an untidy knot at the back of her head.

"You caught me early. I didn't have much time to get myself together."

Wade thought she looked just fine. She motioned for him to follow her.

"Come on. I have coffee waiting for us."

Sandy led him through a small corridor past the two bedrooms and into the kitchen and dining area. He took a seat at the table while Sandy poured their drinks and brought them to the table.

"What did you want to talk about?" Sandy asked. "I hope Holly and her gang aren't causing any trouble."

"No. It's not about Holly."

"Oh, thank God," she said, relieved. "That girl has been giving me a lot of grief lately. I was worried." Sandy stirred her coffee and waited for Wade to continue. He hesitated. "So, what then?" she asked.

"It's about Emma."

Sandy didn't say anything at first, she just kept stirring. "Jesus, Wade," she said, finally.

Wade knew Sandy might not react well to another conversation about Emma. There'd been so many over the years, and she had expressed her frustration with him whenever he raised the topic. "When is this going to stop?" she'd asked him the last time they talked about it. "It's been so long. Why can't you let go?" Wade knew she missed her friend. And like him, she was frustrated that they didn't have any answers. Bringing it up over and over again was reliving the pain and sadness of it, but things had changed. He hoped Lily's situation would temper the tone of the discussion.

"I know you don't want to hear it," he told her. "But there are some new developments. And there's Lily."

Her face softened. "All right," she said, halfheartedly.

"You heard about the girl they found on the beach."

"Of course. Everyone is talking about it." There was concern in her voice, but less than she would've had if she'd known the full details. "I told Holly to be careful."

"Is there anything familiar about it? What you've read or heard?"

Sandy shook her head. "Not that I can think of."

"Do you remember that girl they found under the pier, back in '73?"

Her jaw fell open. "Oh my God. Lisa Harrington. She was the same grade as my cousin. They were friends."

"That's right. There are enough similarities that it got me thinking. Two girls taken right here from our own backyard. Two girls left dead at the beach. If there were two, could there be three? Or more?"

She closed her eyes and shook her head to try and rid herself of the thought. "Why are you telling me all this? Should you be telling me this?"

Wade knew he probably shouldn't, but this was information Sandy already had. He was just refreshing her recollection. And there was a more pressing concern. One closer to both of them.

"I admit, that's a big supposition, but here's why I'm bringing it up with you." Wade touched her arm to make sure he had her full attention. She looked at him, her eyes reddening. "I've always believed the person responsible for Emma knew her. More recently, I've come to suspect that maybe that person got rid of her to keep the truth from coming out."

"The truth?" she asked. "What truth?" There was a break in her voice.

"The truth about Lily. The truth about her father."

Sandy got up and walked to the sink. She filled a glass with water and drank about half of it in a couple of gulps. Wade gave her a minute to collect herself, then began again.

"I think it's more important than ever to find out who Lily's father is. Maybe it's all for nothing. Best case, we find out who he is and that he had nothing to do with anything. Worst case, we find out who he is and that he's responsible for Emma and maybe these other girls too."

Sandy regained her composure and sat back down at the table. "Does Lily want to know?" she asked him.

"I'm not sure yet. I'm going to talk to her about it soon."

"What do you want from me?"

"You were here. You knew who she was running around with. You know who it might be."

Her eyes narrowed. "Do you want me to say the names just so you don't have to?"

She was right. He knew the names. "Brad Wilkerson and Reid Esham."

Sandy sat back in her chair. She pulled one arm tight into her midsection and began chewing at her thumbnail.

"Is there anything else? Anyone else?" Wade asked.

"Those were the only two I knew about around that time. Once you went missing, we kept close. Me, Emma, the rest of the gang. And Paul. Then we found out she was pregnant."

Wade finished the thought. "And she never told you or anyone about the father."

Sandy shook her head.

Lily slid next to Teri in the back of the Smiths' big, green Oldsmobile Cutlass Sedan. The girls nicknamed it The Hulk because of its size and color and because the muffler roared and growled like Lou Ferrigno from the television show. Alicia was driving, as usual. Tammy was easily distracted, especially with guests in the car, and after a broken headlight, smashed fender, and dented rear bumper in less than a year's worth of driving, the girls and their father decided it was best if Alicia served as the designated driver whenever possible. That suited Tammy just fine. Riding shotgun let her focus on the radio or the friends in the backseat or the boys pulling up next to them at a stoplight. The girls clicked their seatbelts and Alicia backed the lumbering automobile down the pitched driveway. The metal of the undercarriage scraped against asphalt when they reached the bottom. Alicia turned the wheel to angle the car onto the road but cut it too soon and drove the front left tire onto the grass and then off the curb. They bopped up and down and Lily could feel the shot springs in the seats punching against the upholstery. Alicia straightened out the car and then nearly backed into the mailbox before putting it in drive and swerving down the road. Lily happened to look back at the house. Mr. Smith was peering out from behind a pulled curtain, shaking his head, probably wondering whether he should allow either of his daughters to get behind the wheel of a car ever again.

Alicia had the front seat pushed up as far up as it would go to reach the steering wheel. For the first few months after the twins turned sixteen, they had to bring a small pillow to sit on to see over the dash. It reminded Lily of those little old ladies she'd see on the road sometimes. She'd look over from her car and all she could spot was a piece of forehead, a shock of bluish-white hair, and two hands firmly planted on the steering wheel.

Tammy turned up the volume of the radio and started singing to a Bon Jovi song blaring from the speakers. They all joined in at the chorus, with Tammy giving each of the girls the opportunity to sing into the phantom microphone she was holding in her hand. They got to the school a few songs later. Alicia was inches away from taking a chunk of metal out of a Toyota Celica when she parked. They walked to the stadium and through the gates and made their way to the senior section of the bleachers. Jake and a couple of his friends were up near the top of the stands. Holly was in the row in front of Jake waving her arms above her head to get Lily's attention. Lily made eye contact and waved back.

Tammy tugged at Lily's sweater and pulled her in close. "What's up with that? First it was lunch. Now this?"

The school band was already sitting in another section of the bleachers playing "Don't Stop Believin'" and the girls could hardly hear over the crowd and the music. Lily wrapped her arms around her friends' shoulders and hugged them into a tight, little circle. She had to yell over the music.

"Holly is going to be our friend again!"

"What?" Tammy yelled back. Her face twisted in a state of disbelief.

"It's gonna be fine!" Lily assured them with another shout.

The girls maneuvered through the crowd and slid their way down the row and into a small space next to Holly. Holly grabbed hold of Lily and gave her a welcoming squeeze before addressing Teri and the sisters.

"Thanks for letting me hang with you tonight," Holly said. "We're gonna have a blast." Alicia and Tammy stared at her skeptically. "You two look cute tonight, by the way," Holly told them.

Lily was happy to be here with all of them, Holly and Jake included. It felt the way it was supposed to be. If there was anything positive about the fallout from her uncle's death, and she hated even thinking about it that way, it was that it had provided Lily with an opportunity to start fresh. She was beginning to see her world differently and she was ready to live a new life. She had no ties or obligations. She was shedding the shackles of grief and guilt and the past. She was ready to move on to something new and different, something optimistic, something happy. New friends, new relationships, college, and more. She was starting to embrace her freedom.

On the field, two cheerleaders were holding a large paper banner with a painted Seahawk mascot at the far end by the goal posts. The players ripped through the paper and charged across the grass. The sudden slack of the ripped banner sent one of the cheerleaders to the ground, feet straight in the air, exposing her navy bloomers, as the players rushed by her and to their bench. The kids in the stands saw it all happen. Jake and the boys behind Lily were laughing and whooping and hollering but settled down once Alicia shushed them.

Jake bent forward between Lily and Alicia. "Sorry, Alicia." He was wearing a sly grin and carrying a little bit of a slur. "We'll behave from now on."

Alicia waved her hand in front of her nose. "Jeez, Jake. You smell like a distillery. When did you guys get started?"

A boy next to Jake edged in. "Just a few shots of Jimmy Beam to warm us up. No need to worry though," he told her as he patted her back. "Brian over here is our designated driver."

Lily and Alicia looked over to the third boy in the group. He was slumped in his seat with his head leaning against the hip of the girl standing next to him, barely conscious.

Jake's arm was still resting against Lily's shoulder. She grabbed his hand and pulled him close to her. "Hey, listen, you three idiots be careful tonight. If you need a ride, let us know."

Jake smiled at her. "Will do." He lingered for a moment. "Hey, are we good?"

Lily turned to meet his eyes. Those eyes used to make her happy, but now they also made her a little sad.

"Yeah, we're good." Though she realized that what they meant to each other now was different, she understood that it was okay.

The kids settled in and enjoyed the game, which was going well for the Seahawks. Jimmy Franklin, Holly's now ex-boyfriend, had already thrown for a touchdown and run for another. Lily watched Holly whenever Jimmy made a play, good or bad. Holly seemed genuinely happy and excited for him and didn't give any indication she was upset about Jimmy's successes or that she delighted in his failures. She was acting like any other fan.

There was a timeout on the field, and the band played again. The cheerleaders performed a pompom routine on the sidelines that ended with a couple of them sprinting down the track into back handsprings and somersaults. Teri tugged at Holly's sleeve.

"Stacy is shooting daggers at you," she told her.

Lily looked down and saw Stacy, hands on her hips, standing with a couple of other cheerleaders. She was staring right back up at Lily and her friends, and at Holly in particular. Stacy mouthed something to the girl next to her, flicked her hair to the side, and spun back to face the field.

"Yeah." Holly sighed. "Stacy knows how to hold a grudge."

The second half began, and the game was turning into a romp. Most of the juniors and seniors in the stands left at halftime to get a head start on the night's parties. Jake and his friends snuck out with another group of boys, and Lily hoped at least one of them would act responsibly for the night. The girls had had enough by the middle of the third quarter and decided to leave. Lily convinced Holly to ride with them to J.D.'s place. Holly grabbed a bagful of wine coolers and a bottle of vodka from the trunk of her car, and the girls piled into The Hulk and headed to the party at the Cropper farm twenty minutes away. Lily had gotten clearance from Wade and Ginny, even though Wade was a bit reluctant considering the news about the girl they found on Assateague. She assured him she'd be with a group of friends and that they'd be careful.

They drove back roads through farmland and woodland and a couple of unincorporated small towns that weren't much more than a post office and a gas station and a few shack-like houses lining the cross streets. They turned on another road running parallel to train tracks that used to run grain and feed and other cargo from Cape Charles to Wilmington but were now overrun by weeds, grass, dandelion stalks and, in some spots, small bushes and trees. After a mile or so, the road curved east across the tracks and ended at a t-intersection that was anchored on one corner by the abandoned St. Martin's Church. Alicia slowed the car as she approached the stop sign.

The church was a simple square building, made from dark, rust colored brick, with a gable roof that was sagging in the middle. Most of the wood from an old picket fence was lying at its perimeter, stained with black rot, broken and splintered apart. A solitary street-lamp on the corner lit the front of the church in a faded, yellow light, the *No Trespassing* signs posted on the front door and the black spray paint graffiti that looked like devil horns and a pentagram barely visible from the street.

It was well known that St. Martin's Church was haunted by the spirits of generations of dead who were buried in an overgrown cemetery at the back of the property, but it was the ghost of Martha Tippet that was a particular nuisance. According to legend, Martha was left at the altar by a boy who'd found better prospects. For Martha, shame and a broken heart was a powerful motivator. Still in her wedding gown, she found that boy and his new girl in a barn on his father's farm and stabbed them through with a pitchfork. Martha fled the scene, blood stained from head to toe, and made her way back to the empty church under the cover of darkness. When the preacher came by in the morning to prepare for Sunday services, he found Martha hanging from the rafters. More than one of the girls' classmates claimed to have seen the ghost of Martha Tippet on church grounds, even though there was no historical record of a Martha Tippet. That didn't stop any of them from believing that the church was haunted, and none of it deterred the girls from their ritual.

"One, two, three, go!" Tammy shouted from the front seat.

The girls opened their doors and sprinted in a line to the church. They ran up the broken cobblestone walkway and hopped over pieces of dilapidated fence and other debris littering the yard. They ran counterclockwise, screaming and shrieking in a mad frenzy around the church, with Tammy, Holly, and then Teri ahead, and Lily and Alicia trailing behind. It was darkest in the rear, and Lily lost sight of the other girls for a moment. She turned the corner and raced toward the giant weeping willow near the front of the church. She caught sight of three shadows under the tree and then saw them disappear behind its trunk. Lily reached the tree and made a final dash for the car but tripped on a thick root. Lily flew out and landed hard. Her head hit something solid, and Lily saw a flash of light and heard a sharp ringing in her ears. Alicia didn't see Lily fall and ran by her unaware. Lily turned on the ground and opened her eyes. Standing over her was an image of a woman dressed in white, but it wasn't Martha. It was her mother, and the vision frightened her.

Lily screamed, and the image of her mother disappeared. She got up to her knees, crying. The girls rushed back to Lily when they heard her. They quickly gathered her up and dragged her to the car, then sped away from the intersection with heavy breaths and a little regret.

Holly was sitting next to Lily in the middle of the back seat. "Oh my God. That was crazy." She leaned in close and examined Lily's head. "I don't see a cut or anything." She ran her fingers through Lily's hair and along her scalp.

"Ouch!" Lily winced and backed away. She wiped the remaining tears from her face with the sleeve of her jacket.

"Sorry. You've got a nasty bump."

Lily touched at the spot gently and winced again.

"What happened back there, Lily?" Tammy asked.

"I don't know. It felt like something reached out from the ground and grabbed my foot."

"You think it was Martha?" Holly asked.

Lily could see the whites of her wide-open eyes but could tell she was just joking around. Holly reached into the paper bag on the floorboard and pulled out a bottle. She opened the twist top and passed it to Lily. Lily took a drink and then set the cool bottle against the knot on her head. Holly pulled out three more bottles, passed one each to Tammy and Teri, and kept one for herself.

Tammy turned up the radio. "All right ladies, it's time to party."

The girls pulled up to a line of cars parked on the side of an access road leading to the Cropper farm. They got out of the car with their alcohol and walked down the path toward the chatter of the crowd and the thumping bass of a stereo. A bunch of kids were huddled outside of a lighted barn and standing around a keg set in a trash can full of ice. A few others were lingering about, and the rest of the crowd was out in the middle of the harvested cornfield where a giant bonfire was lit and already raging. The girls were about twenty yards away, but Lily could feel the heat of the fire.

Lily was still stunned by her fall and the shock of seeing the image of her mother. Maybe she had knocked herself out temporarily and it was a dream, but it certainly felt like she was awake and that her mother was standing over her. Lily decided to drown out the pain and the confusion with alcohol. She chugged down the last of her wine cooler and reached into the bag Holly was holding for the bottle of vodka.

"Let's get drunk," Lily told them.

By the time the football players trickled in, the girls had worked through half the bottle. Jimmy and a few of his teammates found them by the bonfire. Lily, Holly, and Tammy were locked at the shoulders, rocking side-to-side and singing along to a Lynyrd Skynyrd song that was blasting from the barn. Teri and Alicia were huddled with Jake, Brian, and the other boy from their group. He had his arm wrapped tight around Teri, who was burrowed deep under his fur-lined jean jacket seeking some warmth and affection.

"It's about time you got here," Holly yelled out.

"It looks like you're doing fine without us," Jimmy called back.

Holly hooked her arms around Lily and Tammy at the neck and squeezed them closer to her. "Me and my old friends are new friends again. Isn't that nice?"

"I think that's great," Jimmy said, lifting a red Solo cup in their direction.

Holly released Lily from her grasp and nudged her toward Jimmy. "Here. Help Lily. She fell and hurt herself tonight and needs some attention."

Lily stumbled toward Jimmy. He reached out and grabbed her at the elbow to steady her.

"You okay?" he asked.

"Yeah," Lily answered. "I'm just a little drunk. And my head hurts."

"C'mon. Let's get you some water."

Jimmy led Lily away from the bonfire and toward the house on the other side of the access road. They walked around the house until they found a spigot. Jimmy emptied the remaining beer from his cup, rinsed it, then filled it with water and handed it to Lily. Lily took a few sips and handed the cup back to Jimmy. Her head was throbbing, and the pain and dizziness was making her unsteady. She clutched Jimmy at the bicep to maintain her balance.

"I think I need to sit down," she told him.

Jimmy put his arm under Lily's jacket and around her waist and guided her to the front of the house. He sat her down on the front steps and went back to refill his cup with water. He returned and handed her the cup, and she took a few more sips.

"Thanks. I'm already feeling much better."

"No problem, Parker." He stuffed his hands in his blue and white letterman jacket and sat down next to her. "What did you guys get into tonight?"

"We did the church run and I fell and hit my head like an idiot." Lily made a pouting face and rubbed at the side of her head. "I've got a big bump. See?"

Jimmy took her head into his hands, gently, and felt at the spot. His hands slid down the side of Lily's face and lingered for a moment. Her head was still a bit cloudy, but it was clear enough to tell her that this was more than an accidental caress, and she knew that she liked it.

"That's a pretty nasty knock, but I think you'll live."

Jimmy lowered his hands and stuffed them in his jacket again. He leaned back, but his eyes were still on hers. His face was lit by a dim incandescent bulb hanging naked on the porch ceiling. His eyes were sea green on most days, especially in the faded light and under the cover of darkness. In the brightness of the day, though, they often shifted to a crystal blue. She remembered the first time she noticed his eyes on a sunny, spring day on the playground at recess in the first grade. A bunch of kids were playing tag and Jimmy was *It* and he'd chased her down by the swing set. She dashed around a post and changed directions to slip away from him. He miscalculated and stumbled into the post, hitting his head hard against it, knocking him onto the ground. Lily started to run away, thinking Jimmy would be down for only a second, but she stopped when she heard him crying. She went back and kneeled next to him and asked him if he was okay. He nodded and opened his eyes, which were wet with tears, and when the light hit them, the green dissolved to blue and she thought he was magic.

Lily took another drink from the cup. "Do you remember when we were friends?" she asked him.

"We're still friends, Lily."

"Once upon a time we were *really* friends. We used to play at recess. You used to invite me to your birthday parties."

"You still come to my parties. But now, instead of cake, there's beer," he told her.

Lily turned away from him and looked out to the bonfire. Jake was out there somewhere. Holly too.

"Jake and I are done. Did you know that?"

"Yeah. I heard something about that."

Lily turned back to face him. "What about you and Holly? Are you done?" she asked.

"*She* thinks we're done."

"What about you?"

Jimmy shrugged his shoulders. "It depends, I guess. She did send me out here to take care of you. So, tonight, we're done."

Lily's eyes felt heavy, like she was falling into a dream, and she wondered whether it was the effects of the alcohol or the hit to her head or maybe it was just Jimmy. They'd gone out in middle school. They'd kissed, the open-mouth kind that meant they were really girlfriend and boyfriend. Their relationship was short lived, but there was an affection between them that lasted for a time after, and she felt a little of that again now.

She sighed, as if exasperated or exhausted or both. "I think I want you to kiss me," she told him. Her words were slow and slurred, but she knew what she was saying.

He placed his left hand on her shoulder and his right hand gently behind her head. He twisted her ever so slightly and dropped his head towards hers. She watched his lips. They were full and hungry and when they touched hers, they were soft and warm. He tasted like beer and spearmint gum, but he smelled like smoke and Ivory soap. He held her tighter and kissed her more deeply, and then he slid his hand slowly down her back and along her hip and squeezed at the flesh of her thigh over the black tights she was wearing under her skirt. She kissed him back and moved her hands under his jacket. She grabbed two fistfuls of flannel shirt and pulled herself into him and then kissed him some more.

Lily was vaguely aware of her surroundings. There was yelling, and she heard gravel shooting out from under spinning wheels. They pulled apart reluctantly and with heavy breath and saw kids scurrying about and away from the barn and the bonfire. They scattered in all directions but mainly away from the red and blue flashing lights of police cars that were heading up along the access road. Jimmy shot up off the steps and pulled Lily up with him.

"Let's go. My truck is on the other side of the house."

They ran around the house to Jimmy's truck. Another set of flashing lights were heading their way. Jimmy started the truck, put it in gear, and tore away from the house and the party just seconds before the police car pulled up the driveway, blocking the exit of a few other vehicles trying to sneak their way out.

Lily was a little out of breath, but the excitement of their escape sobered her up a bit. She turned in her seat and looked back at the farm. The glow of the fire and the pulsing strobe of the lights rose above the shadow of the farmhouse.

"I hope the girls aren't looking for me," she said. "I hope they got to the car and made it out."

"Where are you staying tonight?" Jimmy asked.

"I'm staying with the twins."

"You want to take a little ride before I take you there?"

"Sure."

Jimmy drove the same roads the girls had traveled to get to the party. They turned at St. Martin's Church and Lily felt at the bump on her head. It still hurt, but not nearly as bad. They cut across the main road leading to the beach and headed south toward Assateague. They turned east and drove across the bridge to the island and then turned south again and past the main entrance. The road narrowed and Jimmy slowed down and pulled into an unlit parking lot. The truck headlights hit a sign posted at the back of the lot, which marked the on-beach access point. There was also a chain hanging between two posts blocking their way. Jimmy stopped the truck and got out. He unhooked the chain and dropped it to the ground. Lily got a little nervous, wondering for a second whether they should be out here on the island all by themselves with a killer on the loose, but Jimmy was standing out there in the lights, tall, handsome, available, and she forgot all about it. Jimmy got back into the truck and drove onto the beach.

"That was easy," he said with a smile.

The path cut through thick, weather-worn dunes with peaks and valleys stabilized by beach grass that shifted in the breeze like the whiskers on the face of an aged island fisherman. The sand on the path was packed and made for relatively easy passage onto the beach. Once through the dunes, the sand softened but was still drivable, especially in a lifted four-wheel drive pickup with oversized off-road tires. Jimmy drove a little farther down the beach, then stopped and backed in against the dune line. He cut off the engine and they sat for a moment, adjusting to the darkness of a moonless night. The sky had cleared during the day, and there wasn't even a wisp of a cloud lingering to hinder the canvas of stars painted across the black sky. They could detect only the slightest evidence of the ocean in front of them, a reflection off the crest of a rippling wave and the gentle rattle of water against sand. Jimmy shifted in his seat and started to say something, but Lily was beyond words. She leaned over and kissed him, hard and long. They tore off their jackets and pulled at each other's shirts. Their hands worked across their bodies. Their breaths grew heavy and hot and steamed the windows.

Lily pulled away suddenly and sat back in her seat. She'd already committed to her new path forward. She was ready to be free. She was ready to live. Jimmy would be a good place to start.

Jimmy rolled open his window to cool the cabin. "Are you okay?" he asked her.

"I'm perfectly fine," she told him.

She reached under her skirt and pulled off her tights and dropped them in a ball on the floor. She climbed on top of him and grabbed the back of his seat and kissed him again. She reached under his shirt and felt the ridges of the muscles on his stomach and his chest and dug her nails into his skin. She felt his fingers and hands on the bare skin of her body. She felt him under her. She felt him everywhere.

Chapter 17

Saturday, October 24, 1987

WADE DROVE DOWN A long, graveled driveway through rows of chicken houses and a harvested cornfield to the front of a stately white farmhouse. The Wilkerson farm was a landmark of sorts, mostly because of the red barn that anchored the property, a massive, thirty-foot-tall structure with a turret-like tower topped with a tin roof shell. For tourists traveling along Route 50, the farm and its barn served as a guidepost. If they were heading east, in twenty minutes they'd be at the beach. If they were heading west, it was a chance to stop on their way back home to make a memory. They'd pull off the highway and drive up to the little country store at the edge of the property to grab an ice cream cone or purchase some fresh produce and maybe take a picture or two.

On clear summer days, when the sun fell at the right angle, the steel grain silos at the edges of the vast cornfield burned silver, orange, and yellow like a freshly struck match against a bright blue sky. It was a living painting, like an artist's rendering leaping off the canvas and settling itself on a parcel of land in the real world. On a cool October day like today, the greens were replaced with browns, ambers, and other tints and hues that signaled the end of one season and the beginning of the next. To most, it was still a beautiful sight. To Wade, though, the farm was an eyesore, ugly not because of how it looked but because of what it represented. It was the place that bore his rival, the boy who stole the heart of the girl he loved. Every time Wade drove by, he couldn't help but recall memories of Emma with Brad. When he approached the house and saw Brad Wilkerson standing on the front porch, more than a little bit of that animosity filtered through the layers of time that had passed between them. Wade parked and got out of the patrol car. He put on his hat and touched the brim with a nod.

"Good morning, Brad."

Brad remained on the landing, indifferent, hands stuffed in the pockets of a canvas jacket and cowboy hat perched on his head, a generous helping of chewing tobacco stuffed between cheek and gum. He walked down the stairs and kept moving past Wade, across the driveway and toward another building that stood opposite the side of the house.

"We'll talk in the office," he said, without looking back at Wade. "Mindy and the girls are still asleep in the house."

Wade followed him to the building, a small mobile home fixed atop a concrete block foundation. Behind it was a long row of stables, where men were already tending to the livestock that filled the stalls, pens, and coops. They walked up a short set of stairs and entered the makeshift office. Brad took off his hat and jacket and hung them on a rack by the door. He pointed Wade to a chair in front of a desk that took up almost a whole side of the room.

"Coffee?" Brad asked.

Wade nodded. "Sure."

There was a small counter in the back corner that held a microwave and a coffee maker. A pot was brewed and ready for them. Brad filled two mugs and handed one to Wade. He didn't offer cream or sugar, and Wade wasn't going to ask. The rest of the office was sparse—just a couple of file cabinets and a few shelves that held boxes of files and office supplies. A muscle car calendar was the only thing hanging on the wall.

Brad took his seat and sipped his coffee, the tobacco still lodged against his cheek. "So, what's all this about?"

"I wanted to let you know that I've decided to reopen Emma Parker's case."

"What's that got to do with me?" Brad asked, the wrinkles at the corner of his eyes now more visible.

"I'm reviewing evidence, looking for new leads. I'm reaching out to friends and acquaintances. Conducting new interviews to see if anything was missed."

Brad didn't react. At least not externally. If there was anything that concerned him, he wasn't showing it. "I said all I had to say about it back then. It's all in your file."

"I read it," Wade told him.

"Then you know I wasn't here when she disappeared. I was back at school."

"I'm not looking for what's in the file. I'm looking for what's not in it."

That got Brad's attention. He leaned up in his chair, his arms crossed and resting on his desk. His eyes focused back on Wade.

"Are you accusing me of something, Sheriff?"

"Not at all. There are just some things missing. Things that might be relevant."

"Like what?"

"Like the identity of Lily Parker's father."

Brad chuckled.

"Something funny?" Wade asked.

Brad used a finger to pull the chaw out of his mouth, disposing of it in a paper cup that was already sitting on the desk. He took another sip of coffee, this time swirling it around in his mouth to rinse any residue, and then spit it all back into the cup.

"No. There's nothing funny about any of this." Brad got up and walked back over to the coffee pot, topping off his mug. "I've got a good life and two beautiful little girls. I don't much appreciate you coming in here now, after all these years, to turn it all upside down."

Wade twisted in his chair to watch Brad, who spoke with little emotion.

"Maybe this has something to do with our history, you and me. I still don't like you much. I'm pretty sure you don't like me. But you trying to ruin my family is crossing the line."

"That's not why I'm here," Wade said. "I'm just trying to find out what happened to her. You can understand that, can't you?" Whatever his faults, Wade knew that Brad had once loved Emma. Back then and maybe still. If Brad didn't have anything to do with Emma's disappearance, Wade believed that he would want to know the truth almost as much as Wade did himself.

Brad walked back around his desk and sat down again. He glanced out the window and stroked the stubble on his chin and cheeks, then turned back to face Wade. "I want to be clear," he started. "I didn't have anything to do with Emma's disappearance. I loved that girl, no matter what we went through. I would've never hurt her."

Wade nodded, though he wasn't sure he believed him just yet.

"When I was home from school the summer after my sophomore year, Emma and I got back together." He paused and ran his hand through his hair. "You were reported missing a couple of weeks later. She didn't want anything to do with me after that. I don't know if she felt guilty, or what, but we didn't talk again until I heard that she was pregnant. I called her from school, asked her if the baby was mine. I told her I'd make it right, but she told me I wasn't the father."

"Did you believe her?" Wade asked.

"I don't know. I was twenty. I know I wanted to believe her. I wasn't ready for that."

"Did she say anything?"

"She told me I didn't need to worry about it. I asked her who the father was. All she said was that it wasn't me."

They both sat quietly for a minute. Wade had always thought it possible that Brad was Lily's father, but he was never sure whether Brad knew it or suspected it, one way or another. Wade's read was that Brad was being truthful. That he was told he wasn't the father. Wade also believed that Brad might now be doubting whether Emma was being truthful with him. Maybe he'd always doubted it.

"How's Lily anyway?" Brad asked. "I heard she moved in with you after her uncle passed."

"That's right. She's making her way, getting used to the new surroundings. All of it has been tough on her."

"Well, good for you for taking her in, with no family or anything left for her."

"I don't know about that," Wade said. "The father could be out there somewhere. We owe it to her to find out, don't you think?"

Brad looked out the window again, where he could catch just enough of the house in his line of sight. He was thinking about his family, Wade guessed, trying to decide what to do next.

"Do you think you could keep it from Mindy?" he asked, finally.

"Keep what from Mindy, Brad?"

"Well, you're asking me to take a paternity test, aren't you?"

"If you're willing, yeah, I guess I'm asking," Wade told him. "I'll do everything I can to keep it quiet."

Wade watched as Brad worked through it in his head. After a long silence, Brad spoke up again.

"People have been looking at me funny for a long time. Talking about me behind my back. There's plenty of 'em out there who think I'm that girl's father. Some of 'em still think I had something to do with Emma disappearing. You're one of those people, and I'm about sick and tired of all of it." Brad jabbed at his desk with his finger. "I'll do this thing. But let me be clear, I'm only doing it for me. I'm ready for some peace and quiet. I don't think I'm that girl's father, and I damn well know for sure I didn't have anything to do with whatever happened to Emma."

Chapter 18

Monday, October 26, 1987

W ADE WAS SITTING AT his desk, staring out the window at a sky painted like dishwater, when he heard a knock and turned to see Deputy Johnson filling every inch of the open doorway to his office.

"Sheriff, you got a minute?"

"Sure, come on in, Garrett." Wade waved him in. "What do you have for me?"

"I followed Reid Esham around like you asked me. There was the normal back and forth between his place and work. Trips to the grocery store and a couple of restaurants. He had a few visits to one of those gated homes near your neighborhood. I think it's his father's house."

"That's right," Wade told him.

"He was out there yesterday, and he came out driving a big, brown Suburban. It was pretty beat up. It looked like something they might use on a farm or for hunting."

"Where was he heading in that?" Wade asked.

"The lumber yard. He filled the truck with two-by-fours and four-by-sixes and went back to his father's place. A few hours later, he left in his own car."

"Anything else?"

"He has a lady friend," Johnson told him.

It wasn't a shocking revelation to Wade based on Reid's reputation. He'd been divorced for a few years and was back to his old ways, though it wasn't like marriage had put much of a damper on his activities in the first place.

"I trailed him into Ocean City after he left his office on Friday. He pulled up to an apartment building on Dorchester Street. I saw him walk up, knock on the door, and then walk in." Johnson dropped a piece of paper on Wade's desk. "That's the address. Second floor apartment. He left after an hour or so. I followed him back to his house and then called it a day."

Wade stared down at the piece of paper. He knew the place but didn't know the resident. "You know who it was?"

Johnson nodded. "Vicky Brittingham."

Wade heard it and almost laughed out loud. A convergence of pricks. Maybe that's why Frank Brittingham was so pissed.

Johnson shifted on his feet. He didn't say much on most days, and he wasn't one to show his emotions. He was a serious fellow and rarely questioned an order or assignment. Wade could tell that there was something on his mind.

"Is there something else?" he asked him. Johnson's face pulled tight. "It's okay, Garrett," Wade told him. "What is it?"

"I don't really understand what I'm doing. Why am I following Reid Esham around? Have we opened an investigation on him? Is there something I should know?"

Wade got up from his chair and closed the door. He came back and leaned against the front of his desk.

"You're the only one in the office who isn't from this area," Wade told him. "You're the only one who doesn't have a connection to Reid Esham or his father or his friends. The rest of us are compromised."

"Okay," Johnson said. "But I still don't understand why we're looking at him."

"You know about the Emma Parker disappearance, right?" Wade asked.

"Yeah, you've talked about it before."

"Reid Esham knew her. It's my understanding that he had some sort of relationship with her before she disappeared."

"So, he's a suspect?"

"I wouldn't go that far just yet."

"I still don't get it. Why are we looking at his activity now?"

"Esham was engaged when he was having his affair with Emma Parker. He was married when Emma had her daughter. Maybe that baby was Reid's and he was afraid his wife would find out."

Garrett's face was still screwed in a knot. "Even if that was true, I don't see it as a reason to kill."

Wade took another shot at persuading Garett. Maybe he was trying to convince himself. "I've seen men kill for less," he told him. "If he was the father, he had a possible motive, and plenty of opportunity. If he was in any way connected to Emma Parker's disappearance, maybe that's reason enough to look at him for Hillary Dent."

Deputy Johnson may not have been convinced by Wade's line of thinking, but he'd heard enough to satisfy his concerns. "What's next?"

"I think we can take the tail off him. Nothing else for you on this right now."

Wade patted Garrett on the shoulder. Johnson got up and left the office. Wade tapped his fingers against the top of his desk. Then he had a thought. He picked up the phone and called Rick Hampton.

"Rick, it's Wade. I need you to set up a meeting with your FBI contacts. I have some information they need to hear."

⇪

Holly was leaning in close. She had her elbows on the cafeteria table and her chin propped at the crest of her clasped hands like a camera on a tripod. She was recording every expression and reaction.

"So, are you gonna tell us what happened after the cops came?" she asked Lily. Teri and the twins were there too, angling in and fishing for information.

"I already told you what happened. Jimmy was getting me water. When we saw the police cars pull in, we got in his truck and drove off."

"But you didn't get back to my house for another couple of hours," Tammy pointed out.

"Like I said, we took a ride and talked," Lily told them.

"Yeah, I've been on a few rides with Jimmy myself," Holly said playfully.

The other girls giggled. Lily was a little embarrassed and a little uncomfortable. Holly had figured it all out already, and she seemed fine about it. It was an easy choice for Lily to make at the time, under a cloud of alcohol and maybe a slight concussion. Two days later with the benefit of sobriety, she considered whether it was a good choice or the right choice. She wasn't sure either way, but what she did know was that she didn't feel guilty about it. She knew what she was doing, and she was glad she did it. But it didn't mean she was ready to talk about what happened. At least not quite yet.

Lily was about to change the subject when she noticed Kevin Brittingham walking by their table. He didn't pay Lily or any of them any mind, but Lily was certain he knew she was there. Him ignoring her felt almost more frightening than an acknowledgment.

Her heart rate accelerated and her palms got sweaty, and it wasn't until he walked out the double doors of the cafeteria that Lily realized she'd been holding her breath the whole time. Alicia noticed.

"I don't think you need to worry about him, Lily," she said. "He's a bully. He thinks he's something bigger than he is. He won't bother with you anymore."

Lily nodded, but something inside her was less than convinced.

It was later than Wade would normally stay on an otherwise slow night, but the file marked *Parker, Emma H.* that was spread open in front of him had monopolized the last few hours of the afternoon and evening. Before he knew it, he'd missed dinner and forgotten to call Ginny. She'd rung him to make sure he was all right. It wasn't unusual for Wade to work late. That happened more in the summer, when the county was littered with college students and bikers and other rowdy tourists getting drunk and starting trouble or finding it. In the fall and winter, things usually went quiet, or relatively so, but he knew she still worried for him. Tonight, she sounded more anxious than usual. And she hadn't been feeling great, either. Her stomach turned when the toast burned or the coffee brewed, and this morning she rushed to the bathroom to throw up after catching a whiff of bacon. She wrote it off to the worrying, about Wade and Lily now too, and he felt some shame that his preoccupation and selfishness might be affecting Ginny's health.

Wade rubbed his eyes and gathered up the loose papers and open folders. There was nothing left for him to find in them. He needed real evidence, and that meant tracking down the identity of Lily's father. Rick had already called back. The meeting was set for the day after tomorrow. The FBI was willing to listen.

Chapter 19

1968

"TAKE A SEAT, CORPORAL."

The captain pointed to an empty chair in front of his desk. A lit cigarette dangled at the edge of his lips, weighed heavy by a long trail of ash at its end. Wade leaned his rifle against the chair and sat with his helmet in his lap. His sergeant, an ornery Texan named Rodriguez, met him as he was coming off patrol and ordered him to the captain's tent directly, so he didn't have time to unload his gear. The captain flipped a pack of Lucky Strikes to Wade.

"Light up," he told him.

Wade emptied a cigarette from the pack and tossed it back to the captain. He slid a matchbook from the band around his helmet and struck a match. Wade took a few puffs to ignite the cigarette, then sucked in a deep breath and held the smoke in his lungs for a few long seconds. Whatever this was about, it had to be serious. Most of Wade's visits to Captain Lewis's tent resulted in a special detail or some other high-risk mission. He took another drag from the cigarette. The captain circled back behind his desk and picked up a folded piece of paper. He opened it and evened out the creases.

"We got this today," he said, handing it over to Wade. "I'm sorry, son. Your father had a heart attack. He didn't make it."

Wade looked up at the captain. "I don't understand," he mumbled. He was trying to process the words. *He didn't make it.* That didn't make sense. His father was a strong, healthy man. Wade read over the telegram, but there was nothing else there. It was a clinical transmission:

We are writing to inform you that George Thompson, father of Cpl. Wade Thompson, died as a result of a heart attack on 12 November 68.

"Unfortunately, these things happen," the captain said, matter-of-factly. "Life back home doesn't stand still for us."

The captain pulled open a drawer and brought out a bottle of bourbon and two shot glasses. He filled the glasses to the brim and handed one to Wade. Then he raised his glass in a toast.

"To your father."

The captain emptied his drink and motioned for Wade to do the same. Wade tipped back his glass and drank it down.

"You're taking a hardship leave effective immediately. Get your gear together. You leave in an hour." The captain grabbed an envelope from the desk. "Here are your orders. We'll see you back here in a couple of weeks." Wade stood up, still disoriented. The captain patted his shoulder. "My condolences, Thompson."

"Thank you, sir," Wade answered, still in shock. He flashed a quick salute, picked up his rifle, and turned and exited the tent.

It took Wade more than forty-eight hours to get to Delaware. He stopped in Hawaii to board another plane and then in California to board a third before finally landing at Dover Air Force Base a couple of days before Thanksgiving. Paul drove the hour or so north from Maryland to pick him up.

"Good to see you, brother," Paul said, reaching for the duffle looped at Wade's shoulder. Wade let it slide off his back and Paul grabbed it and threw it in the back of the truck.

Paul never had much to say, and there wasn't much Wade needed or wanted to say to him or anyone else about his time in the jungle. Wade knew that Paul was glad to see him alive and well, and he knew the rest of it didn't even register with him. They stood by the tailgate long enough for tears to form in the corner of Wade's eyes. Paul pulled him into a tight hug and held him as he wept into his older brother's chest.

Wade collected himself after a minute or so and climbed into the truck. Paul put the truck in gear and drove out through the main gates of the base and onto the highway. He looked as tired as Wade felt, and they didn't talk much on their ride to their parents' house. Wade had gotten the important information from Paul earlier that day. The family hadn't heard from Wade in the days that followed his father's death, and they couldn't be sure if he'd received the message or would even be able to come stateside to attend the funeral. The truth was that on any given day, they weren't sure whether Wade was even alive. After almost a week, they decided to hold the funeral and bury their father. The first time any of them had spoken to Wade since he'd left for Vietnam was about eight hours earlier that day, when Wade called from Oakland Army Base to let them know he was on his way.

"What happened, Paul?" Wade had asked him over the phone.

"He was working on his truck. He finished up and walked to the porch where mom was waiting with some iced tea. He told her he wasn't feeling well, then dropped to the ground right there in front of her. He was dead before he hit the grass."

The church overflowed with people for the funeral, according to Paul. Friends, relatives, old classmates. George Thompson was a well-liked and well-respected man. "Not a more honest man on the whole shore than your old man," is what people would say to Wade whenever he accompanied his father on his errands.

Their mother was not taking it well, Paul reported. She had fallen into a deep depression, and even the news of Wade's return home was barely enough to rouse her from her bed.

"Has she seen a doctor?" Wade asked in the car.

"Dr. Esham came by one day and dropped off some pills. Some to calm her and help her sleep and others to manage her mood and help her feel better."

"Are they working?" Wade asked.

"Not really."

Wade and his mother had always shared a special bond. When Wade was young and Paul wanted to be alone and his father was hard at work, his mother would pack a basket of food and drive them across the bridge to the inlet and spread a blanket on the cold sand to watch the late-year seas churning against the jetty and the beach. Sometimes she would call Hettie Parker, and she and Emma would accompany them to the shore, but usually it was just Wade and his mother. She liked coming to the beach on days when the sun was out, when she could feel its heat through the chill of a late autumn day, especially after a storm had passed through, roughing the ocean and the sand with its winds and waves. She'd tell Wade how, on those kinds of days, she could feel all four seasons at once and that it made her feel most alive to be part of the full cycle of the earth's turn around the sun in one day rather than a whole year. "That's how I feel sometimes, Wade," she told him. "Sometimes I'm happy and sad and hopeful and hopeless and full and empty, all at the same time."

Wade wasn't sure what his mother meant, but he didn't care because on that day, she was happy.

Wade remembered how tender his mother could be, especially on her good days, when she'd be cheerfully baking in her kitchen, singing a song she knew as a little girl. It was on days like that when the urge would hit her, and she'd burst into Wade's room to wake him or skip out into the backyard where he was playing and excitedly tell him to get up and get ready because the two of them were off for a little adventure. Those were some of his favorite days.

They'd find a nice spot between the pier and the jetty where they could see across the inlet to Assateague and where they hoped to spot one of the wild ponies that sometimes gathered on that island's northern point. They'd sit and talk and eat and then he'd be off. He'd run along the edge of the water, hopping over the carpets of foam that spilled from the ocean like an overflowing washing machine. He'd dig for sand crabs and razor clams and then run back to his mother to show her what he'd found. She was an enthusiastic audience, marveling at the assortment he'd bring to her, her eyes and mouth wide open in amazement.

Sometimes he'd grab her hand and pull her off the blanket and lead her to the jetty and its huge, black and gray rocks, and they'd stand at the end and wave to the boats that sailed through the channel. The seagulls would hang in the air above them, caught in a gust with wings spread wide and beaks open, crying hopeful cries at Wade as he tossed scraps of bread up over his head. He had laughed as the gulls swooped and scooped, and he swore they were laughing right with him.

Other times Wade and his mother might stroll down and walk under the pier, and his mother would tell him how much fun she'd had as a little girl, going to the ballroom that used to sit at the end of the pier with her parents, when famous bands and singers would visit and play. And she might sweep him up in her arms and swing him around as she hummed out a tune. But the ballroom had burned down many years ago, before his mother could dance on its parquet floors in the arms of some high school sweetheart or with the love of her life, George Thompson.

Wade shook himself back to the present. He pressed his hand against the window of the pickup and felt the cold outside against the skin of his palm. The eastern sky was thick with gray clouds, heavy and serious. From that direction it felt and smelled and tasted like snow. But to the west it was clear, with wispy streaks of white painted across the blues of the sky, and the sun lit like a flash bulb, shining untroubled. The warmth of it penetrated through the windshield. Wade hadn't understood what his mother meant all those years ago about the seasons, but he understood now. On this day, Wade felt the comfort and the cold, the familiarity and the longing, the life and the death, the happiness and the despair.

When they reached the house, they found their mother bathed and dressed and cooking in the kitchen. Wade smelled the pot roast and potatoes in the oven and the fresh bread cooling on the kitchen counter. It seemed the return of her youngest son, her baby, stirred her from the slumber of her depression and provided her with a reason to wake and live, on this day, at least.

She wiped her hands clean on her red striped apron and dabbed at her eyes with a corner of the matching dishcloth sitting on the counter. She waited before turning to see her boy. Of the two of her sons, it was Wade that most resembled George, and the sight of him would bring her joy for his safe return and sadness at the memory of her husband. They hugged and cried and laughed and then cried some more. Wade and his brother sat with their mother and recalled their father and husband. They remembered riding on his tractor as he plowed their fields. They remembered chasing a young Blue through six-foot-tall stalks of corn. They remembered Sunday drives west to the Chesapeake and south to Chincoteague. They remembered his stories and his jokes.

They had a pleasant dinner and afterwards Paul told Wade that it was the best he'd seen his mother in the couple of weeks following their father's death. Wade was especially tired, and after a long, hot shower, he was ready for bed. His room was as he left it except for the fresh linens his mother had washed and placed earlier that day. There was a model airplane sitting on a bookcase, a P-51 Mustang he'd built in junior high and painted in great detail. He spun the propeller and smiled sadly at how naïve he'd been about war. He wasn't naïve anymore.

He crouched down and ran his finger across the spines of textbooks and novels: *The Great Gatsby, Adventures of Tom Sawyer, The Sun Also Rises, Of Mice and Men.* There was a stack of comic books on the bottom shelf: *Superman, The Flash, The Amazing Spider-Man.* He spied his senior-year yearbook and brought it with him to his bed. The inside front and back covers were full of messages and signatures from friends and classmates. Sandy's note covered half a page. She talked about *all the good times* and told him to stay healthy and to be careful and then added a bunch of little hearts and a line of *X*'s and *O*'s under her name. Timmy just wrote *Timmy*. Emma's message was almost as short: *To my best friend. Come home safe. Love, E.*

He flipped through to pictures of him and his friends in the cafeteria and the hallways and then to the action shots of him and his teammates on the football field, basketball court, and baseball diamond. The photographs were all in black and white, but in his mind, they were alive, in color, and in motion. He found the senior portraits, where he and his classmates posed in caps and gowns, some tight-lipped and serious and others with a curled smile or wide-mouthed grin. He lingered on Emma's photograph. She was looking over her left shoulder, her face angled slightly, catching a glimmer of light in the corner of her eyes. It was the knowing, confident look she'd had when she was younger, when she'd boss Wade around the backyard and in the marsh and on the beach. It was the Emma he grew up and fell in love with.

Wade was asleep by eight o'clock and didn't wake up until after noon the next day. He didn't budge at the smell of bacon and biscuits wafting from the kitchen. He stirred but wasn't bothered when their cat found him alone in the room she'd taken over and decided to curl up on his chest for a late morning snooze. The old girl was always partial to Wade, like most animals were, and she didn't mind the company. It was the vigorous knocking on the front door and the sound of a woman's voice calling out his name that finally shook him awake. He rubbed the sleep from his eyes and shooed away the cat. He slipped on a pair of old jeans he pulled out from his dresser and then walked into the living room. Emma was standing near the front door with a hand on her hip and a frown on her face.

"Wade Thompson, you have a lot of nerve showing up like this without telling me," she said, almost angrily. But after a beat, she smiled and rushed in for a hug. "I missed you," she said, with a tight squeeze. "I missed you a lot."

They held each other for about a minute, neither of them willing to let go. He breathed her in like she was oxygen. Finally, they separated.

She cocked her head and clicked her tongue against the roof of her mouth.

"Well, look at you," she told him. "You're a little skinnier than I remember, but you still look pretty good, all things considered."

He always liked the playful Emma. The girl who jabbed him with a teasing slight or insult. And he liked to jab back.

"Is that the best you could do?" he asked, motioning up and down at her with his hands.

She was wearing a loose-fitting, tattered brown turtleneck sweater and bell-bottom blue jeans that were patched on the right thigh and left knee with red denim squares.

"I could wear the ugliest suit in your closet and still look better than you," she said, and he knew it was true. He stood there a second and took her in. She was every bit as beautiful as he remembered.

Wade's mother came to the door and invited Emma to stay for a late lunch. Wade went to the bathroom to splash some water on his face and then joined them in the kitchen. He took a seat at the table across from Emma while his mother prepared their food. Emma told him she'd enrolled in the nursing program at the community college, and he was excited for her. Wade didn't talk much about the war. He lied and told them that he wasn't in much danger, but these women could see the truth behind Wade's eyes. They knew him better than he knew himself, but they let him lie and told him how thankful they were that he was safe. Emma provided updates about some of their friends. Timmy was still around, but Claire was off at school, though she was back for the Thanksgiving holiday. Sandy was getting serious with her new boyfriend, and Tiffany was working as a secretary in a law office in town. None of them had heard from Dave in months, though. Emma told Wade to plan on a night or two out with the gang, and he agreed. Tomorrow the Parkers and the

Thompsons would celebrate Thanksgiving together, so they decided on Friday night.

After lunch, Emma convinced Wade to walk with her to the bay. They followed the same path they used to take as children, down the road to the edge of the marsh and across the laid-out boards that reached all the way to the beach now. It was a cool day, but the sun was warm, and it was enough to temper the chill in the air. Wade plopped down on the sand and scooped a handful of it in his palm, then watched the grains slide through his fingers. Emma stood at the edge of the water. The sun was behind her, and her shadow cast out to a marker that was posted about twenty feet into the bay.

"This is where we found our arrowheads," she said. "Do you remember?"

"Of course, I remember." He reached under the collar of his flannel shirt and the t-shirt under it and pulled up two necklaces, one holding his dog tags, and the other holding the arrowhead.

"I can't believe you still wear it," she said.

"I never take it off." He slid the necklaces back under his shirt.

Emma rubbed at a spot on her sternum. "I've tried to wear it," she said. "But it's always so cold against my skin. It's so cold it burns. You know what I mean?"

He did know. He'd felt it too.

"I couldn't wear it anymore, Wade. Once you left, it was always just so, so cold." She shook as if to fight off a shiver running through her and then sat down next to him. "Once you left, it was like a piece of me went missing." She started crying. "I was afraid I would lose you forever."

Wade pulled her close and held her. She wiped at her tear-stained cheeks with the sleeves of her sweater and bounced up.

"Enough crying," she said. "You're here now and that's all that matters."

Emma took Wade's hand and walked him along the thin strip of beach that curled around the edge of the marsh. Streaks of orange, yellow, and red from the setting sun splashed across the blues and greens of the water. A cluster of gray and white shorebirds huddled in and around some brush growing from a sandbar island offshore. A small boat navigated through the channel between the island and the mainland, the spits and sputters of its motor echoing across the bay, sending the birds into the air like a celebration of confetti.

Their mother had woken early and prepared a hearty breakfast. They'd planned for a morning visit to the cemetery, and by the time Wade made it out of the shower and to the kitchen his brother was already sitting at the table behind stacks of food.

"Goodness, Momma," Wade told her as he approached the table. "There's only three of us eating, right?"

"Well, look at you, son," she said. "You're skin and bone. I have to fatten you up while you're here with me."

While the sadness lingered among them, the sights, sounds, and smells of home brought Wade great comfort in his grief. He found it difficult to reconcile those feelings of contentment and happiness with those of guilt and despair. Wade was always full of internal conflict, and he'd become an expert in managing and hiding his emotions.

After their visit to the cemetery, Wade and his mother returned home to finish their Thanksgiving preparations, and Paul drove back to the marina. The Parkers and the Thompsons met later that day for a Thanksgiving supper, though Paul was conspicuously absent. He'd told Wade and his mother that he had a problem with the motor on his boat he needed to take care of before it got dark, and that he would be over later for leftovers, but he never showed up.

The next day Wade visited his brother at the marina, where the familiar stench of diesel fuel and fish guts consumed him. He found Paul working at a coil of rope at the front of his boat. He was wearing a sun-bleached, navy-blue sweatshirt that was stained by sea-salt spray and motor oil, a pair of denim blue jeans that were frayed at the pockets and worn at the cuffs, and Wade's yellow American Legion baseball hat cinched tight around his head.

"Did you steal that from my room?" Wade asked, pointing to the hat.

Paul laid the rope on the deck of his boat and hopped onto the dock. "You weren't using it."

Wade didn't really care about the hat. Paul probably just needed one the day he took it from Wade's room. He was always a man of utility and need, not one of want. Or maybe, Wade thought, his brother wanted to keep a piece of him close while he was away.

"Why didn't you eat supper with us yesterday? I don't have too many days left."

"I had too much work to do around here."

Wade didn't believe him. "That's bullshit. What's going on?"

"I didn't feel much like being around Emma, to tell you the truth."

Paul brushed by his brother and opened a storage crate that was sitting on the dock.

"Oh yeah?" Wade huffed. "What's that all about?"

"She thinks she knows what's best. For her and everyone else. I guess I don't agree."

"Everyone else?" Wade asked. "Does that mean you? Is there something I should know?"

Paul threw a rag he'd just picked up back into the boat. "I guess I wasn't too keen on her telling me what to do and how to act, all things considered." His voice was pitched. Whatever was said or done was still nagging at him, for sure.

Wade pressed his brother. "Did she do something? Was it something about you and Sophia?"

"Actually, Wade, there is no me and Sophia anymore."

"You aren't with her?"

Paul turned his back to Wade and jumped onto his boat.

"What happened?" Wade asked.

"She's there, and I'm here."

"What does that have to do with Emma?"

Paul didn't answer. Wade sensed there was more to the story, but Paul was through talking. He picked up a couple of buckets and carried them back off the boat before walking down the dock. Wade followed him.

"I'm meeting Emma and a few others at the Sink or Swim tonight. I guess you and Emma aren't the best of friends right now, but I was hoping you'd meet us out. I want to spend as much time with you as I can."

"I don't think so. You be with your friends tonight."

"C'mon. If you don't want to hang out, just stop by for a drink. We need to raise a glass up to dad at least."

Paul thought about it. "Okay. Maybe one drink."

Sometimes you walk into a place and it's like time doesn't exist. Or at least the passage of time. When Wade walked into that bar with Emma, they were back in high school again. Old fishermen and dockworkers hunched over the bar drinking their drafts and shots of whiskey, trying to put an end to what seemed like an endless day. Underage high schoolers huddled at tables looking guilty about sneaking a few beers in a place that still didn't care how old you were as long as you didn't start any trouble and could pay your tab. A couple of older single ladies in tight clothes and too much makeup were talking and laughing a little louder than necessary, maybe hoping to round up a companion for the night. And a few college kids back from school for the holiday lingered about and caught up with old friends. For Wade, it was the sights and sounds of his adolescence. The smell of spilled beer and greasy food. The clinks of glass pitchers and thick mugs. The irritated grunts from the graybeards at the bar.

Wade and Emma found Timmy, Claire, Tiffany, and Sandy already gathered at one of the tables with a couple of half-empty pitchers and a few plates of french fries spread out in front of them. There were hugs and kisses and more than a few tears, even one or two from Timmy. Sandy's new boyfriend was there too. He was a thick, strong-looking guy, maybe a couple of years older than the rest of them, and he reminded Wade of his friend Dave. This guy Billy was big and lovable and looked like someone who could handle himself in a scrap. He liked a beer or two and made quick work of the whiskey shots they put in front of him. He had a casual, fun-loving attitude that made it easy to like him. Wade was happy for Sandy, but seeing her here with Billy made him realize how much he missed Dave. They hadn't heard much from their old friend since he left for Parris Island and then for East Asia. Wade knew Dave was in the middle of the rough stuff, just like he was, and he worried for him.

Paul walked in and made his way to their table. He looked irritated and tired. Maybe his leg was hurting. He was limping more than usual. Or maybe he was bothered by the crowd or the noise or just about being there. But he said his hellos, took a seat, and poured himself a beer from one of the pitchers. Wade was sitting across the table from Paul, who was quietly listening to their conversation but not paying particularly close attention until Emma went at him.

"When is Sophia getting home?" she asked him. She knew Paul and Sophia weren't together anymore. Wade wondered why she was needling him.

Paul's disposition didn't change much, though Wade did detect a slight furrow at his brow and a clench in his jaw.

"Sorry. I forgot that she isn't talking to you anymore," Emma added.

The coldness of the comment surprised Wade. "That's enough, Emma," he told her.

"It's all right, Wade," Paul interrupted. "This is how Emma and I talk to each other."

Emma gave Wade a little shove on the shoulder. "Don't be so serious all the time, Wade. I'm only playing with him. He doesn't like it when I give him relationship advice."

Paul bit back. "Maybe I don't think you're qualified to give it."

Wade got the gist of that comment. Paul didn't approve of Emma's dating history, at least. Maybe he didn't approve of her current dating activity. None of it was something Wade wanted to talk or hear about.

Emma clutched at her heart. "I'm sorry, big brother. Do you forgive me?" she asked, mockingly.

Paul lifted his mug to her and took a drink. The table livened up again, but Wade could see that Paul was uneasy. Wade rose from the table and motioned for Paul to follow him to the bar.

"Two shots of whiskey," Wade told the bartender, a sullen, skinny man, with sunken cheeks and cloudy eyes. The bartender dropped the shot glasses on the oak planks of the bar and poured in the brown liquid.

Wade lifted his glass. "To Dad."

"To Dad," Paul repeated.

They drank the liquor in one swallow and slapped their glasses down when they finished. The bartender collected the glasses and wiped down the bar with the dirty rag that had been slung over his shoulder. Wade watched him turn circles across the wood. He could see tendons stretching and pulling under the paper-like skin of his hand and the blue blood pumping through a vein that looked like a tree root risen from the depths of a shallow yard. *There isn't much life left in that hand*, Wade thought.

Paul laid down a few bills for the shots. "I think I'm gonna get going," he told Wade.

Wade was distracted and barely heard him. He was looking back at their table. At Emma. He was curious about what was going on between them.

"Why are the two of you like that?" Wade asked.

"Me and Emma?"

"Yeah."

"Haven't we always been that way?"

"I don't know. Maybe. I just don't understand why you're this way now." Wade made a sweeping motion with his hand.

"It's just the way it is, Wade. She and I have a different type of relationship than the two of you. You see her differently and she sees me differently, and that's okay."

"Do you hate her?" Wade asked.

"No. I don't hate her." Paul followed Wade's eyes to Emma. "I love that girl. It hurts me to see her do some of the things she does to herself. It hurts me to see what she does to you."

Wade didn't understand. "What does she do to me?"

"That," Paul said, angling his head in Emma's direction.

She was laughing at something. She was so bright and alive and beautiful. It was all he said, but Wade understood this time. Wade didn't just love Emma as a sister. He loved all of her, and it was something he would never be able to escape from.

They walked back to the table together. Wade sat down while Paul gathered his jacket from his chair. Someone else approached them. Wade knew the man. It was the doctor's son, Reid Esham, a private-school kid a little older than Wade and his classmates. He never liked that kid much, and he was with a couple of other guys from his crew that he recognized, including Ken Meehan, who he liked even less than Reid.

Reid put both hands on the back of Emma's chair and leaned over her. Wade felt an itch of jealousy and maybe a little rage creep up in him.

"Hello, everyone," Reid announced to the table. They all went quiet. "It's nice to see the old gang back together."

Emma looked up at him and scanned the room. "Where's that fiancé of yours? She let you off the leash for a night?"

Reid didn't seem bothered by the comment. In fact, he had a wide, mischievous grin. "I'm out with the boys tonight. We're looking for a little trouble."

Wade was putting it together. Reid and Emma had some history. Maybe this was why Paul was upset with her. Maybe this was what Paul was trying to protect him from.

Reid slid his hands onto Emma's shoulders and started rubbing them, and Emma didn't seem to mind. In fact, Wade saw Emma reach back and touch Reid on the wrist, affectionately, it seemed.

The itch Wade had felt turned into a hot streak that rose up through him until it burned his face. He looked up at Paul, who had replaced his jacket on the chair. Paul had a little history with Reid and Ken and their private-school friends himself. There were more than a few brawls between them in their high school days. Paul eyed Reid with a squint and tightened his grip on the back of the chair, unintentionally gathering the fabric of his jacket in a bunch in his fingers. Reid noticed Paul staring at him.

"Uh oh, Ken," Reid said. He took his hands off Emma. "Looks like we riled up the cripple."

Wade heard some laughter from Ken and their other friends and then the crack of knuckle against cheekbone. Paul had thrown the first punch, catching Reid flush against his face and sending him stumbling back into the table next to them. Wade threw a quick left of his own that landed square against Ken's fat nose, busting it open and sending a spray of blood all over Ken's white shirt. It didn't take Timmy and Billy more than a second to leap from the table, and in no time the four of them were pounding Reid and his boys into the beer-soaked barroom floor. A couple of bartenders and a few others corralled them pretty quickly, though, and pushed them out the front door and into the parking lot.

Paul and Wade were breathless, still angry and full of fire, but Billy and Timmy were laughing.

"Oh, man!" Timmy said excitedly. "That was just like old times!"

Wade caught his breath and started laughing, and then Paul started laughing with him.

"C'mon, fellas," Paul said. "We can walk to my boat from here and have a nightcap."

Billy dusted himself off. "What about the girls?" he asked.

"Oh, shoot, man," Timmy said, wrapping his arm around Billy's broad shoulders. "Don't worry about them. This ain't their first rodeo. We'll catch up with them later."

Billy shrugged his shoulders and followed along. The four of them stumbled down the road and headed toward the marina. They were sitting on the deck of the boat finishing up a second round when they heard footsteps. It was Emma, and she was alone.

"I thought I might find you here," she said. She showed them a tired but contrite smile. It was a peace offering, to Paul and Wade.

"Where are the girls?" Billy asked, suddenly concerned.

"Claire took Sandy home," she told him. She noticed his worried look. "It's okay, Billy. Sandy understands." Emma looked at Wade. They'd all been through something like this before, after all.

"You want a beer?" Paul asked her, pulling a can out of the cooler as a peace offering back to her.

"No, thanks, Paul. I was just checking on you guys. I'm heading home."

Wade got up from a bench on the boat. "I'll come with you."

Wade wasn't going to let his anger and jealousy affect his short stay home. He wanted to be with Emma, and he didn't care what had happened or what was happening. None of it mattered until he was home for good. They walked back to the bar and drove to her house.

"Thanks for the lift, and sorry about the fight," he told her. He got out and started walking to his house next door.

"Wait," Emma called to him.

Wade turned and found Emma right in front of him. She took his hand and rubbed her thumb across his fingers. She was staring at him with her wide, moonlit eyes, and he saw her again. There was the girl from the marsh, mud-stained and full of adventure. He could smell the salt on her skin, and when she leaned in and kissed him, he could taste it too. He kissed her back and pulled her into him and kissed her again. This time she didn't pull back or run away. This time she let him kiss her and she kissed him, and it felt right. He took her hand and led her to his house. He walked her through the hallway and to his bedroom and closed the door.

Wade stayed awake long after she'd fallen asleep, their bodies twisted together under a single sheet, an arm and leg draped across his body. He ran his fingers through her hair and over her shoulder and down her side. Her breathing was easy and warm against his skin. When he finally closed his eyes, she was still in his arms. He felt the heat of the sun on his cheek. He heard the gentle flow of the tide and the calls of shorebirds in flight. He breathed in the salt air and was overwhelmed.

Emma left before Wade or his mother had awakened. He could still smell her on his sheets and missed her already. He didn't see her at all that day or through the rest of the weekend. He spotted her for a second when she was leaving her house on Monday morning, on her way to work, he figured. She waved and pointed to her watch, got in her car, and drove away. It sure seemed like she was avoiding him. Wade assumed their night together was too much for her and that she couldn't face him. He was almost mad at himself about it. Almost.

Another day passed and still no Emma, so Wade walked over to the Parkers, but she wasn't there. He spent an hour or so with Mr. and Mrs. Parker and they reminisced a bit about summers at the beach and the family trips they took together, which Wade remembered fondly. Emma was working a couple of jobs and going to classes at night, they told him, but maybe he could catch up with her tomorrow.

It was about midafternoon the following day. His mother was at the hairdresser, and he was alone reading his high school copy of *The Catcher in the Rye* in the living room, when he heard a knock at the door. He found Emma on the front step with her purse hanging from her shoulder.

"You want to come in?" Wade asked her. He wanted to rush out and grab her and pull her to him. He wanted to smell her hair and taste her skin. He wanted to take her to his bedroom again, but he knew it was all over just by looking at her. She waved him off.

"I can't. I'm heading to work over at Bailey's. They give me hours on the register and sometimes I work the lunch counter. It isn't anything special, but it gives me some spending money, and I'm saving as much as I can for school."

"That's great," Wade told her.

"I know you've been trying to catch up with me," she said. "Sorry. I've just been so busy."

"Yeah, yeah. I understand," Wade offered, though he wasn't sure he did understand. He yearned for her, and she'd barely acknowledged him since their night together. "I thought we should talk about what happened before I leave. You know?"

"Yeah. I know. You're right." She checked her watch and then reached into her purse for her car keys. "Let's spend the day together tomorrow. Can we do that?" she asked him. "We can grab breakfast and walk on the boardwalk and then maybe head into town for lunch and ice cream. That sounds like fun, doesn't it?"

Wade nodded approvingly. "It sure does."

"Great." She backed down the brick steps. "I'll come by around nine," she said as she scurried back across their yards and to her car.

Emma arrived at nine the next morning, as promised, dressed in a sharp black coat over a black turtleneck sweater and white denim jeans. Her hair was gathered in a black headband, and she was wearing thick, black plastic sunglasses. She'd decided they'd spend the day as tourists in their own town, and Wade let her lead them on their adventure, one more time.

They took her car, stopping first for their breakfast at the little coffee shop by the marina. After they ate, they drove to the beach and parked in the big lot by the inlet. They strolled down the boardwalk and to the pier and walked out on it over the Atlantic. They touched hands but didn't hold them. Wade had some loose change that he fed into one of the coin-operated binoculars, and they spent some time looking up the coast and down to Assateague and then back west across the bay and over the mainland. They laughed when a seagull flew between them for a stray french fry on the ground.

Most of the shops were closed and boarded up for winter, but the Playland arcade was still open and so was the Five and Ten up near Division Street. They played a few games at the arcade and then went over to the Five and Ten where they found the owner, an ancient wisp of a man with ghost-white hair and thick caterpillar eyebrows, perched on a stool and greeting customers near the entrance. Emma bought Wade a conch shell with a blue wave painted on the side and

Wade bought Emma a pair of cheap, seashell earrings. They walked south and back to Emma's car arm in arm, and it felt good to Wade to have her all to himself for the day.

They drove back over the bridge, ate lunch at the Main Street Diner, and topped it off with some ice cream from the shop down the street. On their way home, Emma decided they'd finish their adventure with a walk out to the marsh.

"Maybe we'll see her this time," she said, whimsically. She reached under her turtleneck and showed him her arrowhead, and he knew that it was a possibility.

They got back home and instead of skipping or running down the road like they used to, they strolled at a much more leisurely pace. Wade looked over at the empty field and wondered whether another farmer would do it justice. They'd decided to rent out the land to provide his mother with the income she'd need for her living expenses, and Paul and Wade figured it would be enough for her to live a comfortable life for the foreseeable future. He thought about his old dog Blue and how happy Blue seemed to be when he accompanied them on their adventures. Or maybe it was Wade who was happy to have Blue and Emma with him. They walked down the path and along the boards across the marsh to their spit of beach on the bay. Emma pulled Wade down to the sand by the hand and let out a heavy sigh.

"I'm sorry, Wade," she told him.

"About what?"

"About me," she said. She released his hand and dropped her head into her open palms. "It isn't fair to you."

"I don't understand."

"It isn't fair that I don't love you the way you need me to love you. I'm not sure I have that kind of love in me."

Wade wasn't necessarily surprised, but it still hurt to hear it. "Did you really ever give me the chance?" he asked her. "Did you give yourself the chance?"

"Maybe it's how we started out together. Maybe I couldn't overcome that."

What was wrong with our start? Wade thought. He'd loved her from the first second he knew her. From their beginning. He'd love her to their end. There was always something inside him that told him that much.

"You were always the only thing that mattered to me," Wade told her. "You *are* the only thing that matters to me. If you would have let me love you, you would have been my world."

"That's what hurts the most," she said through a sniffle. She wiped at a tear with the back of her hand. "That I've let you down."

He sat there looking over that water one more time, and he found himself drawing little circles in the wet sand again with his finger, like he did as a little boy.

"We'll always be together," he told her. "Even if we live our lives apart." He reached for her hand and turned it, palm up, and rubbed at the scar. She reached for his hand and did the same.

"Blood sister," she said to him.

"Blood brother," he said back, though this time it didn't feel like enough. He wanted more, and possibly for the first time in his life, he knew it was never going to happen.

Chapter 20

Wednesday, October 28, 1987

W ADE TRAVELED THE THIRTY minutes from his house in relative silence. There was no music on the drive today, just the sound of tires running through water and rubber scraping across the windshield glass. He needed the time to think. It had all come in a rush. Tom's death. Lily's arrival. Hillary Dent's murder. And with all of it, memories of Emma and the mystery of her disappearance were suddenly, once again, at the top of Wade's mind.

Wade arrived at State Police Headquarters and walked into the building. A young woman Wade hadn't seen before was stationed at an intake desk in the lobby. She greeted him when he walked up and pointed him to a chair while she called Rick to the front. A minute or two later Rick emerged through a set of security doors.

"Hey, Wade, back here."

Wade walked over and greeted Rick with a handshake. Rick guided Wade through the doors and into a hallway leading to offices, conference rooms, labs, and other restricted areas.

"I guess you noticed Ken's HR handywork up front?" Rick asked with a sly smile, thumbing in the direction of the receptionist behind them.

"Not really," Wade said.

Rick must have taken it as a cue to shut up, which is about how Wade meant it. They continued down the hallway and stopped at a closed door with a frosted glass window. Rick held out a hand. His eyes narrowed.

"Just a heads up. Ken didn't want this meeting, but the FBI wanted to talk to you. They found the Harrington info compelling."

Rick hesitated. Wade waited.

"They've also heard about your own investigation."

"How did they find out about that?" Wade asked.

"Ken came back from your little meeting the other day pretty fired up. He told me you were reopening the case, and how you thought all the cases might be connected. I might've mentioned something about it to the FBI. By accident, of course."

Wade couldn't help but smile.

"Now look, man. Ken isn't your friend in this. He doesn't want you to know anything. He doesn't want you to do anything. He doesn't want your help. He doesn't want you to exist." Rick set his eyes on Wade's. "What the hell did you do to make him hate you so much?"

"You'll have to ask him," was all Wade said back.

Rick opened the door. The room was set up with a table at its center and ten or so rolling desk chairs circling it. Ken was at the head of the table at the far end. There were a couple of manila folders and a notepad in front of him. The two agents, a man and a woman, were seated in chairs facing the door, their backs to the wall of windows behind them. The blinds were pulled all the way up to brighten the room, but in the dreariness of the day it simply dulled the color and contrast of the surroundings. Rick rolled two chairs back from the table opposite the agents, and he and Wade took their seats.

Wade assumed Ken would begin with introductions, but it was one of the agents who spoke first. He looked to be the older of the two, with dark black hair that was grayed along the temples and over the ears and slicked back close to his scalp.

"Good morning, Sheriff." Wade recognized a Baltimore accent. "I'm Special Agent Bruce Reynolds. This is my colleague, Special Agent Jessica Chase."

"Nice to meet you," Wade said.

That was the extent of the small talk. Chase slid a folder across the table to Wade. Wade opened it and flipped through pages and pictures.

"That's Deborah Mansfield. She was a University of Delaware senior. Disappeared after attending a fraternity party with a few of her girlfriends. They said she had a couple of beers and left early. She told them she was going back to her apartment to study, but she never made it there."

"That was four years ago," Reynolds said. "She was sexually assaulted. No semen. No fingerprints or traces of hair. Wiped clean with a household cleanser. Posed at the scene."

Wade looked at the photographs of the girl in the file. There was a picture that looked like it had been taken at a college formal or wedding. She had brown hair and brown eyes and clear, smooth skin. She was pretty, and she looked happy. He flipped to a crime scene photo and it immediately reminded him of Hillary Dent. Wade looked up at the agents and then over to Rick and Ken.

"Looks familiar, right?" Rick asked.

Wade returned to the photographs. Her body was propped against a post on a dock overlooking a body of water. She was dressed only in a short white nightgown or pajama top, and even in the photograph, Wade could see through it. The hem of the gown fell short above her hip, leaving her naked from the waist down. Her legs were pulled in toward her body with her knees gathered to one side twisting her lower half so that she was almost sitting on her feet. Her hands were folded neatly in front of her and laying on her right hip.

"How was she killed?" Wade asked.

"Manual strangulation," Reynolds told him.

Chase slid another file over to him.

"Eve Francis. Another college student, three years before Mansfield. This one at Temple. She was working nights at a convenience store. She disappeared after a shift. Same story."

Wade opened the folder and looked over its contents. Another brunette with brown eyes. Young and attractive. *He has a type*, Wade thought.

"No one saw anything," Reynolds remarked. "The killer may as well be a ghost."

Wade reviewed the photographs of the crime scene. There were differences, for sure, but enough similarities to at least suspect a link. Like the others, she wore a simple white garment, this time a short sundress, and she was otherwise naked. She was found near the water, but this girl was lying down on the grass, and she was holding yellow daisies in her hands across her abdomen. The contrast of the yellow against the white of her shirt and the chalk of her skin reminded Wade of those old black-and-white movies they tried to colorize. The backgrounds were usually bland and washed out, with one or two features that were sharp and bright. Here, it was the flowers, and they drew Wade's eyes right to them.

"Yellow flowers," Wade commented.

"That's right," Reynolds responded. "Just like Hillary Dent."

Chase interrupted. "We're looking at Lisa Harrington now too as a possible fourth related case, thanks to the information you provided to Rick and Ken."

Wade settled in the chair and eyed the folders in front of him. It was time to make his move. "I believe you're aware of a potential fifth victim from 1970."

Ken slapped an open palm against the table. "I told you this was a bad idea. This has nothing to do with Emma Parker."

Reynolds lifted a hand in Ken's direction. "Wait a minute, Ken. I want to hear this." He turned his attention back to Wade. "Tell us about the Parker case."

Wade went through the details. He knew the file front to back and could recite most of the interview reports verbatim. The room was quiet for the most part except for the occasional grunt or puff from Ken, who had grown increasingly agitated throughout Wade's report. Wade argued the logic of the possible connection between Emma and these other girls and explained his theory about the unknown father. Wade hoped he'd given them enough. In Wade's mind, this was a legitimate lead, one that the FBI couldn't ignore considering the lack of other tangible evidence connecting them to a suspect.

Chase and Reynolds listened dispassionately, processing the information Wade provided without asking a question or making a comment. After a few minutes, Wade finished his presentation. "If my theory is correct, and Emma Parker is victim number one, then finding the father of her daughter should be a priority."

There was no immediate reaction from any of them, though Ken was still fidgeting in his seat. Wade thought he'd lost them. Then, Reynolds broke the silence.

"You have some names?"

Wade was encouraged. "I have two. One of them, Brad Wilkerson, has already agreed to provide a blood sample. He wants to know if he's the father. Either way, I'm not sure I like him for this. He was allegedly back at school when Emma disappeared. The results could eliminate him as a suspect altogether."

"What about the other one?" Chase asked.

"Reid Esham."

Ken nearly lost his seat when he heard that. "Are you serious, Wade?"

Wade tried to keep his composure. "He was seeing her back then, wasn't he, Ken? And he was engaged at the time. He was married in '70 when she disappeared. If it was his kid, he might've wanted to keep it quiet."

Ken's face went red, and Wade could tell from the itch in his chin that he wanted to say something. But Wade had compromised him, and a wrong word might get him kicked off the investigation altogether. Wade figured he might pay for that later, but it was worth it if he could get the FBI behind his theory, and he felt like he'd given Chase and Reynolds enough information to get them at least curious. Reynolds confirmed his suspicion.

"You think the girl will cooperate?" Reynolds asked.

"I think she will," Wade answered confidently, even though there was no way yet to know for sure.

Chapter 21

Thursday, October 29, 1987

G INNY HAD SET UP a dinner for the family, and the family now included Lily. She was more than a week into it, living with a husband and wife, being treated as part of this family unit and not as a guest. She was still getting used to the idea, feeling more like a distant cousin, perhaps, than a daughter or even a stepdaughter. There was no pressure from either side to force it into something it wasn't. Whatever it was, or whatever it might become, it was going to be a natural, organic thing. If it worked out, great. If not, she was fine with moving on. None of this was her idea anyway.

Paul and Mrs. Thompson arrived a little after six o'clock. Lily was setting the table in the dining room but could hear them in the foyer. She peeked out and watched them at the door.

"Whatcha got there, Ma?" Wade asked, pointing to a dish in her arms.

"Chocolate cake. Lily used to like it," Lily heard her say.

Lily suddenly remembered sitting at a table with Mrs. Thompson and her grandmother when she was little, eating cake and drinking milk while the ladies drank their tea. She remembered the gray and white cat that would curl up next to her on the living room carpet, and the smells of sugar and lemon coming from the kitchen. She remembered the music that played from a record player in the front room and the birds that sang through the screen door at the back. Most of all, she remembered feeling safe and happy. Lily realized it was the first time she'd seen Mrs. Thompson in years, probably not since she moved in with her uncle. Mrs. Thompson wasn't at her uncle's funeral. She'd been sick and unable to attend. Seeing her again now, after so long, recalling those memories, was like traveling back in time.

Paul squeezed by Wade and his mother. He was holding a paper bag full of something. "Mom made a batch of biscuits and packed up some preserves and jams for you," he said, gruffly.

Even here, in Wade's house, a place where he should be comfortable, Lily thought Paul looked anything but. She found it so unusual, she couldn't help but watch him. It was like something was itching under his skin. When he caught a glimpse of Lily in the dining room, he quickly cast his eyes downward and shuffled back toward the kitchen, the bag of biscuits still in his hands.

Wade came up behind his mother and pulled gently at her coat. She twisted with him and turned out of the coat, freeing herself from the weight of it. She brushed out the wrinkles in her top and felt at her hair, which was modestly styled and still a thick salt and pepper. She walked into the foyer and saw Lily. The sight must have surprised her.

"Lily, dear. Oh my, how you have grown."

"Hello, Mrs. Thompson."

"Do you remember me?"

"Of course I remember you, Mrs. Thompson."

Mrs. Thompson took Lily's hands and squeezed them gently. She raised them above her waist, looked her over, and let out a whisper of a sigh. "So beautiful. You are your mother's daughter."

Lily couldn't recall the last time anyone called her beautiful. That's not to say she thought she was ugly. No. She regarded herself as cute. Pretty, even. Maybe. She never really had any trouble catching a boy's eye, but she never felt she met the measure of her mother's beauty.

And her mother was her standard of beauty. Many people had told her how beautiful her mother was. "More beautiful than Natalie Wood," someone had said once. They might say something to Lily about a resemblance. The eyes, usually. Sometimes the mouth. The older she got the more she thought there was a likeness. But beautiful? She wasn't sure about that.

Ginny walked into the dining room carrying a bowl, which she set on the table.

"Mom brought cake," Wade told her.

Ginny greeted Wade's mother with a kiss on the cheek and took the cake dish and placed it on the buffet table. "Dinner is on the way," she told them.

Ginny finished bringing in the dishes and Wade handled the drinks. He brought in a bottle of wine, opened it, and went back into the refrigerator for a couple of beers for Paul and himself. The five of them gathered around the table. Wade said a quick prayer, they finished with an *Amen*, and then they filled their plates.

Lily poured herself a glass of water from the pitcher on the table and took a sip. Wade grabbed another empty glass and poured in a small amount of wine. He slid the glass over to Lily, who was sitting to his left. She looked at him curiously and noticed a similar expression from Ginny. He raised his drink in a toast.

"Now that we have all the Thompsons here tonight," he started, "I wanted to formally welcome you, Lily, into our home and our family."

Wade and the other adults took a drink. Lily hesitated and looked over at Ginny.

"It's okay," Ginny told her. "I won't call the cops on you."

They all laughed. Even Paul, who'd been cool and awkward with her since he'd arrived. He avoided her up until they sat for their meal.

He hadn't even said hello. Lily took a sip of her wine, wondering as she drank whether Wade's older brother acted like that around everyone, or if it was only something he did around her.

They spent the next few minutes eating and drinking with some casual conversation before Mrs. Thompson brought up a more sobering subject.

"I heard about the missing girl they found on the beach on Assateague. Are you working on that case, Wade?"

"Not really, Mom. The state police are handling that, and the FBI is involved."

"My goodness. What a terrible thing."

"This really isn't dinner conversation, Ma," Paul interjected.

"You're right," Mrs. Thompson agreed and changed the subject. "Lily, dear, I wanted to apologize for not attending your uncle's funeral. I'd been ill, unfortunately. I am so sorry for your loss. Your uncle was a good man."

"Thank you, Mrs. Thompson." Lily quickly refocused her efforts on the ham on her plate. She wouldn't have minded if they'd left that subject of conversation as well.

"But you, dear? How are you?" Mrs. Thompson asked her.

"I'm holding up fine, thank you." Lily cut up another piece of ham and bit it off her fork.

Mrs. Thompson watched her and then let out a little laugh. "I'm overwhelmed looking at you. You were such a tiny baby. I remember holding you and thinking how much easier it would have been to carry *you* around instead of these two." She waved a finger at Wade and Paul. "You were barely seven pounds when you were born."

"I didn't know that," Lily said.

"You were there, Paul. You remember, don't you?"

Paul shrugged. He didn't seem to remember, or he didn't much care to talk about it. Lily was surprised. She figured Wade might be there, but not Paul.

Mrs. Thompson turned back to Lily. "When you finally got home, though, you thrived. Your mother loved you so."

The table grew quiet. The comment was innocent enough. Lily didn't mind hearing it. She knew it was true. Mrs. Thompson must have realized that maybe she shouldn't have said it, though. Wade and Ginny were wearing uncomfortable smiles. Paul's mouth was twisted in a knot.

"I'm sorry, dear. I hope I didn't upset you."

"It's all right, Mrs. Thompson," she told her.

Lily looked around the table. All their faces had tightened. They were the ones that looked uneasy and upset, especially Wade, who was playing with something around his neck.

"What's that?" Lily asked, pointing at Wade's chest. He'd pulled a necklace out from under his shirt and was rubbing at something hanging from the end of it.

"Wade hasn't told you about that?" Mrs. Thompson asked her.

Lily shook her head.

"Your mother found that and gave it to him."

"Really?" Lily asked with interest. She leaned across the corner of the table to get a closer look.

Wade reached behind his neck and untied the leather cord. He gathered it in the palm of his hand and offered it to her. She took it and studied it.

"Your mother used to take Wade out on little adventures," Mrs. Thompson told her.

"She pulled that arrowhead out of the bay," Wade said. "Actually, she pulled out two. She kept one and gave that one to me."

Wade turned to Paul. "Paul was supposed to come with us that day. Maybe if he had, your mother would've found three of them, but Paul didn't like coming out on our expeditions," Wade said to her. "He didn't like being bossed around."

"By you?" Lily asked him.

"Oh, no," Wade said, shaking his head. "By your mom. She liked to do things her way."

Paul got up from the table abruptly. "Excuse me, folks. I'm gonna step outside for some air."

Lily watched him walk into the kitchen and heard the snap of the screen door behind him as he exited out to the back deck. It was a strange reaction to what Lily perceived as a harmless comment.

"Is he okay?" Lily asked.

"He's fine," Mrs. Thompson answered. "Paul isn't one to reminisce about the past."

Ginny stirred from the other end of the table. "I'm going to get a pot of coffee going."

Mrs. Thompson stood up after her. "I'll help you."

The two women gathered the dishes and left for the kitchen, leaving Wade and Lily at the table. Lily wasn't sure if it was the flood of memories or dreams that had come to her recently or being around all of them together like this and hearing the story about the arrowhead, but Lily felt she was ready to talk to Wade. She was ready to hear some things she might not want to hear. Things that no one had told her before. Things she'd had no control over but had shaped her life from the moment she was born. Lily set the necklace on the table and slid it in front of Wade.

"Wade, what happened to my mother?"

Wade's expression didn't change. Not even a blink or a twitch at the corner of his mouth. It was almost as if he was expecting the question. "We really don't know, Lily."

Lily wasn't sure she believed him. There had to be something. "I've never heard anything about her disappearance. Only that they found her car by the side of the road and that she was gone. I'd like to hear what you think. I'd like to hear the truth."

This time Wade did react. He leaned up in his seat and propped an elbow on the table, his hand at his mouth, his thumb holding the weight of his head like a hook at the chin. After a long pause, he answered.

"I think someone who knew your mother killed her."

He'd said it so matter-of-factly that the horror of the possibility barely registered with her. It might've been the most honest thing anyone had ever said to her, and she realized that she wasn't surprised by it. Maybe she'd believed it her whole life. Maybe she'd even suspected that her father might be the person responsible.

"I've wondered about who my father might be," she told him then, saying it out loud, implying the worst possible truth. "I don't like to spend too much time on that. It feels like the answer might disappoint me."

In fact, she'd thought about it more over the last few days than she had over the last several years. She decided she was ready to know. She was ready to hear his name if Wade knew it.

"Wade, do you know who my father is?"

Wade didn't say anything right away. He crossed his arms on the table and angled forward. Lily supposed he was trying to read her, trying to determine how much she was ready and willing to hear.

"There are a couple of possibilities," he said, finally. "Nothing we can know for sure. It doesn't mean they had anything to do with what happened to your mother, but finding out might answer some questions."

Ginny and Mrs. Thompson returned with cups, dessert plates, and the coffee. Mrs. Thompson must have seen something in their faces or sensed something in the room.

"Is everything all right?" she asked.

Wade was quiet. Lily felt compelled to say something.

"We were talking about my mom."

"Oh, I see."

An awkward silence passed over them. Ginny poured everyone a cup of coffee and sent around the cream and sugar. Mrs. Thompson cut the cake and handed out slices. Lily wanted to hear more.

"When was the last time you saw my mom?"

Wade played at some icing with his fork before answering. "I was back in the States the Thanksgiving before she disappeared. I saw her then. That was the last time."

"Back from where?" Lily asked.

"From the war, dear," Mrs. Thompson interjected. "He was in Vietnam. He came back when his father died suddenly."

"Oh. I'm sorry. I didn't know."

"That's okay," Wade told her. "There was no reason for you to know." He took a sip of coffee. "I had to go back right after that. I never saw your mother again."

"We thought we'd lost him too," Mrs. Thompson said. "After he went back, we didn't hear from him much. They were sending him out on special missions, and he wasn't in contact with us for months at a time. Then we got word that he was missing in action."

"Really?" Lily asked.

"Yes. We were all very worried. Your mother too," Mrs. Thompson told her. "We feared the worst. We assumed the worst. Then months later, out of the blue, we got word that he'd been found alive."

"What happened?" Lily asked.

Mrs. Thompson and Ginny looked over at Wade. So did Lily. Wade tensed. His brow creased.

"I was sent on one of those missions with a small team. We were ambushed and I was injured. The rest of my team were killed," Wade said, unemotionally. "I crawled into some brush and passed out. When I woke up a few days later, I was in a POW camp."

Wade's mother finished the story.

"He was sick and injured, but there was another prisoner, an American doctor, who helped him recover. Otherwise, he might not be here today. A patrol finally swept through and freed them. He'd been missing for almost a year."

Ginny got up from the table. "I'm sorry," she said. "I'm not feeling well all of a sudden. Will you excuse me?"

"Are you all right?" Wade asked.

"I'm feeling a little off again," she told him. "I just need to lie down. Don't worry about me."

Mrs. Thompson eyed Wade and then Ginny. "How long has this been going on?" she asked.

"Just a couple of days," Ginny told her. "I think I caught a little bug."

Ginny actually had been sick for more than a week, but Lily didn't feel compelled to correct her, at least not in front of Mrs. Thompson. She didn't know if Ginny's condition now was related to her illness or the topic of discussion. It must've been hard for Ginny to hear about Lily's mother all the time, especially now with her own daughter living under Ginny's roof. Lily had the sense that Wade and her mother were closer than anyone had let on, and if that was the case, Ginny's reaction could be related to that. Lily decided it was enough for tonight.

"I'll take care of the dishes," Lily told her.

Ginny thanked her and then disappeared down the hallway and into her bedroom. Lily started collecting the rest of the plates and silverware.

Mrs. Thompson turned to Wade. "Just a couple of days?" she asked him.

"Yeah, Ma," he said. "I don't think it's anything to worry about."

Wade's mother didn't seem convinced. She lifted from her seat with a sigh and helped Lily with the dishes. She pointed to a slice of cake that had been left for Paul.

"Take that out to your brother. Lily and I will clean up."

Wade did as his mother instructed. He found his brother sitting out on the back porch and handed him the plate. Paul didn't say anything. He sunk his fork into the deepest part of the cake and took a bite. Wade sat down in a chair next to him.

It was a dark, starless, night. Cool, but not cold. The smell of marsh and wet autumn leaves carried across the yard on a gentle sea salt breeze. Wade felt the weight of his conversation with Lily in his body, to his bones. He was tired, exhausted from almost twenty years' worth of unanswered questions. He was ready for those answers, and maybe Lily was too. She wasn't a child. She didn't need protection from that kind of truth. She wanted to know, and she needed to know.

Paul interrupted his thought. "Mom can bake a hell of a chocolate cake."

"A cake like that can take your mind off things," Wade told him.

"Yeah. Unfortunately, it can also bring back memories, good and bad."

That was a strange comment, coming from his brother. "What do you mean?" Wade asked.

"Seeing her is a little unsettling. That's all."

"Lily?"

Paul nodded and took another big bite. "She reminds me of Emma."

As much as Paul would've denied it, Wade knew Paul loved Emma almost as much as he did. She was every bit of a little sister to him. Wade probably never acknowledged Paul's own grief. That was selfish. He rarely, if ever, talked to him about her. Not the way he probably should've talked to him about her, at least.

"Imagine living with her," Wade said, almost under his breath. "But it's good to have her in my life."

"And Ginny?" Paul cut in. "How is she handling all of it?"

Wade considered the question. Things may not have been going as well as he'd thought. "She hasn't been herself the last few days. Something doesn't feel right. Maybe Lily moving in has something to do with it."

"It has to be tough for her too. There was always the shadow of Emma hanging over you. Hanging over both of you."

Wade couldn't help but agree. That shadow had overwhelmed them these last couple of weeks. It was all out there for Ginny, surrounding her, suffocating her, perhaps. Lily was with them every day. And Ginny could probably see the obsession of his investigation sweeping over him. Maybe she didn't know exactly what was going on, but she could surely feel it. She was probably doubting herself again, doubting him, wondering if their love was second best, or worse, wondering if he loved her at all. He hoped she knew. She was his reason for living after he got home from the war. She helped him fight off the demons. She showed him love and compassion again. She showed him how to deal with loss and overwhelming grief. He needed her much more than she needed him. He loved her more than she probably even knew.

It was quiet except for the sounds of the night around them. There were a few crickets out, and some frogs calling from the pond. Paul ate the last few bites of his cake and then stood up and walked over to the railing of the deck. He seemed on edge, nervous, like there was something gnawing at him.

"You got something on your mind?" Wade asked him.

Paul reached into the front pocket of his shirt and pulled out a pack of cigarettes. He lit one and rested his forearms against the railing. "I was just thinking about some things. Mistakes. Regrets."

Wade wasn't sure where this was coming from. Emma? Lily? Something else? Ken's inquiry in the Dent matter, maybe? "Anything I need to be worried about?" he asked him.

Paul stared out into the darkness, and between puffs on his cigarette, started talking.

"I was thinking about a trip I had on my boat a few years ago. I was all by myself, finishing up a good day of fishing, and I see a ripple in the water, not too far off in the distance. Then I see that ripple move toward me. I think to myself, that's a pretty large animal heading my way. My boat's big, right? I've taken it into the deep ocean, up and down the coast. I've ridden her through winter storms and battled the heaviest seas, and she's always done right by me. She gets me where I need to be. Takes me to my spots, gives me my reason for living. Gets me home at night. But I know the ocean can be unkind and unforgiving. Better men than me have been taken by her without cause or consideration. An unsuspecting storm, a rogue wave, some undeserved bad luck. But they've seen me through the worst of it, my boat and our ocean, that's for sure. They've made me what I am, I think."

"What are you getting at, Paul?" Wade asked him.

"Nothing. I'm just telling a story."

Wade wasn't so sure. Paul didn't tell too many stories, especially about the past. Last week it was Sophia, and now this.

"Anyway, there I was on that day, under an endless blue sky, with calm, welcoming seas, and a boat already full of fish. Perfect conditions. Content and satisfied. I'm thinking to myself, this is how it's gonna end? On a day like this? When nothing could or should go wrong? I'm gonna get rammed by a whale in the middle of the open ocean?"

Paul turned around to face Wade. He wasn't agitated anymore. He was calm. His eyes were relaxed, a hint of a smile on his lips.

"She was coming fast, and I'm wondering, do I have time to get to the wheel? But I already know the answer. I wrap my arm around the railing at the stern, bracing for impact, hoping the boat stays afloat and I stay dry. It's just yards away now, and it isn't a ripple anymore. It's a wake. I whisper a little prayer and hang on for dear life. Then it's gone. Under the boat, I assume. A last second decision to spare my life. Or maybe she was playing games with me."

"I've never heard this story," Wade told him.

Paul nodded. Wade knew no one had heard this story before. Paul took one last drag from the cigarette and ground the butt of it against the railing.

"I spin around to try to catch a glimpse of her. I'm hanging over the side scanning the water below me, and I see her shadow coming to the surface. Slowly this time. Gently. I can see the notches around her mouth and on her chin and the ridges in her thick skin that looked like a fingerprint stamped on paper. And then she opened her eye and looked right at me, Wade. It took my breath away. I was sure she saw me."

There was a chuckle and a grin. He tapped the edge of the railing and pointed at Wade.

"You know how that feels, right? When someone or something eyes you and it's as if they can see straight through your flesh and bone and into the depths of your soul? That's what it felt like to me. She drifted past me, and I could see the scars on her back. The markings of a life lived. Kind of like me, you know? Like us." Paul waved a finger back and forth between them.

"Everything we've done, everything we've experienced—it marks us. We wear it like a skin. Sometimes it's comfortable, and sometimes it isn't. For us, most of the time, it's not."

Wade was surely scarred, physically and emotionally. His shoulder had been torn apart by machine gun fire. His heart had been torn apart by grief. He got up from his seat and joined his brother at the railing. They stood there together for a bit longer before Paul stirred again.

"I wasn't afraid to die that day, Wade. Not out there. Not on the water. That's basically where I was born, and that's probably where I'm going to die."

Paul left the rail and walked back inside. Wade followed him. His mother was sitting at the dining room table with Lily. They were chatting and seemed to be enjoying each other's company. She saw Paul walk to the front door and understood that it was time to leave.

She gathered her things and let Wade help her with her coat. She gave Lily a long hug and kissed Wade on the cheek.

"Go check on your girl," she told him, before walking out of the house with Paul.

Wade did just that. Ginny was already in her pajamas and asleep in their bed, Shadow curled at her feet. Wade felt her forehead. She was a little clammy, but she didn't have a fever. She stirred when he kissed her and then turned away from him. He left her to rest and walked back to Lily, who was seated at the dining room table toying with his necklace. She was pulling the cord across the table, dragging it from side to side like a snake on a hot highway. He sat down with her.

"Are you okay?" he asked her.

"Yeah," she answered. "It's a lot, you know?"

"I do."

Wade watched her pull the necklace along. He thought back to the day Emma found the arrowheads. "Did anyone ever tell you that your mother thought she could talk to ghosts?"

Lily was caught off guard by the comment. She stopped playing with the necklace and stared back at Wade. "What are you talking about?"

"Your mother swore that she could see and talk to ghosts. And I believed her."

"*You*?" she asked, surprised. "*You* believed her?"

"Yeah. Me." Wade reached over and picked up the necklace. "When we were in the marsh that day, your mother told me she heard a whisper that led her to the arrowheads." Wade rubbed at it. "How would a ten-year-old girl know to stick her arm in the water in that spot? How could she know?"

Lily's expression changed. "You still believe her, don't you?"

Wade shook his head and let out a long, heavy breath. "I'm not sure what I believe. There are things we can't see. There are things we feel but don't understand. Things that happen that we can't comprehend. The day your mother pulled this out of the sand, she told me that if I wore it, it would protect me. I've been in situations that maybe I shouldn't have made it out of. I mostly chalked it up to training and experience or just luck, but there were a couple of times I wasn't so sure."

Wade stood and walked behind Lily before draping the necklace around her neck. "I think this really belongs to you."

Lily touched it and then stopped. "I'm ready," she said, determined.

Wade didn't understand. "Ready for what?" he asked.

"I'm ready to find out the truth. All of it."

Chapter 22

Saturday, October 31, 1987

I T WAS A CRISP, bright morning. Wade was out early with Shadow for a walk to the Mumford Trail, which gave him the opportunity to clear his head and think. Rick had reached out to him to let him know they'd approached Reid about obtaining a blood sample, and that Reid had agreed to provide it without a warrant. That was at least a little bit of a surprise to Wade, who figured Reid would make it difficult on them whether he believed he might be the father or not. The fact that Wade's two main targets openly volunteered to get tested also didn't look great for his theory or his credibility. Wade guessed that Ken had given Reid a heads-up about what was happening, and that Reid may have already spoken to his lawyer about all of it. Without Emma's blood, there would be no way to confirm paternity with one hundred percent certainty, so even a potential match could be discredited to some degree. A negative test could clear Reid altogether and effectively eliminate him as a person of interest for Emma and Hillary Dent and the others.

Wade's walk took him right by Dr. Esham's house, which was in a neighborhood of homes that sat on multi-acre plots of waterfront property. The homes were mostly surrounded by fences and monitored with cameras, clear indicators that the common folk were not welcome there. Wade slowed as he approached the property. He looked through the open gate and down the driveway and saw a person standing near the front of the house, but he couldn't make out if it was Dr. Esham, Reid, or someone else. Another figure appeared and immediately Shadow took interest. It was Dr. Esham's dog, Toby. Shadow turned and jogged toward his brother. The dogs met about halfway down the drive, greeted each other enthusiastically, and continued together back toward the house. By the time Wade reached them, they were chasing each other around the large stone fountain out front, and Reid was there with them. The last thing Wade wanted, today of all days, was to run into Reid.

"It's nice to see you, Wade." Reid almost sounded like he meant it. To Reid's credit, whatever concerns he might have had about Wade and his inquiry hadn't affected his demeanor.

Wade was eager to rustle Shadow and be on his way. "Sorry, Reid. He saw Toby and got away from me." Wade whistled and Shadow finally came over to him. He hooked a leash to Shadow's collar and pulled him close.

"I'm sure it was all a happy accident," Reid said. A condescending smartass to the very end. "Just a coincidence. Like that deputy you had following me the last couple of weeks."

Wade was in the middle of it now. There was no turning back. "It's my responsibility to track down every lead."

Reid laughed. "I'm not sure staking out my lunch is going to do a lot for your investigation."

Wade bit back. "You never know, Reid. Sometimes lunches turn into lunch dates. Things can get interesting."

Reid wiped the smirk off his face. "Harassment. That's all this is, Thompson. You've got my blood now, and when the tests come back, you'll see the truth. You're nothing but a jealous schoolboy chasing the ghost of the girl who broke your heart. Just because she wouldn't have you doesn't mean the rest of us are guilty. It wasn't like she didn't want it."

Every bit of Wade wanted to punch Reid in the mouth, but he wasn't nineteen anymore. He took a second to calm himself before responding. "I never understood why the last person who dated Emma before she disappeared got so little attention in the sheriff's report. For someone like you who loves attention, I found that unusual. It was almost like somebody was trying to hide something."

Reid narrowed his eyes, staring back at Wade like he was wishing he was nineteen again, too. But better judgment prevailed, and he backed off. He snapped his fingers, bringing Toby to attention. "C'mon boy," he told him. "Let's leave Sheriff Thompson alone with his delusions." And he walked away.

Wade stood there for a moment with Shadow next to the fountain. It was beautiful but not necessarily extraordinary. He was drawn to it, and he didn't quite know why. At its center was a large stone bird with wings spread out feeding water into the pool below through its mouth. A flock of smaller birds hovered above on one side, looking down with interest. On the other side was a young woman on bent knee, her stone hands held out into the falling water, which deflected off her palms and into the basin.

Wade closed his eyes and took a long, deep breath, feeling the sting of it in his lungs and chest. When he opened them, he saw a goldfinch standing with the girl and the bird's stone brothers and sisters. She was bathing in the falling water and drinking from the pools gathering in the girl's open hands.

By the time Halloween arrived, Lily hadn't had much time or energy to think about a costume. It was a senior class tradition to rent out the amusement park on the pier for a Halloween party. The expectation, of course, was that you'd be dressed appropriately for the occasion, though there were sure to be a few kids who were too cool to play along or too lame to make an effort. Lily didn't want to be associated with either of those groups and was planning to skip until Ginny convinced her to go. Ginny found a pair of denim overalls she'd worn in her younger days and some old work boots that happened to fit Lily's feet. She brought home a hard hat and a weathered leather tool belt from the hardware store, and the next thing Lily knew she was heading out as a construction worker or a member of the Village People; she hadn't decided which one quite yet.

Holly picked her up in her blue Ford Escort. She was dressed as Madonna, the "Desperately Seeking Susan" version and not the "Like a Virgin" one. She'd probably be one of twenty. Holly leaned over and rolled down the passenger window, spilling J.J. Fad's "Supersonic" into the neighborhood streets.

"Get in here, girl, we got a party to go to," she yelled over the music.

Holly's energy was contagious. As soon as Lily got in the car, Holly had her bouncing in her seat and singing. They drove to the inlet and spotted The Hulk parked in a strip of cars closest to the beach. Teri and the twins were getting out when they arrived.

Alicia and Teri were dressed as cats. Tammy was a nurse. When Holly ran up behind her and pinched the back of her thigh, Tammy squealed.

"Dang, girl," Holly told her, playfully. "The boys are gonna be all over you tonight with that outfit."

Lily spotted a tiny smile from Tammy and maybe a touch of redness in her cheeks. Holly was winning them over, and Lily was glad about it. She'd squeezed herself into their tight, little friend group and brought some life to it. They were even better now as a fivesome.

Ten bucks bought their way in for amusement park rides, carnival games, and endless cotton candy, funnel cake, and soda. They met up with Jimmy and a few of his friends at the ring toss.

"My dad needs some help building a shed in our backyard," he said when he saw her coming. "You looking for work?"

Lily laughed a little and looked him over. He was wearing a pair of blue jeans and his letterman jacket. "What are you supposed to be?" she asked him.

"Just your everyday high school football player."

She should've known. Too cool for a costume. He got close and leaned into her. His hand rubbed against her leg. He pulled her in and whispered in her ear.

"I've been thinking about you. I've been thinking about our drive out to Assateague."

Lily had been thinking about it too. They'd talked little since that night. Mostly hallway chatter. She was still trying to figure out what they were, but she wasn't sure it mattered. Maybe it would have been better if they weren't anything at all. Maybe they could just be and let whatever was going to happen just happen. She touched his hand gently.

"I haven't thought about it much at all," she whispered back. She couldn't see his reaction to her flirtation, but she felt it. He kissed her neck and then her ear, and she felt his breath as he whispered again.

"Are you sure?" he asked, then followed with a gentle bite to her earlobe. Lily would've left with him right then if he'd asked.

A big cheer rose up next to them. A ring on the lone red jug won Alicia a stuffed teddy bear. Jimmy and Lily separated when they heard the noise, a lingering finger hooking one of Lily's as Jimmy backed away. He gave her a little wave before joining his friends in line at the roller coaster. If Holly and the girls had seen their interaction, they didn't much care. They were already pulling her to another game on the other side of the pier.

After a half an hour or so of food and games and rides, they decided to head to the main attraction, the pier's haunted house. It was a big, black box of a structure, built to look like it was leaning to the side, with wooden vampire bats hovering about a circled window at the top, an animated stuffed werewolf menacing from the second-floor balcony, and giant paper mâché spiders plastered up the wall. A woman in zombie makeup waved them in and closed the door behind them.

The first room was a holding pen. It was dark with fake candles perched in corners casting only enough light to see a few closed doors and no obvious place to walk through. The doors sprung open without warning, and a couple of people dressed as monsters emerged growling, sending the girls in a screaming frenzy through an open hallway. They crept ahead cautiously to eerie music and recorded sounds of howling wolves, squealing mice, and a witch's cackling laugh. They climbed up a flight of stairs to the second floor and a long hallway where hands shot out from holes in the wall, grabbing at them as they scurried along into another small room. The walls in this one were covered in projected images of spinning hypnotic wheels, which made Lily dizzy. She closed her eyes and let her friends guide her out the back and down another flight of stairs into the last room of the house, where life-sized animals stood in the corners and the heads of others were mounted on the walls. There was an opening at the end of another hallway and light at the end, showing the exit. She relaxed a bit, assuming it was all over, but then she heard the sound of a spitting engine and saw a man leap out in a hockey mask holding a running chainsaw. He revved it and came after them as they sprinted down the last corridor and out of the house. The girls emptied to an outside patio surrounded by black, six-foot-high walls. They were laughing and out of breath and ready to head back around to the main area of the pier when Lily heard a voice coming from the top of one of the walls.

"Surprise," the voice said.

It was a boy, dressed in all black and wearing a black mask, sitting on the wall directly across from them. He was holding something out in front of him. A balloon, maybe. Then Lily noticed the others. Three more boys, all in black, also holding what looked to be liquid-filled balloons.

"I told you I'd get you back, Parker."

Lily recognized the voice this time. It was Kevin Brittingham. As soon as he said it, and before the girls could move, one of the other boys launched his balloon. That first one fell short, hitting the ground in front of Lily and sending a splatter of red liquid all over them. The next one flew by them and did little damage, but the third one caught Tammy in the shoulder, and the last one hit Lily square in the chest. The liquid was sticky. It was all over her clothes and on her face and in her hair. She could taste it. Blood. Deer or pig, probably.

When Lily looked back up, they were gone. She was so angry she couldn't muster a sound. Tammy, though, was running through a stream of cuss words Lily had only heard coming from angry fishermen at the docks. Alicia was the only one crying, a soft sniffle and a catch in her breath, clutching her blood-soaked teddy bear close to her chest. Teri put an arm around Alicia, and Holly grabbed Lily's hand.

"Let's get out of here," Holly said.

They circled out onto the pier. It was quiet, and Lily thought maybe she'd gone deaf with rage. But she realized that the activity had all but stopped and that every single eye was on them as they walked down the pier. A couple of teachers who were chaperoning and some of the amusement park workers met them almost immediately and shepherded them to a utility room. They wiped themselves with towels and washed with soap and water and some chemical cleaner, but the blood wouldn't come all the way out. Holly suggested they head back to her place, which was only a few blocks away, to clean up, but Alicia wanted to go home. Teri offered to drive the twins back to their house, and Lily agreed to ride with Holly to her place.

"What a piece of shit." Holly's teeth clenched when she said it. She had a tight grip on the steering wheel and was driving a little faster than she probably should've. "I knew he was a piece of shit," she said again. "But I didn't know he was that kind of piece of shit."

Lily didn't even know how to answer. Kevin Brittingham was pretty much the worst human she knew. None of it was a surprise to her.

Holly's mother met them at the door when they arrived. Her mouth dropped open. She reached out and took Holly's face in her hands.

"Are you all right? Are you hurt?"

Holly delicately shrugged her off. "We're fine, mom. It was only a prank."

They changed out of their clothes and did their best to shower off the remaining blood. Lily was going to call Wade to come and pick her up, but Holly and her mom convinced her to stay the night. Mrs. Mitchell reached out to Wade and Ginny to let them know what was going on.

After some hot chocolate, they went into Holly's room and got ready for bed. They'd made a spot for her on a trundle, and Lily was lying there now, watching the glow of a lava light ripple, roll, and float across the ceiling. Holly popped her head over the edge of her bed and looked down at Lily.

"I want you to know something." Her tone was serious, sincere. "I want you to know that you can count on me." She reached down and squeezed Lily's shoulder, and then laid back onto her bed.

The urge to cry was sudden and unexpected. Lily pushed her face into her pillow to quiet her sobs and drown out her tears until she finally wore herself out and fell asleep.

Chapter 23

WADE GOT UP EARLY to take Lily to the clinic for her blood draw. She was quiet but nervous, adjusting and readjusting herself in her seat, fidgeting with the cuff of her sweater, playing with the lock on the door. She still seemed willing to go through all of it, though Wade thought she might back out after what happened on the pier over the weekend. She'd been pretty shaken up, Wade could tell, even if she didn't want to talk much when he asked her about it. Ginny tried too, but nothing. "I'm fine," was all they could get out of her. But Wade didn't think she was fine. She'd spent a good part of Sunday at the marsh and then the rest of it in her room.

Wade didn't have the skills required to navigate the emotional complexity of a seventeen-year-old girl. His default was to leave her alone and give her space, which seemed like a sound strategy to him until they were in the tight confines of his patrol car. They were about a mile from the clinic before she spoke a word.

"What's going to happen if we get a positive test?" she asked.

"That's going to be up to you," Wade told her. Although he was thinking that the answer might depend on who provided the result.

"These guys just agreed to do it?" There was a trace of skepticism in her voice.

"Yes," was all he said back to her. Now wasn't the time to get into the details. Wade had provided her with a limited amount of information, and he wanted to keep it that way for the time being. All she knew was that a couple of men whom he'd identified as potential candidates were approached, and they'd agreed to participate. But he didn't give her the why or how, and he didn't mention anything about the possible connection to Hillary Dent or the other women.

"And you won't tell me if I know them?" she asked, testing him once more for that piece of information. She'd brought it up a couple of times since the dinner, and he'd shrugged her off on each occasion.

"I don't think that's a good idea," he replied, simply.

She didn't say much more than that while they were at the clinic or on the way to school. She asked him to drop her off in the supermarket parking lot across the street, and even though she didn't give Wade her reasons, it was safe to assume she was embarrassed by the thought of her getting out of a cop car in front of the whole school. Wade parked and she got out. He watched her cross the road and then sat there for a few minutes, thinking.

They'd already obtained the samples from Wilkerson and Esham, and now that Lily's was in, they'd be able to process the tests and get the findings soon, maybe even by the end of the week. Wade was running scenarios through his head, none of which resulted in particularly good outcomes. A lot of doubt was creeping into Wade's mind—about his methods, his motivation, his purpose. He was possibly only a few days away from finding Lily's father and perhaps getting some answers about what happened to Emma, but it didn't necessarily feel like a tangible, obtainable thing. In fact, Wade was beginning to fear that it was just as likely that nothing would come of this, that they'd be right back where they started with no answers, no truth, nothing.

The other thing that was bothering him was this mess with Lily and Kevin Brittingham. What little Wade and Ginny heard about it was thirdhand from Sandy. Holly told Sandy about what happened at the haunted house and mentioned a previous confrontation with Kevin at school a couple of weeks earlier. Wade was concerned enough that he decided to pay Vicky Brittingham a quick visit before heading into his office.

He drove to Ocean City and pulled up to Vicky's place just in time to see Reid Esham skipping down the wooden staircase from her second-floor apartment. Reid had his sportscoat hooked at the collar with his index finger and slung over his shoulder. A morning pit stop before work, Wade supposed. He watched Reid get into his BMW and drive away. Wade was tempted to follow, but he decided to continue with the business at hand. He got out of his car, climbed the stairs, and knocked on Vicky's door.

"Did you forget something?" Vicky called out. She opened the door. Her face tightened when she realized it was Wade standing there and not Reid. "Oh, it's you," she said.

Wade tried not to let on that he'd seen Reid leave her apartment. She poked her head out and scanned the area, then refocused her attention back to Wade.

"What are you doing here?" She was dressed in a red bath robe. Her hair was messy, and she wasn't wearing any make-up.

"Sorry to bother you so early, Vicky. I wanted to talk to you about Kevin."

Vicky scowled and pulled the robe tight to her body. "What about him?"

Wade tried to keep it friendly. "I'm not sure you heard, but Kevin and a couple of his friends were involved in a prank at that senior day party at the pier on Saturday. They threw some balloons at a group of girls."

"So?" She was indignant.

"They were filled with animal blood."

She pushed her shoulders back and cocked her head to the side. "Are they pressing charges?" she asked, with a little bit of concern.

"No, that's not what this is about," Wade told her.

"What then?" she asked, still on alert, her eyebrows arched and her lips crooked.

"One of the girls was Lily Parker. Her uncle just died and she's living with me now. I was hoping maybe you could talk to Kevin and ask him to cool it. She's been through a lot and doesn't need this."

"He's a teenage boy doing stupid, teenage things." She shrugged. "He doesn't listen to me."

"Well, if he won't listen to you, maybe I'll have a conversation with him."

She understood. If she wouldn't do something about it, he would.

"Okay. I'll talk to him," she said, and then she shut the door in Wade's face without so much as a goodbye.

There were more than a few stares and giggles and outright laughs when Lily walked through the halls at school. The kids were relentless. They weren't going to pass up the chance to have some fun at someone else's expense. It took her two days' worth of showers to get the last traces of blood off her skin and out of her hair, which Lily found ironic considering she'd just donated her own blood that morning. She wondered whether there might be a trace of animal that got mixed in by mistake, and she started daydreaming about matching with some half-man, half-pig creature out of an H.G. Wells novel. By lunch, most of the kids had had their fill, and things got back to normal. All five of the girls took their share of abuse though, including Holly, who'd heard some nasty Madonna-related comments herself.

"They were calling me the bloody virgin," she told them. "I think one kid was waving a tampon at me."

Alicia pinched her face. As usual, it was Tammy who put it all into perspective.

"Most of those idiots don't even know how those things work or where they go."

They laughed a little, but they were still angry and embarrassed, and a weekend wouldn't be enough to wash the filth of the experience off them.

Lily scanned the cafeteria, taking stock of her schoolmates. Most of these kids didn't have the functional intelligence to think for themselves. A bully had tripped a kid and left him on the floor injured, ridiculing him just for fun. Most kids stood back and watched it happen and laughed with him. That same bully attacked Lily and her friends for committing the cardinal sin of standing up to him, and most of these kids spent half of their day making fun of the victims. It amazed her that one evil person could poison them like that. It wasn't like they didn't know what he was and who he was. They all hated him, but that didn't stop them from going along with it.

Alicia must have noticed Lily looking around and assumed she was searching for Kevin. "I heard he's getting suspended," she said.

Lily wasn't following. She was still distracted. "What?"

"Kevin. He's getting suspended. For a week."

That's the least they could do, Lily thought. If there was a way to suspend him off the face of the earth, the world would be a better place.

Just then, Jimmy walked over and sat down at their table. He playfully nudged in next to Lily, but she wasn't in the mood for teenage flirtations. His lack of awareness bothered her. If he'd known what they'd been through that morning, he wouldn't be acting so cavalier. Or maybe he just didn't care. Either way, Lily was annoyed and shrugged him off.

"Whoa. Did I do something wrong?"

Holly threw a french fry at him. "Jimmy, you're an idiot."

He looked around the table and must have finally sensed their humiliation and irritation. He turned his hands up in surrender. "Sorry," he said. He scooted over to give Lily her space and got back to what brought him over in the first place.

"We've got a big thing brewing for Friday night after the game," he said.

"Oh yeah?" Tammy chimed in. "Working on a party already? What a surprise."

Jimmy scowled at her and got back to it. "We're gonna have a huge blowout at Stinky Beach. Kegs, bonfire, booze. I wanted to make sure you were gonna make it." He looked right at Lily when he said it.

"We'll think about it," Holly told him with a backhanded wave, sending him on his way.

As he was leaving, he turned back to Lily one more time. "I hope I see you there," he said, and then he walked away.

After a busy morning, Wade was counting on a quieter afternoon. An hour or so after lunch, though, he got a call from Ginny. She'd finally decided to see a doctor after more than a couple of weeks of not feeling well. When he heard her on the other end of the handset, he knew something was wrong. Her voice was shaky, and it sounded like she'd been crying.

"Can you come home?" she asked, with a sniffle.

Wade was worried. "Of course, I can," he told her. "What's wrong?"

She took a breath, and it sounded like she was trying to hold back a sob.

"We can talk about it when you get here."

Wade grabbed his hat and practically ran out the door. He didn't say anything to anyone. He raced home and tore into the driveway, sending broken oyster shells into the grass in his front yard. He pushed through the front door and found Ginny sitting in the dining room, a box of tissues by her hand, a dozen or so spent ones balled up on the table and on the floor. Now Wade was scared.

"Ginny, what's going on?" he asked as he moved toward her.

She got up and hugged him, bawling into his chest. Wade stroked her hair, trying to calm her.

"What did the doctor say? Are you okay?"

She was huffing and trying to catch her breath. She pulled back and he looked at her. Her eyes were red and swollen. Her nose was puffy and raw. Wade was sick to his stomach.

"I'm pregnant," she said, her voice still choppy.

Wade wasn't sure he heard it right. "What?"

She slowed down, caught her breath. "I'm pregnant," she said again, calmly.

This time he heard it clearly. Pregnant. He thought she was sick. He thought she might be dying. There was an immediate sense of relief. He was ready to celebrate and laugh about it. Then the weight of it hit him. She was in shock. She was terrified.

He moved her to the couch in the living room, then went into the kitchen to start a pot of water. He came back in, circled behind her, and rubbed her shoulders. She reached back and caressed his hand.

The kettle whistled, and he left her for a moment to prepare her tea. He handed her the mug, sat in the armchair, and waited for her. She took a few sips and set her cup on the table.

"I don't know if I can do it, Wade." Her voice was steady, if not resigned. "I don't know if I can go through that again."

Wade got up and sat next to her. He pulled her in close and kissed her on the top of her head. "It'll be different this time," he said to her, knowing full well that he couldn't predict such a thing.

She looked up at him. Her face was determined but not angry. Her eyes were clear. She'd cried herself out. "We can't be sure. You know that."

She was right, of course. It would be a hard road for both of them, but especially for her. He didn't want to put her through anything she didn't want to go through.

"I'll support you in whatever you decide. I'll be here, no matter what."

She laid her head in his lap and closed her eyes. He touched her cheek and let her rest and thought about the little girl in his mother's dream.

Chapter 24

1970

THERE WAS AN AMERICAN Army doctor at the prison camp who'd been allowed to set up a makeshift medical clinic for other wounded soldiers. The clinic operated out of a crude hut with little medicine or supplies. Surgeries were performed with no anesthesia, equipment was as sterile as it could get absent electricity and running water, and the only help the doctor received was from a couple of fellow prisoners he'd trained as nurses in the most basic sense of the definition. It was a cruel trick played by the captors, though, because as soon as the wounded were just healthy enough, the guards would beat and torture them to the edge of death and it would start all over again.

Wade spent the first couple of months in the camp fighting infection and fever. He slowly recovered and grew stronger over time, but the infection and constant pain had sapped his stamina, and the relentless beatings continued to take their toll. He was still weak months later, and his shoulder had not healed properly, notwithstanding the doctor's best efforts. Absent a miracle, Wade knew he was already dead. Luckily for Wade and the others, an American patrol came through and liberated the camp. A couple of days later, Wade was transported to a mobile hospital unit somewhere in South Vietnam. They cleaned him up and flew him out to a Navy hospital in Honolulu a week or so after that.

As soon as Wade got to Hawaii, he called home. Paul answered. Wade asked about Emma. Paul broke the news calmly.

"She's missing, Wade. No one knows where she is or what happened to her."

Wade went numb. He didn't say anything for a while. He'd spent months in the jungle and in that camp thinking about her, dreaming about her. She was the only thing on his mind when he got rescued, and now Paul was telling him that she was gone. Now that he was safe and alive and on his way home.

"Is there anything else you can tell me?" Wade asked his brother.

"There's nothing more to say."

That was the last time Wade talked to Paul until he got home. Every other call was with his mother, who'd gotten well enough to come home from her own hospital stay by the time he'd made it to Honolulu. Every time he spoke with her, he asked about Emma. And every time, there was nothing. And yet, he held out hope that she'd be found safe and that she'd be waiting for him at his house when he got back, but that wasn't the case.

It was another six weeks before Wade was deemed healthy enough to be released from the hospital and discharged. He'd undergone a surgery to repair his collarbone and scapula and clean up a mess of scar tissue, and they put him through a rigorous physical therapy regimen to help him regain full use of his arm and shoulder. He didn't get back home until August. By then, Emma's investigation was all but closed.

His first night back was quiet. Paul and his mom picked him up from the Air Force base in Dover. Wade slept in his room, in the same bed where he'd spent that night with Emma. He dug his face deep into the sheets and pillow and breathed in heavy breaths, hoping to pull out the last traces of her, but she wasn't there. He spent the next few hours playing with the necklace around his neck and staring at the ceiling, wondering how he'd live the rest of his life without her.

The next morning after breakfast, Wade decided to walk over to visit the Parkers. It would be difficult, but it wouldn't be the hardest thing he'd been through. When Emma's mother opened the door, they both started crying. She pulled him in and hugged him tight and they stood there for a few minutes sobbing into each other's shoulders. They would have stayed there longer if not for the crying coming from the other room. They separated, and Mrs. Parker led him to the living room.

The baby was lying on her back in a crib that was set up in a corner. Mrs. Parker picked her up, and she stopped her fussing. She was a tiny little thing with curly brown hair and big brown eyes, and when Mrs. Parker put her on the carpet, she crawled right up to Wade and tried to climb up his leg. She was a sweetheart from the first moment he met her. Mrs. Parker picked her up again and they walked out the back of the house to the porch.

Mr. Parker was sitting in a rocking chair staring out at nothing. He heard them approach and stopped rocking, then turned to Wade. His face was thin and tired, his hair now a shocking bright white. When Wade looked into his eyes, he didn't see the happiness that used to live in them. They were empty and sad and defeated. Wade had seen that look before in soldiers who'd accepted their fate and abandoned their lives even before they hit the ground dead. He was living just enough, though, to shed a tear at the sight of Wade, and he got up slowly from his chair to greet him with a handshake and a hug.

Wade spent the next few days catching up with Sandy and Timmy and some of his other friends. He signed up for a few classes at the local community college, criminal justice and basic accounting, trying to figure out some future for himself while he settled back into civilian life. Mr. Parker offered him a job at his seed and supply business and Wade took him up on it, managing enough time for class between shifts at the warehouse and in the store.

The first time he saw Ginny McCabe was about a month after he got back. He was doing some work around the house and drove out to the hardware store to pick up some tools and supplies. Ginny was at the counter when he walked in, but he didn't recognize her.

"Wade Thompson. Is that you?" she asked when he walked through the door.

He looked at her for a good minute before he figured it out. The sharp, pale blue eyes. The wheat-colored blonde hair. But she wasn't the shy, sixteen-year-old girl he knew from math class, the one Emma said had a crush on him. No, she wasn't a girl anymore.

"Ginny McCabe?" he asked, just to make sure.

She walked over and hugged him. Her hair smelled like flowers.

"I heard you were back," she told him.

They talked for a good hour before Wade finally left, forgetting half the supplies he was supposed to get. Maybe it was by accident, or maybe it was on purpose. There were several visits over the next few weeks, until one day he finally asked her to join him for lunch at the diner next door. They both had cheeseburgers and chocolate milkshakes and split a plate of french fries because Ginny didn't think she could eat a whole order by herself. Two years later they were married.

Chapter 25

Friday, November 6, 1987

HOLLY POURED OUT OF the passenger side of Teri's Beatle with a four-pack of Bartles & Jaymes in one hand and a big bottle of Boone's Farm in the other. She stumbled when she landed but held on, gathered herself, and then slithered her way across the sand to the group assembled around the bonfire.

"I've got the wine coolers!" she yelled at the crowd, and a cheer rose from the girls who were scattered about.

Holly handed out the smaller bottles. She saw Lily standing with Tammy and tossed her the last one. Lily let out a scared little yelp as the bottle flew toward her. Her hands were covered by the sleeves of an oversized sweatshirt, one of Jake's that she liked to wear when the nights started to chill. The bottle almost slipped through her grasp, but she snagged it before it slid to the ground.

"Nice hands Parker," Jimmy yelled at her. He was walking from his truck, which was parked in the sand along with the usual assortment of four-wheel drives and jacked-up pickups, and he was carrying a case of Budweiser and a bottle of Jack Daniels. "We could've used you in the game tonight."

One of Jimmy's friends grabbed the handle of Jack, and Jimmy emptied the cans of beer into one of the coolers near the fire. When he bent over to pick one out, Holly pushed him, sending him to the sand in a heap, inches from the pit. Red liquid from Holly's Solo cup flew at a cluster of girls who scurried away to avoid the spray.

Teri leaned into Lily. "What's going on over there?" She pointed to Jimmy and Holly. "They're looking pretty chummy."

Lily was watching. Jimmy was still sprawled out on his back, but Holly was now standing over him. They were talking to each other. Jimmy had a sly little smile curling at the edges of his mouth, and it looked like Holly was getting ready to lean in for a kiss. Instead, she leaned in and gave Jimmy a playful smack across the cheek. He rubbed at the spot and lay there for a minute while Holly casually backed away and started hopping around in a drunken dance to a New Order song playing from someone's boombox.

Lily didn't know what to make of it all. Holly had passed off her old boyfriend to her like it was no big deal. She had all but encouraged it. If Lily had known there was still something there between them, she never would have done it. At least that's what she was telling herself. There was a twinge of regret, sure. But Jimmy was a good-looking boy and Lily was searching for something to take the edge off. One night with Jimmy was a good start. She wasn't invested enough in a relationship with Jimmy to care much anyway. That worried her more than anything. She took a drink from her peach-flavored wine cooler. It was enough to cover the taste of alcohol and make it damn easy to drink five too many and find herself face-down in a ditch somewhere. She saw a group of kids heading her way and heard someone calling to her.

"Hey, Lily."

It was Jake. He was walking over with the Smith twins and one of Jake's teammates from the soccer team. Jake was wearing a denim jacket and a red, white, and blue trucker hat with an STP Motor Oil logo on the front.

"Hey," she called back. Lily looked down at the sweatshirt. She raised the one hand she had in the front pocket, lifting it to attract his attention. "I guess I should give this back you."

"Nah, I think you should keep it. It looks better on you anyway." He winked at her, smiled, and walked away.

The friends gathered in a circle and talked and drank from their bottles and red plastic cups. Holly snuck up behind Lily and hugged her around her stomach.

"Loosen up, Lily," she whispered through the thick cotton of the sweatshirt hood. "All Jimmy's been talking about all week is this party and you. I was making sure he knew you were under my protection."

Lily turned to face Holly, thinking perhaps all of this was some joke they were playing on her, but Holly was serious. There was no anger or resentment. She was just stating the truth. One, it seemed, that Holly was not only willing to accept, but that she'd embraced. Holly didn't like or love Jimmy enough anymore to keep their thing going. She was mature enough to realize that things had ended, and it was time to move on. She gave Lily the confidence to move on too.

Holly pecked Lily on the cheek and let out a loud *Woohoo!* and danced through their little group. She grabbed Alicia's hands and pulled her into the middle of the circle. Together they twisted and turned to the guitar riff and drumbeats of their favorite new R.E.M. song. The beach was getting crowded. Bodies were bouncing off of each other, drinks were spilling, and words were starting to slur. Lily was happy to be there with her friends, laughing and singing and dancing. It was another slice of a normal life.

Wade was sitting in the kitchen eating a piece of the apple pie his mother dropped off for Ginny earlier in the day. Ginny and Wade had debated whether to tell his mother and her father about the baby, but they felt they owed it to them. Their parents had been through the highs and lows of the first two pregnancies with them, after all, and they'd suffered almost as much. His mother came over to check on Ginny every day after they told her, bringing some kind of dessert with each trip. Wade figured he'd gained at least five pounds already, but he wasn't too worried about it. He couldn't resist his mother's desserts and they were the perfect complement to happy eating or stress eating or worry eating. He was doing a little bit of all three right about now.

The phone rang, interrupting his last bite, and Wade reluctantly got up and answered. It was Rick. Wade's first thought was that the blood test results had come in, but that wasn't why he was calling.

"There's been a shooting in Ocean City," Rick told him.

Rick wouldn't be reaching out if it wasn't someone he knew. His mind went to Lily for some reason and his stomach dropped.

"Who is it?" Wade asked. He stiffened up to ready himself for the answer.

"Reid Esham. Someone shot him outside of Vicky Brittingham's apartment."

"Holy shit," was all Wade could muster. There was a great sense of relief that it wasn't someone close to him and guilt that he felt any relief at all. He gathered himself. "Is he gonna make it?"

"Yeah. It looks like it. It was a little twenty-two pop shot. Didn't do much damage."

Wade's first thought was revenge. "Was it Frank Brittingham?"

"Don't know. Someone heard the shot and the police found him bleeding in the street. They're working it but don't have anyone in custody. Anyway, I thought you should know."

Wade hung up and the worry he'd felt before that piece of pie came back to him. Something in his head was telling him to go find Lily and make sure she was all right. He'd overheard her talking to Ginny that morning about going out with her friends after the football game, and Deputy Johnson had reached out earlier after receiving a complaint about a party on Stinky Beach. Loud music and a big crowd, Wade figured Lily might be there. He grabbed a jacket and told Ginny he was going out on a call. When he got to his car, he radioed Johnson to meet him there.

Wade drove down the highway and turned onto the road that ran past the marina. He looked over to where Paul's boats were moored but couldn't spot them. Lights on stanchions filled the docks with an eerie and dull yellow glow, but it was still too dark to see much beyond the first few rows of boats and the view was obstructed anyway by masts and nets. He slowed and turned onto a gravel path that cut through overgrown brush and low-lying evergreen. Cars and trucks lined the path on either side. A few kids scattered when they saw him approach and then pass, and he caught more than a couple of them in the middle of a kiss or grope with the headlights of his patrol car. He parked where the gravel ended and the sand began, and he got out of his car, flashlight in hand.

A thin sliver of the moon hung in the sky like a cut fingernail, guarded by a solitary, bright star. The glow of a bonfire danced behind a line of brush and trees. Wade could hear the thumping bass of music and a chorus of laughter and conversation, but it really wasn't much of a nuisance to anyone. The noise would be barely a whisper by the time it reached the nearest house. Wade figured the complaint came in from a frustrated busybody looking to spoil a little teenage frolic and fun.

A small group of kids emerged from an opening in the brush and froze when they saw Wade standing in front of them. Wade flashed the light in their eyes, smiling a little on the inside at their terror-stricken faces, and decided to toy with them a bit.

"What's that you got in your hand, fella?" he asked the youngest-looking of them.

The kid glanced at his red plastic cup and then back up at Wade. "Nothing, sir. Just water." He sounded as unconvinced as Wade was.

"Water, huh?" Wade walked closer to him and flashed the light into the cup. "That looks a little too yellow for water, son. Don't you think?"

The kid hung his head, assuming the worst was yet to come. Wade lifted the flashlight and scanned their faces.

"Do you all have a ride off the beach? Someone who hasn't been drinking the, uh...water?"

The kids all looked at each other, confused, then a girl near the back raised her hand.

"I haven't been drinking. I can drive."

"Good. Y'all tip those cups over, empty them out, and get out of here. Safely."

The kids tipped their cups as instructed and scurried down the road behind him. Wade laughed to himself and then headed over toward the cut-through onto the beach.

Lily was standing next to Jimmy by the bonfire. Holly and the girls were singing and dancing. Jimmy was in the middle of some crazy story about his uncle's ostrich farm out in California and then stopped midsentence. Lily laughed.

"Well, aren't you going to finish your story?" she asked him.

Jimmy didn't say anything and then Lily realized that none of them were talking or laughing or singing anymore. She followed Jimmy's eyes to the dark figure in the shadow behind her. He was wearing a black sweatshirt with a hood over his head, and she couldn't make out his face. All she could focus on was the gun in his hand that was pointed right at her.

"I told you I was going to get you," he said.

Lily closed her eyes and saw her mother. She was a young woman, happy and smiling. She reached out and touched Lily's hand and Lily felt it like the cold burn of ice against her skin. She leaned in close, and Lily could feel her mother's hair against her cheek. The scent overwhelmed her. Lilacs again, sweet and sugary, like breathing in threads of cotton candy, and she thought she heard a whisper. *If you wear it, it will protect you.*

Wade poked through the brush and spotted a group of five or six kids standing near the bonfire. He recognized Lily and Holly and walked toward them. He stopped for a moment, ready to call out to them, and then he saw the boy with the gun.

The impact and the sound of the shot were almost simultaneous. Lily was hit from the side by a large object. It was muscle and bone, she thought. Bigger than one of the boys. A man. She didn't feel the shot, she just heard it. It must have missed her.

Lily opened her eyes. Kevin Brittingham was face down in the sand with a man lying on top of him. It was Wade. She sat up and turned to see who had taken her to the ground, but the man was facing away from her. She reached for his shoulder and felt something warm and sticky on his jacket. The man grunted as he rolled himself over. It was Paul Thompson.

Another man, this one in uniform, reached Kevin and kicked the gun away. He pressed a knee in Kevin's back, wrenched his arms behind him, and slapped on a pair of handcuffs. Wade stumbled through the sand and fell next to Paul.

"Paul. Are you okay?"

Paul grunted again and tried to sit up. Wade helped him. Paul clutched his arm at the bicep.

"The little prick shot me in the arm," he said through clenched teeth.

"Lily. Are you hurt?" Wade asked.

"No, I'm fine," she told him. "He jumped in front of me," she said, looking back down at Paul.

"Hang on, Paul," Wade told him. "Let's get you to the hospital."

Chapter 26

Saturday, November 7, 1987

W ADE STAYED WITH PAUL at the hospital for most of the night. The doctors performed a short, uncomplicated procedure to take out the bullet, which had nestled in a fleshy part of Paul's upper arm. They kept him overnight for monitoring. Wade left for a few hours and came back the next morning with some clean clothes for Paul. He found Rick Hampton waiting outside Paul's room. He was holding a cup of coffee in one hand and a large brown envelope in the other.

"Is that what I think it is?" Wade asked, pointing at the envelope.

"Yup." Rick wasn't giving anything away. "I wanted to catch you before you went in."

"I'm guessing you had that yesterday. Why didn't you say anything when you called last night?"

"It wasn't the right time."

Rick handed Wade the envelope. Wade's heart started pumping a little faster. He put down the bag of clothes, opened the envelope, and pulled out the documents. The first report was for Wilkerson. He skimmed down the page and found the only line that mattered.

Paternity: Negative

He rubbed away a trail of sweat that had formed at his temple with the back of his hand and flipped to the next report, this one for Esham. His heartbeat filled his ears. He traced his finger down the page and found it.

Paternity: Negative

He was angry. Angry that it might be Esham. Angry for wanting it to be Esham. Angry that it wasn't Esham. But he realized he wasn't surprised.

This doesn't mean anything, he told himself. *He still could've killed her*, he reasoned. *He still could've done it to the others.* But he knew the truth. It wasn't Esham. It wasn't Wilkerson. The investigation was over, at least as it related to Emma's case.

Wade handed back the envelope and picked up the bag.

"I'm sorry I put you through this, Rick. I really thought there was something there." There wasn't much more he could say.

Rick gave Wade a light slap on the arm. "I know, buddy."

"I guess Ken had a field day over all this," Wade added, trying to lighten the mood. Trying to lighten his mood, really.

Rick didn't react to the comment as Wade would've expected. He didn't laugh or make a joke. He was stoic. Maybe it was because of what happened to Reid. Maybe it was something else. But Wade knew there was more.

"What's going on, Rick?"

Rick leaned in close to him. His voice was low, almost a whisper. "Ken was here today too. He convinced the FBI to investigate Paul. For real this time."

Wade stepped back. He had to be joking. Rick's expression told him he wasn't. "Paul didn't have anything to do with those girls or Emma. You know that."

Rick put his hand out. "Paul was seen with Dent. He was here when Emma disappeared. We heard some stories."

Wade didn't know what he was talking about. "What stories?"

"People are saying they were close. Maybe closer than you knew. Maybe these people told us things they wouldn't or couldn't tell you."

Now Wade was getting angry again. "That's complete bullshit, Rick. This is all bullshit."

"Could be," Rick answered. "We'll know one way or another soon. Ken is on his way to see the judge. We're getting a court order for Paul's blood. He wouldn't agree to do it without one." Rick patted him on the shoulder again and walked away.

Wade stood there, trying to get a handle on all of it, but his head was spinning, and he couldn't get it under control. He had to figure out what he was going to say to Lily. Finding her father now was pretty much a dead end. He had to come to grips with the reality of never finding out the truth about Emma. His wife was in the early stages of a high-risk pregnancy, and his brother was a target in a serial killer investigation.

He gathered himself, and after a minute or two, walked into Paul's room. Paul was sitting on the edge of his bed, waiting for him. His IV was out, but he was still in his gown and his left arm was in a sling. Wade placed the bag on the bed and took out Paul's clothes. Paul put on his underwear and pants, one-armed, and then let Wade help with the rest of it. Wade gently slipped Paul's arm out of the sling and through the arm hole of his shirt. Then Paul sat back on the bed and let Wade put on his socks and shoes.

"I guess you talked to Rick?" Paul asked.

"Yeah, I talked to him." Wade was tying up the laces. "It's a bunch of bullshit is how I see it. Ken's still playing his high school games."

Paul didn't respond. He sat quietly and let Wade work. None of it seemed to be bothering him, so Wade decided he didn't need to worry, either. There was nothing there. They would test Paul and it would come to nothing and all this would be over. For good this time. For all of them. He finished the last knot and patted his brother on the knee.

"I guess now both of us have a bad arm," Paul joked.

Wade laughed a little. "I guess so."

Paul slid off the bed and Wade remembered something he wanted to ask him. "I didn't get a chance to ask you last night. Why were you at the beach anyway?"

Paul stood still as Wade helped with the sling. "I don't even know," he said. "I was sitting on my boat drinking a beer and staring up at the moon and I could hear the kids laughing and the music playing and something in my head told me to take a walk over there. I can't explain it."

Wade didn't need to hear anything else. That made sense to him. It was the same reason he was out there. A feeling.

Wade drove Paul to his house and helped him get settled. As Wade prepared to leave, he realized he hadn't shared the news about Ginny with his brother. He felt like Paul deserved to know, and he just came out and said it.

"Ginny's pregnant."

A little grin widened over Paul's chin. That was about as much of a smile as he could muster. "I'm happy for you, Wade. I'm happy for both of you."

That meant a lot for Wade to hear from his older brother. He choked up a little and tried to hide it the best he could. As he was walking out the door, Paul called to him.

"You make sure to tell Lily that I'm glad she's all right. You tell her that taking that bullet was the best thing I've ever done in my whole damn life."

Chapter 27

Tuesday, November 10, 1987

W ADE WAS CLEANING OFF his desk, getting ready to leave for the night. He called Ginny to let her know he'd be home soon.

"Your brother stopped by," she told him. "He left something for you."

Paul didn't mention anything about coming by the house when they talked earlier in the day. Wade had been in touch to ask him about the court order. Tomorrow was the deadline for Paul to provide the sample, otherwise Ken and his boys would come and arrest him, and Wade was sure that Ken would make a show of it.

"I'm not worried about any of that," Paul had said. Still, Wade hoped that Paul wouldn't be his usual stubborn self and just get it over with.

Emma's file was the last thing on his desk, even though he'd promised himself that he'd put it away for good. He opened it one more time and flipped to a page about a third of the way through, to the interview report for Sally Jenkins, the nurse who was supervising Emma's clinical rotation at the hospital the night she disappeared.

Parker received a call at the nurses' station at approximately 10:30 pm. Jenkins didn't hear the conversation but heard her start crying before she hung up the phone. Parker said, "I have to go," and then grabbed her coat and left the floor.

Wade slapped the file closed and pushed it across the desk. That was enough. He turned off the lights to his office and headed out to his car. He got home and found Ginny and Lily in the living room. They'd already finished their dinner and were sitting in their pajamas talking and drinking coffee.

"I left your dinner in the kitchen," Ginny told him.

He walked in and saw an envelope propped up against his covered plate. It was sealed and had his name printed on the front. His brother's handwriting. He opened it and emptied it onto the table. A leather necklace, wrapped in a coil. Wade picked it up until it fell open, the weight of Emma's arrowhead pulling it down in a straight line.

It hit him suddenly. His heart raced, pumping blood through his veins, quickening his pulse. It pounded in his head. The room started spinning. He put his hands on the table to steady himself and knocked over one of the chairs.

Ginny called out from the living room. "Everything okay in there?"

He shoved the necklace in his pocket and rushed through the living room. "I need to see Paul." He didn't look back to read Ginny's reaction. He got in his car, peeled out of the driveway, and headed for the marina.

Wade left his car running in the parking lot, his driver's side door wide open. He sprinted down the dock toward Paul's boats. He could see the bigger one, the trawler, but he didn't see the smaller one until he was right up on her. There was Paul, about to lift the last rope from its mooring.

Paul put his hand up. "Stay right there, brother."

Wade was having trouble thinking. It didn't matter that this was his brother. Paul knew something. Maybe he'd done something. He'd lied about all of it. If it was anyone other than his brother, he would've leapt up onto that boat and taken him down. But it *was* his brother. Wade couldn't move. His feet were frozen to the dock.

"You were with Emma that night. You know what happened, don't you?"

Paul had the rope pulled tight to him, in his one good arm, with one foot on the boat and the other on the mooring post. "What do you want me to say?"

"I want you to tell me the truth."

"It doesn't matter now," Paul told him. There wasn't much emotion in Paul's voice, except maybe relief.

"It matters to me."

Wade finally took a step toward the boat. Paul raised his hand again. His face softened.

"Are you sure you want to know?" Paul asked.

Wade didn't move. He didn't say anything.

"We never meant for it to happen," Paul began. "You went missing. We thought you were dead. We comforted each other and mourned you together. One night, we had too much to drink. We knew it was a mistake and it never happened again. Then we found out she was pregnant."

Wade's stomach turned. To think it was one thing. To know it was another.

"We decided to keep it our secret. We didn't think people would understand. I wasn't gonna be much good raising a kid anyway."

"What happened to Emma, Paul?" Wade's voice cracked.

"Mom was at the facility up in Cambridge. She was in bad shape. They tried to reach her to tell her that you'd been rescued and that you were alive, but they got me instead. I was going to drive up there first thing in the morning to break the news to her in person. I decided I needed to tell Emma that night. I called her at work and I told her to meet me at our old hunting cabin so we could talk about it. She wanted to keep the truth about Lily from you forever. I told her I couldn't do it.

"We argued. She said it would kill you if you knew and I told her it would kill me if you didn't. She got mad at me and came after me. She swung to slap me and lost her footing. I tried to grab her, but all I got was a handful of her necklace. She hit her head on the table on the way down and that was it. She was gone."

Wade was numb. He wanted to scream out or cry but couldn't. "You kept it a secret all these years. She died for nothing."

Paul was bobbing up and down with the boat, but he kept his eyes fixed on Wade's. "I wanted to tell you. About Lily, at least. But you would've figured it all out."

"What did you do with her, Paul?"

"I drove her car to that tobacco barn and left it, then walked back to the cabin through the woods. I wrapped her up, drove her to the boat, and took her out to sea." Paul said it so plainly.

Wade slumped over. Tears formed in his eyes. He took a deep breath and righted himself.

"How could you do that, Paul? It was Emma. How could you throw her away like that?"

Paul looked him in the eye. His voice steady, calm. "I know you're hurting, Wade. But that's not fair. I didn't throw her away. I'm out there every day," he said, motioning to the open water. "When I'm out there, she's there with me."

He turned his head for a moment, then turned back to Wade.

"I loved her, just like you. It was an accident, but I couldn't afford any accidents back then. I was taking care of Mom, and you were coming home, and I didn't know what kind of shape you'd be in. I didn't think I had a choice. I made the best decision I could at the time."

"What about the other girls?" Wade asked. "Was that you, Paul? Please tell me that wasn't you."

"I had nothing to do with those other girls, Wade. I swear to you. I don't know anything about that."

Wade thought Paul was telling him the truth about the others, but he wasn't sure what he should or shouldn't believe anymore, and he was sick about what he did know for sure.

"What am I supposed to do now, Paul?"

It was a question Wade was asking, not only to Paul, but to himself. He didn't know what to do. Ignoring all of it wasn't in his character, but this was his brother. And what about Lily? It would surely wreck her if she knew the truth.

"You don't have to do anything, Wade."

Of course he had to do something. He had to decide. Either take his brother in and reveal the truth or lie to himself and everyone else and shut it all away again.

"It was always going to be the ocean," Paul told him.

Wade understood this time. His chest tightened. He was having trouble catching his breath. Paul was going to take care of it. He didn't have to decide. He didn't have to do anything.

"Get off the boat, Paul," he pleaded. "We can figure it out."

Paul didn't say anything right away. It looked like he was thinking about it. Wade hoped he was, at least. But Paul didn't make a move.

"I got close to ending it out there a couple of times," he said. "Especially once I knew you and Mom would be okay. But it got harder and harder to leave that little girl. I was watching her, you know. Now she's safe. She's with you. And it's time."

He pressed his fist to his heart, rope still in hand.

"I've been wearing this like an anchor on my chest, and on most nights, I hoped that it would drag me down and make me disappear. I can't have Lily finding out I killed her mother. I can't do that to her."

Paul unhooked the rope and pushed off the dock. He took off his hat, waved it, and retreated into the shadows. Wade stayed and watched as the boat drifted out of the marina and into the harbor. Right before it disappeared into the darkness, a flash of light caught the stern, and Wade read the name on the back of the boat for the very last time.

Epilogue

1988

N O ONE QUESTIONED WHAT happened that night, not even Ken Meehan. It wasn't unusual for Paul to make an evening run out into the ocean, and there was nothing strange about Wade driving out to see his brother. After a few days, the search for Paul was called off. He was declared lost at sea, and they mourned him.

Wade quietly closed Emma's case shortly thereafter. He put away the file for good this time and locked away Paul's secret with it. The Hillary Dent investigation also went quiet. As much as Wade's gut had pointed him in Reid Esham's direction, there was no evidence to support it. And if the last year had proven anything, it was that Wade's gut was an unreliable witness. But Paul having anything to do with the other girls was not something Wade could wrap his mind around. Until there was some tangible evidence to the contrary, Wade would believe that much about his brother.

Wade moved his mother into their house for a bit to help her get through it, and having Lily around was a blessing. Lily and his mother took a real liking to each other. His mother taught Lily how to bake and it became a sort of therapy for both of them.

The new year came and went, Lily graduated high school, and Ginny gave birth to a healthy baby girl. She had blue eyes like her parents, and they named her Lucy after Wade's grandmother. Lily left for college, November was back again before they knew it, and then it was Thanksgiving.

They gathered around their table for a meal, the four of them, with Wade's mother and Ginny's father as well. They ate and drank and laughed and remembered. Ginny's father drove Wade's mother home. Lily went out to meet up with some of her friends. Ginny took Lucy back to their bed.

Wade found himself alone in the quiet of the house sooner than he'd expected. He poured himself a cup of coffee and walked out to the back porch. The air was crisp and clean, and it washed over him like a wave. There was something about the fall that always called to him. His mother had seen it.

"Autumn is the season when the truth in the world reveals itself," she'd told him one day when she was wasn't feeling quite herself and a young Wade had come to comfort her. "Winter is cold and angry, and it makes you sad. Spring is wet and temperamental. It promises sunshine, but all it does is rain. Summer is hot and unforgiving. It tricks you into thinking that things are wonderful, but it comes with a cost. But autumn, Wade. Autumn doesn't lie to you. Autumn is honest and true, just like you. There's solace in autumn. It gives you comfort. And that's when you can find the truth in you."

Early the next morning, Wade drove out to his old neighborhood. Houses stood where his father's cornfield once lay, the dirt path replaced by a concrete sidewalk. He followed it to a playground, where slides and swings were planted in the ground instead of wild grass and buttercups, trails laid down by children, not deer. He walked along the boardwalk, wider than it ever was, all the way through the marsh and right to the sandy shores of the beach where the creek opened into the bay. He felt a breeze rise from across the water and heard a whisper in the wind. He walked to the edge of the water and stepped into it, up to his ankles at first and then to his knees. He kept walking, farther and deeper into the bay, before stopping and looking down at his feet. He reached into his pocket, pulled out the necklace, and held it in his hand out in front of him. He let it fall into the water and disappear into the sand.

A blue heron rose from the salt grass. She circled him, once, twice, three times, before turning and lifting in the air. She flew up and away. East toward the rising sun. East to the open ocean.

Acknowledgements

I AM DEEPLY INDEBTED to the friends and family who generously agreed to read early drafts of a manuscript that was nowhere near ready for print. Among them, my patient and tolerant friends, Joe Riley, Dirk Hofschire, Carl Schwertz, J.D. Beam, Tiffany Messer, and Kenny Messer; my immensely talented brothers-in-law, Kent Knowles and Richard Knowles; and my very first reader, my mother-in-law, Doreen Knowles.

My thanks to Annie Mydla and Elizabeth Buege for their thoughtful critiques.

My gratitude to Joel Brigham and Andie Smith for their invaluable input and edits.

To my parents, for their unconditional love and support.

To my sister, for her infinite love and kindness.

To Grey and Noah, for always making me proud.

And, most importantly, to my wife, Kai, for her insightful review, revision, and criticism (which was "tough, but fair"), and her constant encouragement and enthusiasm as I navigated my writing journey. I certainly could not have done it without you.

About the author

MICHAEL WAS BORN IN Washington, D.C., and grew up on Maryland's Eastern Shore, spending most of his childhood roaming the beach and boardwalk in Ocean City. Michael currently lives in a suburb of Richmond, Virginia with his wife and two sons. *The Solace of Autumn* is Michael's debut novel.

www.michaeldpappas.com